Readers love
ROWAN MCALLISTER

Green the Whole Year 'Round

"Definitely a heartwarming and wonderful holiday novella!"
—Boys in Our Books

"If you are a sucker for Christmas tales of love the way I am, I can't recommend it enough."
—Prism Book Alliance

Lost in the Outcome

"McAllister did a really wonderful job of giving us fantastic characters and a great plot. Each little twist that happened was believable and had sound reasoning behind it."
—Joyfully Jay

"I like being able to say with complete sincerity that this is a good romantic suspense and not have to add, 'oh yea, it's m/m.' Because it is just a good book!"
—It's About The Book

Never a Road Without a Turning

"…Rowan McAllister is a good author who writes a wonderfully engaging story and fans of this genre will enjoy this sweet novel."
—The Novel Approach

By ROWAN MCALLISTER

Cherries on Top
Cuddling (Dreamspinner Anthology)
A Devil's Own Luck • Never a Road Without a Turning
Feels Like Home
Grand Adventures (Dreamspinner Anthology)
Green the Whole Year 'Round
Hot Mess
Lost in the Outcome
My Only Sunshine
Power Bottom?
A Promise of Tomorrow
Riding Double (Dreamspinner Anthology)

ELEMENTAL HARMONY
Air and Earth
Water and Fire

Published by DREAMSPINNER PRESS
www.dreamspinnerpress.com

POWER
Bottom?

ROWAN McALLISTER

DREAMSPINNER PRESS

Published by
DREAMSPINNER PRESS

5032 Capital Circle SW, Suite 2, PMB# 279, Tallahassee, FL 32305-7886 USA
www.dreamspinnerpress.com

Power Bottom?
© 2016 Rowan McAllister.

Cover Art
© 2016 AngstyG.
http://www.angstyg.com
Cover content is for illustrative purposes only and any person depicted on the cover is a model.

ISBN: 978-1-63477-685-1
Digital ISBN: 978-1-63477-686-8
Library of Congress Control Number: 2016906841
Published September 2016
v. 1.0

Printed in the United States of America
∞
This paper meets the requirements of
ANSI/NISO Z39.48-1992 (Permanence of Paper).

CHAPTER ONE

"ADRIAN, WAIT!"

If Martin hadn't fisted a hand in his jacket, Adrian wouldn't have stopped. His palms were already sweating, his stomach in knots, and momentum was about the only thing keeping his shaking legs moving.

"Are you sure about this?" Martin whispered breathlessly, his eyes flitting nervously between Adrian's face and his destination.

No, I'm not sure about this.

The words would've come out snippy, so Adrian took a breath and swallowed before opening his mouth. "What choice do we have? We're in the middle of nowhere. Neither one of us can get signal enough to call someone, let alone google the number of the closest tow company."

Martin's cherubic features squinched in concern, and Adrian's gut twisted again as he followed Martin's nervous gaze. Despite the flashing blue-and-red Open sign in the window, the building did not seem at all welcoming. The log-cabinesque exterior might have been charming, with its long farm porch just begging for rocking chairs, if not for the Harleys and beat-up pickup trucks with gun racks parked in the gravel lot.

From the relative safety of the tree line, Adrian squinted through the haze of grime on the windows again, but what little he could make out didn't exactly inspire confidence. Very large shapes huddled around pool tables and along a dark wood bar in the dimly lit interior. He could just make out the blue-black outlines of dozens of tattoos on thick, bare arms and lots of black clothing bearing the unmistakable sheen of leather.

Swallowing against another rush of queasiness, he looked down at what he and Martin were wearing and cringed. He had a feeling his beige sneakers, pressed khaki slacks, sky blue polo, and beige windbreaker were going to go over like a lead balloon. But at least his outfit was better than the orange skinny jeans, white boat shoes, and tight orange-and-pink-plaid short-sleeve button-down Martin had on under his white nylon jacket. In this neck of the woods, Martin might as well have a flashing neon sign above his head—"Homosexual here! For beatings, line up to the left!"

Under normal circumstances, Adrian actually admired Martin's flair for style—so much so that he'd let Martin revamp his own dull and dated wardrobe over the eleven months they'd been together. But at that particular moment, Martin's flair was more likely to get them sent to the hospital.

Shivering in the fading light, he removed Martin's hand from his sleeve and clasped it between his own. "Martin, sweetie, why don't you wait out here."

Martin's delicate auburn eyebrows lifted. "Are you sure? I mean, of course, if you think that's best."

Part of Adrian was relieved Martin wasn't going to argue with him, but he couldn't help feeling a little disgruntled that his *boyfriend* hadn't put up more of a fight. After all, he was suggesting going into possibly hostile territory all by himself. With a sigh, he shook it off and managed a reassuring smile as he squeezed Martin's hand and let go.

It made sense for Adrian to be the one to go in. Martin was barely five foot three, and his slender build made Adrian, at a whopping five eight, the more butch of the two of them—not even taking into account the wardrobe issues. If they went in together, they'd draw more attention than Adrian by himself. He was fairly good at being invisible, if his prior experience with bars was anything to go on. And honestly, if there was trouble inside, it wasn't as if either of them would be rescuing the other. They'd probably both get pummeled.

At least if Martin stayed outside, he could run for help if Adrian was being beaten to a pulp. Someone could tell his parents where his shallow grave might be located.

In a last-ditch effort, Adrian fished his phone out of his pocket and lifted it above his head, praying for even one tiny little bar. His hopes and his stomach had just fallen in resignation when a notification popped up with a detected Wi-Fi network.

The bar had Wi-Fi!

Holding his breath, Adrian tapped on the screen, but the network was locked.

"Shit!"

"What?" Martin gripped his arm again and pressed close to look at the screen.

"They have Wi-Fi, but I need the password," he groaned. "I still have to go in."

"Oh."

There was no help for it. The mountain air was getting colder, and cowering in the shadows at the edge of the gravel parking area wasn't going to get them any closer to a tow truck or home. In the hour it had taken them to walk from Adrian's lifeless car to this bar, they'd seen only one vehicle on the isolated mountain road where they broke down, and it hadn't even slowed for their frantic waving. The sun was beginning to dip behind the mountain peaks, so this was their only option, unless they wanted to huddle in his car overnight and hope someone came by in the morning.

Taking a steadying breath, Adrian squared his shoulders and plucked Martin's hand from his arm again. "Be back in a couple minutes."

I hope.

His sneakers might not be biker boots, but they made a satisfying crunch as he strode across the gravel lot and stepped up to the covered porch. He took heart from that. He wasn't exactly going to intimidate anyone inside, but he could put up a front that he wasn't quaking in his khakis.

The heavy oak door swung open on a squeal of rusted hinges, but thankfully the country music was loud enough that only the rough-looking guy behind the bar seemed to notice his entrance. The bartender wasn't much taller than Adrian, but he was a lot broader, a barrel of a man with beefy, tattooed arms protruding from a red T-shirt with the sleeves cut off. As Adrian squinted at him through the gloom, the man didn't exactly seem hostile, but his quirked bushy eyebrow and the amused twist of his lips as he looked Adrian up and down didn't exactly inspire confidence either.

"What can I get ya?" he said when Adrian hurried over to the bar, studiously ignoring the rest of the room. He really didn't want to know what other looks he might be getting.

"Um, hi. Uh, sorry to bother you, but our car broke down a couple miles down the road, and I was hoping you might have a phone I could use to call a tow truck."

Even without looking, he could feel eyes on him now, and a trickle of sweat slid down his neck to his spine. Then, like the sun coming out from behind the clouds, the bartender gave him a surprisingly warm and sympathetic smile, and just like that, Adrian could breathe again.

"Yeah, sure. Come on down to the end of the bar, and I'll get it for you."

On somewhat wobbly legs, Adrian followed the tattooed brick of a man to the end of the bar, keeping his back to the rest of the room and his gaze straight ahead. If he didn't make eye contact, maybe everyone else would forget he was there.

"Here ya go," the bartender said as he lifted a hideous snot-yellow rotary phone out from behind the bar.

The look on Adrian's face must have been priceless, because the bartender laughed as he said, "Hey, no one ever tries to steal it. Let me get the phone book too."

The man didn't look more than twenty years older than Adrian's thirty-two, but after hearing that, Adrian might need to revise his initial estimate.

Feeling a little like he'd gone back in time a few decades, Adrian said, "Oh, you don't have to do that. If you just give me the Wi-Fi password, I can find someone on my phone."

The bartender gave him that amused smirk again and slapped a phone book barely thicker than an IKEA catalogue onto the bar. "There's only a couple of guys close enough to do you any good out here. It'll take you longer to log in to the Wi-Fi than it will to find their page in the book."

"Oh…. Yeah, I see your point. Thank you."

Smiling sheepishly, Adrian thumbed through until he found the page and called the first number. The guy on the other end of the line gave him the number for someone closer, and after telling the new guy the name of the bar and approximate location and description of his car, Adrian hung up and handed the phone back.

"Thanks again."

The man shrugged and smiled. "No problem. Can I get you a drink while you wait?"

"Thanks, but the driver said he wasn't far. He should only be about ten minutes, so I think I'll just—"

Adrian was going to say, "I'll just wait outside." But the words lodged in his throat as he felt someone come up close behind him and put his hands on the wooden back of Adrian's barstool.

"Hey, Jack, I'll have another Maker's on the rocks, and put whatever he's having on my tab too."

The deep bass rumbling from close behind him sent a simultaneous jolt of fear and arousal through Adrian's body, leaving him suddenly breathless. It was an odd sensation, and one he wasn't sure he ever wanted to experience again. While he struggled to breathe, the hairs on his neck and forearms rose in reaction as the man's body heat blanketed his back. Jack the bartender's bushy eyebrows shot up, almost to his slightly receding hairline, and Adrian flushed for no reason.

Feeling ridiculous, he fought down his hormone surges and cleared his throat. "Oh, thank you. That's very kind of you, but you don't have to—"

That was all he managed to get out before he almost swallowed his tongue. While Jack had moved off to fix his drink, the man had slid onto the stool next to him, and as Adrian caught sight of *way* more than six feet of black-leather-clad gorgeousness, he might have forgotten how to speak.

The guy's sleepy hazel eyes swept Adrian from head to toe and back again as his lips quirked in a smile that was pure sin. "Come on. Let me buy you a drink."

Thick, dark brown hair, long enough to brush his shoulders, framed a strong, square face, rugged with what looked like a couple of days' worth of stubble. His sharp features were saved from being too harsh by surprisingly generous lips that widened into a grin the longer Adrian stared. At least Adrian had been startled enough to clamp his mouth shut instead of letting it drop open to dribble drool down his chin.

"I, uh, well, I…." Adrian tried but stuttered to a halt.

Gorgeous, dark-haired, tattooed strangers with miles of muscle encased in leather pants and tight black T-shirts did *not* hit on him in bars. In fact, he could probably count the number of people who had ever hit on him *anywhere* on one hand—not that he was ugly or anything, just average, ordinary, "kinda forgettable," as his college crush had informed him one mortifying night many years ago.

Adrian might have tried to manage another string of garbled nonsense, but Jack the bartender returned, saving him from himself. As Jack handed over the stranger's drink, the guy finally broke eye contact, and Adrian was able to remember why he was there… and where he was.

In sudden fear, he darted a glance around the bar. A couple of the guys at the pool tables were looking in their direction, but they seemed more amused than angry or disgusted. When Adrian turned back to Jack, the man was actually watching the two of them with a knowing smile. Flustered and a bit confused, Adrian ignored the weight of the distractingly gorgeous man's gaze and took another look at his surroundings. It wasn't until he spotted the first rainbow patch on a black leather biker jacket hanging on a hook by the pool tables that he figured it out.

Holy shit. I'm in a leather bar.

Like the parting of the veils, he saw the bar with new eyes. Sure enough, mixed among the wood paneling and antler décor was a movie poster for *Midnight Cowboy*. There were more deer butts than deer heads on the walls, and the two deer heads that were mounted on the far wall were angled toward each other, antlers intertwined, like they were sharing a kiss. Though not lit, he could just make out strings of rainbow party lights tacked to the dark wood trim by the ceiling. And now that he wasn't too afraid to make eye contact, he could see a few of the men at the pool tables were standing a bit closer to each other and touching a bit more often than was absolutely necessary.

He nearly laughed out loud in relief. He was such an idiot. He'd come in here so sure of what he'd find, that was exactly what he'd seen. In his defense, who would've ever thought to find a gay bar in the mountains in Maryland, this close to West Virginia, off a backcountry road Adrian hadn't even heard of until his Garmin had led him to it?

Feeling a little less flustered now that the threat of a bashing was significantly reduced, he turned back to the tattooed man still eyeing him like he was dessert and managed to find his tongue, and a little pride.

"Thank you for the offer, but my boyfriend's waiting outside, and I should get back out there before the tow truck arrives."

He saw a flicker of something in the man's hazel eyes that he couldn't put a name to before the guy gave him another sexy smile, grabbed his drink, and stood up. Jack moved away at the same time after a call came from one of the tables for more beer, and whatever spell Adrian had been under was broken. He started to climb to his feet but froze when a large warm hand landed on his shoulder and the stranger's body heat enveloped him again.

"If you were mine, I never would've let a hot little power bottom like you within ten feet of this place without me by your side."

The warm breath and brush of soft lips against his ear sent an involuntary shiver down Adrian's spine and shut off his brain, until the hand disappeared from his shoulder and the man sauntered off toward the back of the bar.

Too caught up in sensation, the words didn't even register until Adrian was already outside, gulping in a little fresh air.

What did he mean, power bottom? Who says I'm even a bottom at all?

Not that there was anything wrong with that. In fact, he was pretty versatile, though with Martin, he usually topped.

And why was he even worrying about what some stranger in a bar thought anyway?

Shaking his head, he stomped across the gravel lot.

If I were his….

"As if," Adrian huffed.

"As if what?" Martin said as he trotted over, meeting him halfway.

Adrian started guiltily. He'd almost forgotten Martin was there. Shaking his head again, he said, "Nothing. It doesn't matter. The tow truck driver is on his way. He should be here soon."

"Oh, thank God." Martin clutched anxiously at Adrian's arm. "You were gone longer than I expected. I was getting a little worried."

Tamping down on the sudden claustrophobic urge to shrug Martin's hand off, Adrian forced a chuckle. "We didn't have to be so scared. It's a gay bar, if you can believe that."

"Seriously?"

This time Adrian didn't need to force the laugh as he pushed aside the weirdness of his encounter in the bar and focused on his boyfriend's disbelieving expression. "Seriously, a leather bar. I never would've guessed it either, but I actually got hit on."

"Really?"

Martin's speculative glance at the bar rankled less than the patent surprise in his voice, but both took some of the humor out of the moment. Adrian was tempted to give him some shit, in hopes that he might inspire some other reaction, like maybe *jealousy* from his *boyfriend*. But then the loud rumble of what he hoped was the tow truck rounding the bend in the road distracted him, and he decided to let it go. He was tired, strangely off-balance, and just wanted to go home.

CHAPTER TWO

THE HEAVY silence in the cab of the tow truck left Adrian with way too much time to think. He and Martin had both tried a little small talk with the driver on the way to get his car, and then again on the way to a mechanic, but the looks and one-word answers from the crotchety old guy in coveralls weren't exactly encouraging. They'd all fallen silent fairly quickly. While Martin plucked at the fabric of his skinny jeans and stared out the window, Adrian tried to keep as much space as he could between him and the driver on the bench seat as he obsessed over what the man in the bar said and became more offended by the second.

Who did that guy think he was? I mean, sure, he was gorgeous and tall and cut—those arms, God, *and those thighs—but really, who says things like that to someone they don't even know? As if I'd need an escort into a leather bar. As if I wasn't a grown man, perfectly capable of taking care of myself.*

Conveniently forgetting his earlier pique with Martin for not putting up more of a fight over letting him go into that bar alone, Adrian's thoughts ran in a similar loop throughout the wait at the repair shop and the two-hour drive home, particularly after Martin nodded off halfway and left him with nothing else to distract himself. Martin hated the music Adrian liked, and Adrian hadn't been able to do much of a search for his earbuds while he was driving, so all he had was the dark road ahead of him and his thoughts to keep him company.

At least the repairs had been minor, something to do with his battery connections, and they hadn't had to wait long, nor did it cost an arm and a leg. That was a relief. His old Honda was reaching the end of its days, and he wasn't sure he could justify dumping too much more money into it.

By the time he pulled into the parking lot of their apartment building, he was more than tired of the voices inside his head. Grateful for something to occupy himself, he didn't even bother asking Martin to help unload the car. He just sent Martin upstairs to bed while he collected the blanket, cooler, picnic basket, and bag of trash and recycling left over from their romantic alfresco lunch in the mountains.

He smiled as he grabbed the empty wine bottle from the floor where it had fallen. The weirdness in the bar notwithstanding, their little day trip had actually gone pretty well… up until the point where his car broke down. They'd walked a little on one of the easier and more manicured state park trails to the falls, driven a scenic route to a picnic area with a majestic mountain overlook, and sipped wine and nibbled fruit, cheeses, and sausages on a soft cotton quilt Adrian had picked up on clearance just for the occasion. All in all, it had been as perfect as he'd hoped, a chance for them to get out of the rut they seemed to have fallen into and have some fun. Martin had even smiled and laughed and chatted like when they'd first started dating, giving Adrian more attention than he had in months.

Smiling at the quilt and smoothing a hand over it, Adrian shoved the weirdness that had come after out of his mind. So what if his car had crapped out on the drive home and he'd had a very *Twilight Zone* moment at a gay leather bar in the middle of nowhere? He didn't have to let it ruin their romantic day, or their night.

With renewed determination, Adrian slammed the trunk of his beige Civic with a little more force than necessary and juggled his armload of stuff up the stairs. Martin had left the door unlocked, but Adrian still managed to drop half of what he was carrying in his rush to get inside. He dumped the blanket on the couch and dropped the cooler, basket, and bag of trash on the floor. He toed off his sneakers, slipped out of his jacket, and pulled his polo over his head. He almost fell face-first into his dresser as he struggled to shimmy out of his khakis without stopping his headlong dash into the bedroom, but luckily, Martin lay facing away from the door, so he didn't witness that unsexy bit of clumsiness.

Now only in his boxers, his cock beginning to strain against the buttoned opening, Adrian slid across the mattress and spooned Martin's smaller body. He nuzzled the back of Martin's neck as he slid an arm beneath him and tugged him backward.

"Are you asleep?" Adrian whispered playfully as he nipped at Martin's earlobe.

"Yes."

Undeterred by the short answer, Adrian slid his palms over Martin's chest and belly and kissed his neck as he pressed his erection against Martin's pert little ass. "Are you sure? Maybe I could convince you to wake up just a little bit."

After a heavy sigh that sounded more irritated than aroused, Martin said, "I'm exhausted. Can we please just go to sleep?"

Adrian froze. "Oh. Yeah, sure, okay."

Withdrawing his arms and rolling back to his side of the bed, he stared at the ceiling, trying not to feel hurt and disappointed, while Martin's breathing evened out into quiet snores.

He's just tired, like he said. We did get up pretty early for our drive to the mountains, especially for a Saturday.

His erection fizzled along with his excitement as he rolled over and pulled the blankets up to his chin.

Whatever sleep he eventually got was not restful. A vague sense of unease dogged him throughout the night.

ADRIAN HAD cleaned up the mess he'd left by the couch and was on his second cup of coffee by the time Martin shuffled out of their bedroom to grab a cup for himself. As they sat across from each other at the small table he'd been able to squeeze between the couch and the pass-through to the tiny galley kitchen, Adrian worried his lip and waited for Martin to say something, *anything* to break the silence.

After about fifteen minutes in which that didn't happen, he couldn't take it anymore and asked, "Are you hungry? I could make us some breakfast."

Martin looked up from the magazine he was absently leafing through and gave him a tepid smile. "That's okay. Kenny and the boys texted a little while ago. They want to meet me—*us*—for Sunday brunch and maybe a little shopping after. I was just about to hop in the shower."

"But… I thought we were going to continue our romantic weekend together. You know, have a little breakfast, curl up together on the couch, watch a movie, have lunch and maybe dinner in bed." Pushing away his growing unease, Adrian waggled his eyebrows and forced a leer.

The snort Martin gave him showed more animation than anything else Adrian had received so far. And despite feeling just a little bit insulted, Adrian's hopes rose when Martin reached across the table and squeezed his hand—until Martin spoke. "Awww, babe, that's sweet, but we can do that anytime. We hang out together on the couch every night after work. Let's go out and do something fun."

With that, Martin got up, carried his mug to the kitchen, and went to take his shower, leaving Adrian to brood at the table, despite the peck on the cheek Martin gave him in passing.

What? I'm not fun?

Despite the sourness of his mood, Adrian gave in, as usual. He showered and dressed, then drove them both to brunch. Kenny, Jason, and Tyrell had already gotten a table at The Sturges Speakeasy, so all Adrian had to do was slide into one of the open chairs they'd left. Martin and the other boys chatted and laughed animatedly while Adrian sat and tried to will himself out of his funk. Today was like any of a hundred other days when they'd all gotten together, and despite the little friction between him and Martin that morning, he should've perked up by now.

He was halfway through his third slice of bacon, chewing away while the conversation flowed without him, when he froze, the half-eaten bacon pressed against his lips. He'd barely said more than two words since they'd arrived, and not one person at the table had even noticed or tried to drag anything more out of him. As the realization dawned, Adrian sat with the bacon still dangling by his lips and glanced around the table. It was like he was watching a TV show, outside staring in. For all the attention they paid him, he might as well have been a statue.

Maybe I'm not even here. Maybe this is a dream.

Right on the heels of that thought came another, more unpleasant one as he studied each face. These weren't really *their* friends. These were *Martin's* friends, and in that moment, Adrian wasn't even sure Martin gave a damn whether he was there or not. Hell, only a little more than twelve hours ago, a perfect stranger in a bar in the middle of nowhere had looked at him with more interest and intensity than he could ever remember receiving from his own boyfriend. The thought didn't hurt as much as it probably would later, because he was still experiencing that sense of disassociation. Eventually, though, he started to come back to himself, and he swallowed around the tightness in his throat and put the bacon down.

"Uh, Martin, can I talk to you for a second?"

The conversation at the table didn't even pause.

Maybe I am invisible.

Adrian shook his head.

Or maybe he just didn't hear me.

He put his hand on Martin's arm to get his attention and tried again. "I need to talk to you. Can we go outside for a sec?"

Martin frowned, actually looking straight at him for the first time in at least an hour. "Can it wait? Kenny was just about to tell us about his latest hottie."

"I'd really like to talk to you."

After a slight pause and a quiet sigh, Martin nodded and stood up. "We'll be right back."

Adrian ignored the looks Martin's friends shot them as they walked away.

Outside, he said, "I think we need to talk about some things. Can we pay the check and go back to the apartment now, please?"

With another frown, Martin put his hands on his hips. "But we've barely been here an hour, and I haven't seen them all week."

At some point Adrian remembered thinking Martin's pout was kind of cute, but right now he couldn't remember when. "I just want to talk, spend some time together, just you and me. Can we do that?"

"We did that all yesterday on that picnic thing you wanted to do. Why can't we do something I want today?"

"Picnic *I* wanted? You said you wanted to do it too. You went on and on about how romantic the waterfall sounded."

Martin rolled his eyes and waved a dismissive hand. "Well, maybe it sounded romantic, but four hours in a car round-trip for dirt, bugs, water, and some trees was a bit much. I was ready to go home an hour after we got there, and that was way before the whole mess with your crap car that you should've traded in a decade ago."

It was Adrian's turn to sigh. *Not this again.*

"I said I was sorry about that. And my car's not that bad. Maybe I should look into getting a new one soon, but it's been too good a car for me to just throw away."

"You mean you've been too cheap an owner," Martin mumbled under his breath.

Adrian could feel his cheeks getting hot. "What's that supposed to mean?"

Martin blew out a breath and took Adrian's hand. "Nothing. I'm sorry. Look, if you don't feel like hanging out today, that's fine. Why don't you head home? One of the boys will drop me off later, and we can talk tonight, okay?"

Since he was getting too upset to have a rational conversation anyway, Adrian figured that was probably a better idea than continuing to fight about it in public. Honestly, at this point, he didn't exactly know what he was feeling or what he wanted to say anyway.

He'd go home, maybe take a nap, and give his roiling emotions a chance to settle so they might make some sense, and then he and Martin could talk about it without fighting. That was a good plan.

"Yeah. Okay."

Sleep proved as elusive that afternoon as it had the night before, and Adrian spent most of the day puttering around their apartment and fretting. Eventually it got bad enough that he even wished his Sunday were over so he could go back to work, where everything made sense. At least at work he could do something other than drive himself crazy, because today, laundry just wasn't cutting it.

He texted Martin a couple of times but didn't get much response, and by the time six o'clock rolled around, Adrian was starting to get pissed again. He ate dinner alone and must have fallen asleep on the couch, because he almost fell off it when Martin stumbled through the door. Blinking the spots from his eyes at the sudden flare of the overhead light, Adrian glanced down at his watch and frowned when it came into focus. It was after midnight.

"Oh, hey, I didn't think you'd still be up," Martin said, looking everywhere but at Adrian as he dumped his keys and wallet on the coffee table.

"I wasn't. I fell asleep on the couch. Where were you? I thought we were going to talk."

A bit more awake now and remembering his earlier anger, Adrian followed as Martin wove his unsteady way to the kitchen and poured himself a glass of water. "Oh, you know Kenny. You can't call it a day of shopping without capping it off with a couple of cocktails… and you can't have a couple of cocktails without dancing, right?"

That last was said with a laugh and hand wave that sloshed water out of the cup he was holding, and Adrian took a long, slow breath. Martin was drunk. That's why he was being so obtuse. Trying to have a serious conversation about his feelings now would be pointless.

Adrian let out a huff, turned his back, and headed for the bedroom. "Come on. Let's get you to bed. We've both got work in the morning."

"Yup. Work, work, work. That's my Adrian. The workin' machine," Martin singsonged behind him.

What's that supposed to mean?

Scowling, Adrian flipped the switch for the overhead light in their bedroom and began shucking clothes. Down to his boxers, he was about to climb into bed when Martin jostled the dresser, knocking over the bowling pin setup of his egregiously expensive cologne bottles that filled the top.

"Shit. Stupid tiny apartment. Can't even move without bumping into shit," Martin grumbled.

Since Martin was currently trapped in the shirt he was trying to pull over his head without unbuttoning it, Adrian felt it was hardly the apartment's fault, or the dresser's. He hurried over and started undoing buttons before any real damage could be done, but it wasn't easy with Martin wrestling with the shirt the whole time.

"Hold still, please," Adrian finally huffed, and when Martin slumped into the dresser, Adrian was able to peel the shirt the rest of the way off him.

After tossing it in the hamper, he was about to reach for Martin's belt to speed the process along when he froze with the leather end in his hand. Blinking, not quite sure he was seeing what he thought he was seeing, he stared dumbly at a silver-dollar-sized reddish-purple mark on Martin's throat, just above his collarbone, that hadn't been there this morning.

"What's that?"

He wasn't an idiot. He knew what it was, but he couldn't think of anything else to say at the moment, and he really hoped he was wrong.

"What?" Martin blinked at him blearily, his face scrunched unattractively.

"That, Martin," he repeated, pointing at the mark. "What is that?"

Martin turned to the mirror above the dresser and quickly put a hand over it. "Oh," he giggled. "That's just Kenny being stupid. It's nothing. He thought he was being funny."

"He thought giving you a hickey would be funny?"

His patent disbelief must have been obvious enough for Martin to hear through his alcohol-induced haze, because he frowned at Adrian's reflection in the mirror. "Don't start."

"Don't start? What the hell is that supposed to mean?"

Martin stepped away from the mirror and moved to the bed, but Adrian stayed close behind him.

"You come home with a hickey and laugh it off, and what? I'm just supposed to ignore it?"

Now that he was looking, Adrian noticed Martin's lips were a little redder than usual and he had what could be stubble burn on his neck too.

"I told you. Kenny got drunk and a little stupid. That's all."

"Well, if Kenny was the drunk and stupid one, how come you're the one with the hickey and swollen lips?"

Martin froze with his knee on the bed and the edge of the sheet in his hand. Adrian wasn't sure what he expected to happen next, but the long-suffering sigh Martin let out was not it.

"Do you really want to do this now?" His gaze was suddenly a lot clearer and steadier than Adrian was prepared for, and it set him off-balance. Apparently Martin was sobering quickly.

"Do what now?" he asked stupidly.

When Martin sighed again and sat on the edge of the bed, his resigned and slightly annoyed expression made Adrian's stomach clench.

"Okay, fine. It wasn't Kenny who gave me the hickey, all right?"

Uh. Am I supposed to answer that? Because no, it's not all right.

Before he could think of what to say, Martin continued, "I'm sorry, Adrian. It was a guy I've seen a few times at Stallions. His name's Chris. We've fooled around a little. I mean, we didn't really do anything. I didn't really cheat on you. It was just some heavy petting. That's all."

It took a few beats before Adrian's brain kicked in enough to form words. "Uh, how exactly is that not cheating?"

"Oh, come on, Adrian. It was just a little kissing… and, you know, maybe a blowjob. We didn't fuck or anything." He at least had the decency to sound a little guilty when he mumbled that last bombshell.

Outrage finally replaced shock. "How could you?" Adrian cringed at the octave his voice had just achieved. Dear God, he sounded like the jilted wife from every Lifetime movie ever made. His lower lip was even trembling a little, but, dammit, he couldn't help it. They'd agreed to a monogamous relationship before they'd moved in together. They'd had a long and detailed conversation about it. Martin had *promised*.

"Come on, Ade. Don't be like that."

"*Don't be like that?*"

Okay, now he was mad.

That was better.

He so did not like the whole teary-eyed, lip-quivering thing that had been threatening a moment before. "How can you say that to me? You're acting like I'm the one at fault here when you're the one who lied and cheated! And don't try to tell me that bullshit about how a blowjob's not really cheating, because you know it is! You knew *I'd* see it as cheating, and you did it anyway."

Martin climbed off the bed and moved to stand in front of Adrian. He put a hand on Adrian's shoulder and squeezed, but the pitying expression on his face negated any comfort Adrian might have gotten from the gesture.

"I'm sorry, Ade. I'm sorry if I hurt you. I should've been up front with you, but I was trying not to hurt your feelings. I mean, we've got a good thing going here. It just isn't quite enough. So I thought if I could get what I needed elsewhere, without you knowing, everything would be okay."

Wait. What?

Adrian's head was beginning to ache trying to puzzle out what the hell was going on. His anger deflated like a popped balloon in his confusion. He felt like a complete idiot, and he was probably going to regret it, but he had to ask. "What do you mean? What did you need that I wasn't giving you?"

The pitying look came back, worse than before. "Oh come on, Ade, let's be honest. I mean, I'm being honest with you now. Don't you think you should try to do the same?"

The expression on Adrian's face must have communicated his complete cluelessness because Martin's expression hardened into annoyance—which Adrian almost preferred to the pity.

"You really want me to say it for you?" Martin huffed and dropped his hand from Adrian's shoulder. "Okay. Fine. I need excitement. I need fun. Hell, I need *sex*! I didn't lie about that, though. I haven't fucked anyone yet. But it was only a matter of time before I reached the point I couldn't take it anymore. You can understand that, can't you?"

Adrian stood there gaping like a fish until he managed to croak out, "But we have fun, and we definitely have sex, anytime you want it. You're the one who hasn't wanted it lately, not me."

The pitying look returned. "You really don't get it, do you?"

"I guess not."

"Oh, sweetie, how is that even possible?" Martin scrubbed a hand across his face. After a pause and a long sigh, he shook his head. "I don't think we should continue this conversation right now. I think I'm still a little drunk, and I'm tired, and we both have work tomorrow, like you said. We should go to bed, and we can talk about this after work. Okay?"

Oh, hell no.

Adrian was finally recovering a little from his shock, and even though he was still at a loss, he knew he'd never sleep a wink tonight without knowing exactly what Martin meant. He grabbed Martin's wrist as he turned toward the bed. "Stop. I want you to tell me what you mean."

"Adrian, not tonight. Just let it go, and we can talk about it when we're both a little more clearheaded."

Adrian dropped Martin's wrist and put his hands on his hips. "Oh, my head is perfectly clear, and you've made it sound like this is something I should know, something you've felt for a long time, so let's have it. What is it you think I've been lying to myself about?"

Martin's shoulders slumped, and he peered up at Adrian, his delicate auburn brows knit with concern. "You really want to do this? You're sure?"

The warning in Martin's tone made Adrian's stomach quail, but he lifted his chin and took a steadying breath. "Yes."

"Okay." Martin took a deep breath and said, "Adrian, you are a sweet, generous, kind man, but you are also incredibly *boring*. I'm sorry, but you are. I mean, you're an accountant, so that should've probably been obvious. But I never realized just how boring you could be until I moved in with you. I swear, another quiet evening on the couch with you in this sardine can you call an apartment, and I'd just about lose my mind. And that's another thing. You're cheap, *needlessly* cheap. You have a great job. You make all this money, and *this* is where you live? In this crappy little apartment, in this crappy little neighborhood, so far out from *everything* that we have to drive in that junk heap you call a car to get to anywhere fashionable or interesting? I'm embarrassed every time my friends have to come all the way out here to drop me off."

Martin was on a roll now, apparently. He paced the small confines of their bedroom, waving his hands around, and all Adrian could do was watch in stunned silence, possibly bleeding out from the various jabs he'd received so far. But then Martin let him have it with the broadsword.

"…and that's not even talking about the sex." He swung around and pointed an angry finger at Adrian. "You can't tell me you're that oblivious. If you want to lie to yourself, that's fine, but don't lie to me. You know the sex sucks."

"It does?"

Martin stopped in his tracks and studied Adrian for a second with wide green eyes. "You *really* didn't know? Seriously?"

"I...."

Martin clapped a hand to his forehead and dragged it down his face. "Oh, honey. Really?"

There was enough pity dripping from his tone, Adrian couldn't make himself believe Martin was just lashing out. He really meant it.

Adrian almost flinched when Martin put his hands on both of Adrian's shoulders and drove the blade home. "Oh, Adrian, I'm sorry if you really didn't know. It shouldn't have come out this way, but, sweetie, you're a lousy lay."

Before he collapsed into a puddle on the floor, Adrian shrugged off Martin's hands and braced himself in a corner of the room. It took him a couple of tries, but he managed to grate out, "If I'm such a lousy... boyfriend, why are you even with me?"

Martin shook his head, and his green eyes even glistened a little. "I never said you were a lousy boyfriend, Adrian. You're sweet. You're considerate. You're caring and nurturing. You're just not very exciting. That's all. You're *comfortable*, you know, like a favorite pair of sweatpants or an old T-shirt."

Sweatpants?

Seriously? I'm sweatpants?

And then, past the haze of hurt and shock, Adrian got it. The pieces clicked together in his head, and the air rushed out of his lungs. He wasn't a boyfriend for Martin—he was a placeholder, something convenient and comfortable to rely on until someone better came along.

Back in the beginning of their relationship, Adrian had wondered many times why someone as vibrant and pretty as Martin had given him the time of day. Outgoing, charming, ginger-haired, and cherub-faced, Martin always had a crowd around him, was always the life of the party. Adrian didn't get flirted with often, so he'd been flattered by Martin's attention, flattered by Martin's clothing and décor suggestions. He'd thought maybe Martin was ready for something real, someone to settle down with, now that he was in his midthirties. But no, Adrian apparently wasn't that guy. He was the pair of sweatpants Martin kept in a drawer for when he was sick or worn out or feeling run-down. He was the cardboard cutout standing in for the real thing.

He swallowed and then swallowed again. When he could get enough air in his lungs, he said, "I'm going to go sleep on the couch. I think... I think I'm going out tomorrow night after work. And I think you should take that time to start packing up your stuff. I'd rather you not be here when I get home," he said dully, looking anywhere but at Martin. He was drained enough he might actually be able to find a few hours of sleep now, so that was good.

"Adrian, sweetie, I'm sorry. I told you I didn't want to do this now. I didn't want to hurt you."

He actually sounded sincere, and there were tears on his cheeks when Adrian was able to lift his gaze to see them.

Straightening, Adrian shook his head. "No. No. I asked you to be honest, and you most definitely were." He walked stiffly to the bed and grabbed a pillow, staring at it like he'd never seen it before. "But now I really think you shouldn't live here anymore.... I put you on that savings plan, and we've got your debt down to a pretty manageable level in the last eleven months, especially with me covering the rent here. You should have more than enough saved up for first and last month's on a place of your own. You'll probably need to find a roommate if you want to live closer to downtown—where all the action is—but I'm sure you won't have any trouble finding one. You've got so many friends. So, yeah."

He was rambling, but he couldn't seem to stop. He needed to lie down.

"Adrian—"

"Good night, Martin."

After grabbing a spare blanket out of the closet, he walked out into the living room, and thankfully Martin didn't follow. Adrian really couldn't handle any more talking.

CHAPTER THREE

ADRIAN WAS the first employee in the building the following morning. That wasn't exactly unusual, but this time he was early enough that more than two hours passed before he heard any car doors outside or the ping of the elevators. He'd managed to sleep fitfully for a few hours on the couch before waking with a headache and stiff back and neck. Showered and shaved, he'd had to creep into the bedroom to get his clothes, but Martin hadn't moved a muscle, not that Adrian had been expecting him to. The clothing store where Martin worked didn't open until nine, so it was normal for Adrian to be up and out of the apartment long before he woke. The only difference this time was Adrian had left before the sun was up, and he hadn't even bothered to adjust the timer on the coffeepot. Today, he'd splurged for one of those outrageously expensive froufrou coffee drinks on his way to work so he didn't have to be in that apartment one minute longer than necessary.

"Knock, knock."

He looked up to find Beverly Tullman—the other half of Pacciano Bros crack accounting "team"—poking her head through his door.

"Happy Monday, crappy Monday to you, sir," she said, with a brilliant smile that belied the latter part of her greeting.

"Hey," he replied.

Beverly was one of those insanely cheerful morning people, the ones nonmorning people like Adrian wanted to bash in their cheery little faces before ten o'clock. At least Bev had enough consideration to tone it down to suit her audience. Like today, she took one look at Adrian's face and her blinding smile disappeared completely.

"Hey, babe, what's wrong?"

"Long story. I don't think I'm up to talking about it yet, though."

In the three years they'd worked together, she'd gotten to know him well enough that she knew when to push and when to leave him alone.

"Okay, I'll check back in with you later. Just throw a pencil at the wall if you need anything."

Pacciano Bros construction company was doing well enough that their two-person accounting department had a floor to themselves and a fancy internal phone system. They could page each other with just the push of a button, but the wall that separated their offices was thin enough a pencil tap was just as effective and far more satisfying. He could also probably yell whatever he needed, and she'd hear him just fine, but they were accountants. They didn't yell.

By noon, the numbers on Adrian's computer screen were starting to blur, and his headache had achieved throbbing proportions. Still, he refused to quit. He attacked his job with single-minded determination so he wouldn't have to think about anything else. His cell phone had chimed from inside his bag a few times during the morning, but he hadn't bothered to check it. He was pretty sure who the messages were from, and he didn't want to know what they said.

In desperation, he finally broke down and started digging through his desk for some Tylenol when Beverly poked her head through his door again.

"Hey there, want to go get some lunch?"

He followed her gaze to the empty corner cabinet where the insulated bag with his lunch was noticeably absent. He winced and rubbed his temple. He was tempted to say yes, but another throb behind his left eye changed his mind. He wasn't going to be very good company.

"Thanks, but I think I'll just work through lunch today and leave early."

Of course, leaving early wasn't exactly going to do him any good either, since he couldn't go home. He winced again and let out a pitiful little moan.

"You know that headache you have isn't going to get any better with you sitting behind your desk staring at your screen. And it is just possible the reason you have a headache is because you haven't eaten."

"Stop making sense. It's annoying," he grumbled.

She grinned. "Sorry, can't help it. It's a gift, really."

He grunted.

"Come on, Ebenezer. I'll even spring for your lunch."

She was teasing him, the same as she always did, but the "Ebenezer" comment struck a little close to home, and Adrian scowled.

Did everyone think he was a cheap bastard?

It took some effort, but he managed not to snap at her. "I can buy my own lunch."

Seemingly unaffected, she grinned at him. "Excellent! Then we're on for lunch. Let me just go get my jacket and purse."

Not quite sure how he'd gotten there, Adrian slumped into their booth at the diner up the street from their building and took his menu. He remained silent after they ordered, but Beverly didn't seem to mind. She talked a little about the weather, the days getting cooler and shorter, and then about some invoices they were working on, without requiring a response. His headache went away halfway through his soda and club sandwich, and he sighed in relief as he let his head fall against the padded red vinyl behind him. When he looked up, Bev was smiling at him.

"Better?"

He nodded. "Thanks. This was a much better idea than downing another half a pot of office coffee and a bunch of pills."

She nodded. "Now that you're feeling better, do you want to tell me what's going on?"

Adrian sighed and worried his lip. He considered Bev a friend, maybe one of the only real friends he had, but they'd never been confidantes. They did lunch when Adrian felt like splurging instead of bringing leftovers from home. He'd been to her house for a few barbecues. But she had her husband and her kids and the PTA, or whatever, and he had—well, what did he have exactly? He had a boyfriend who wasn't really a boyfriend and friends he hung out with who really weren't *his* friends.

Now he was starting to get depressed.

"I had a fight with Martin last night, and he said some things that… let's just say, weren't flattering. And now I'm trying to figure out what to do or think because I honestly didn't see it coming."

She reached across the table and placed a warm hand over his. "Oh, I'm so sorry, Adrian. You know they say only the ones we love really know how to hurt us."

Did he love Martin?

That was a good question.

After chewing on his lip for a little while, Adrian shook his head. "I don't think I was there yet with Martin. I'm just not sure if he said what he did because it was true, or out of spite, or what."

Even as the words left his mouth, he knew they were a lie. Martin had meant it. He hadn't said it to hurt, not really. He'd even tried to get out of saying anything until Adrian had pushed.

"What did he say?" Beverly's question brought him out of his inward spiral, and he grimaced.

"I'm not sure I want to share that. It's pretty humiliating."

She leaned across the table and whispered, "This morning, my youngest told every other parent at the bus stop that we were both wearing damp undies because I'd had to wash them in the sink and dry them with my hair dryer, because I forgot to do laundry yesterday. Believe me, I know humiliation."

Adrian nearly snarfed his soda. After his coughing and laughing were under control he sent an apologetic look in her direction, but she just smirked. She'd done it on purpose, and he smiled for the first time that day.

"Thanks, Bev. Way to put everything into perspective for me."

"Oh, I wasn't trying to do anything so complicated. I just wanted to see you smile… and the story is true, by the way, so now it's your turn. What happened?"

The smile fell from his face, and he slumped his shoulders. "He came home with a hickey last night."

"No."

If he hadn't been talking about his life, Adrian would've smiled at the way she gasped out the word and leaned closer, over their half-eaten lunch, her brown eyes wide above her glasses. "Yeah. Things had already been a bit off for us the last couple of months, so I planned this romantic picnic thing on Saturday, only that kinda got messed up. And I tried to get him to talk to me, spend some time with just us to figure out what was going on, but he kept avoiding it. Then he went out with his friends and came home with a big old hickey on his neck, and I kind of lost it."

"Yeah? Did you yell?"

She seemed so hopeful, Adrian hated to let her down, but he shook his head. "Not really. I mean, maybe I raised my voice a little."

She clapped her hands and bounced in her seat. "Good. I'm proud of you."

He wasn't quite sure how to take that, so he pushed it aside. Now came the humiliating part. "Except that wasn't the end of our fight. Apparently, I'm not only cheap but about as exciting as watching paint dry."

"He said that?"

"Not in so many words, but yeah… and worse."

"What a dick!" she hissed. "I hope you kicked his freeloading ass to the curb."

Adrian's jaw dropped. He hadn't even told her all of it, and she actually seemed incensed. He could swear he hadn't heard her use this many swear words in the three years he'd known her.

When he continued to stare, she sat back in her chair and frowned at him. "What?"

"I guess I just never realized you felt so strongly about him."

She shrugged. "It's not as if I hated the guy. I mean, I only met him a couple of times, and I thought you could do better, but I didn't think he was this much of an asshole. I mean, he's been sponging off you for what, almost a year now?"

"Eleven months," Adrian mumbled, feeling his cheeks heat.

He hadn't actually viewed it as sponging. Martin had some debts he was trying to clear, and after they'd sat down and reviewed his finances, it had just made sense for Adrian to keep paying for the apartment, given that his income was significantly more than Martin's. Part of him wanted to defend himself and Martin, but he shoved the words down. What was the point? He had been an idiot, a doormat... a pair of sweatpants.

"Sweatpants?" Beverly asked, her brows knit in confusion.

He hadn't meant to say it out loud.

"He compared me to a favorite old pair of sweatpants," he mumbled.

One of her eyebrows shot up as she seemed to ponder this. "But he meant it in a bad way? Like, I have to tell you, sweatpants are one of my favorite articles of clothing—you know, as long as I'm not going out in public... and even sometimes then."

Adrian grimaced and nodded. "But that's it. I think that's kind of what he meant. I think he was trying to make me feel better, but all it did was make it worse. I don't want to be somebody's sweatpants... or, I guess, I don't want to *only* be that, particularly when we haven't even been together for a year yet. Am I really that boring?"

When, instead of immediately leaping to his defense, Beverly paused and seemed to consider her words, he moaned and dropped his head in his hands. "Oh God. I am that boring."

"No!" Bev reached across the table again and squeezed one of his wrists until he lifted his head. "You are *not* boring. I mean, both of us like a bit of order in our lives. And maybe you like a quiet night at home more than a night out on the town."

"Yeah, he said if he had to spend another night on the couch with me, he would've gone crazy," Adrian cut in morosely.

"Jerk. But that doesn't make you boring. It just makes you an introvert. From what you've told me in the past, it wasn't like Martin ever tried to find common ground for the two of you. I mean, he stayed home on weeknights with you, but that's just common sense when you both had to be up for work, or he didn't get home until after his store closed. He still went out and partied most weekends, with you or without you."

Recently it had been more often without, since Adrian could only take so many nights barhopping and clubbing with Kenny and the boys. It was fun every once in a while, but a person couldn't really hold a decent conversation in places like that, nothing meaningful anyway. Talk about boring—same songs, same drinks, same stupid gossip and small talk. He didn't understand how people went to clubs day in and day out. It might be monotony with a kickin' beat, but it was still monotony.

Adrian felt his shoulders relax a little as he pondered this. Maybe he and Martin were just too different. They wanted different things. That didn't make what Adrian wanted bad, just not what Martin was looking for… except that didn't cover the "lousy lay" part of the conversation, but he sure as hell wasn't going to share that with Bev.

"…and about the cheap part," Beverly continued, gaining volume and oblivious to the fact that Adrian had checked out for a few seconds. "You're not cheap. You're financially responsible. You don't like waste. What's wrong with that? And how much debt was Martin in when you met him? I mean seriously, who the hell is he to criticize? Spending within your means is *smart*, not cheap!"

Adrian wasn't sure whether her ire was for his sake or because this particular subject was a hot button. Either way, other people at the restaurant were starting to stare.

"Okay, okay, Bev. You're right. I shouldn't have let it hit me so hard," he placated. "I guess it just felt like it all came out of the blue, and I was blindsided. That's all." He sighed and rested his hand over hers on the table. "Anyway, thanks for listening, for the pep talk and… for being a friend. I really appreciate it."

Her fist unclenched beneath his palm, and her smile was a little sheepish. "At least tell me you kicked him out."

He smiled. "Yeah. I told him I was going to be late tonight, and I would prefer it if he started packing and looking for a new place."

She rolled her eyes. "That doesn't sound anywhere near as satisfying as shoving him out the door and throwing all his shit out the window… but good for you. Just stick to your guns, and don't let him weasel his way back in, okay? You deserve better than that."

"I won't."

He meant it.

His self-esteem may have taken a beating, and it hadn't exactly been all that healthy to begin with, but he wasn't low enough that he was willing to be someone's fallback position. He did deserve better than that, though he wasn't sure if he'd ever find it.

"Come on. We need to get back in case Perretti finishes his eighteenth hole early and actually makes it to the office and notices we're gone."

On the walk back, Bev took his arm, and they bumped shoulders companionably. The physical contact was nice, something new for them, but nice. He couldn't think why he'd never tried to become better friends. They were enough alike. She got him, probably better than anyone else would.

"…a shame, really. It would've been nice to have Donnie so close by," Bev was saying.

"Huh?"

"Are you even listening to me?"

Oops.

"Uh. Sorry. Got distracted."

She glared at him a moment before rolling her eyes. "I'll forgive you this time, since you've had a shitty weekend. But don't let it happen again. I was *saying*, I think they leased that office space my brother was looking at to someone else." She waved a hand behind them, toward the empty building that had had a Space For Lease banner on it for the three years Adrian had worked for Pacciano Bros.

"Oh, yeah. Donnie was gonna try to open an acupuncture or homeopathy clinic or something, right?"

"Naturopathy, but yeah. He's been trying to get a loan for a while now, but I guess it looks like he won't be able to get *this* space. I've seen workmen coming in and out of the building the last couple of weeks, though there's no Coming Soon sign yet and the For Lease banner's still there."

"Maybe they're just sprucing it up to help lease it. He might still have a chance."

Her lips twisted. "I doubt it. They haven't put any money into that place since we've been here. I can't believe they'd bother if they didn't have a client on the hook so they'd know what direction to go in with the reno."

Trying to pull his head out of his ass for her sake, Adrian managed to dredge up a sympathetic smile. "I guess you're right. That's too bad. Donnie's a pretty great guy. He deserves to get his own place."

She shrugged. "He'll find somewhere. I just thought it'd be cool to have him right down the street from our office. I wonder who's going to move in there... maybe a new restaurant. It would be awesome to have somewhere other than the diner and Chinese takeout within walking distance."

"Uh-huh," he replied absently, already feeling the weight of his weekend dragging him down again.

She gave his arm a smack.

"Ow. What was that for?"

"I'm trying to distract you from your problems with my witty repartee, but it won't work if you're not paying attention."

"I *was*."

"Uh-huh."

THE REST of the workday passed quickly enough. He'd actually put in his eight hours long before five o'clock, but he hung around in Bev's office helping her finish up, since she'd insisted on inviting him over to their place for dinner.

"I'm not going to let you eat dinner alone and mope," she'd said flatly, and he really didn't relish the idea so much either, so he hadn't put up much of a fight.

He'd avoided it all day, but trapped in his car on the slow rush-hour drive to her place, he heard his phone buzz again, and he couldn't take it anymore. He had seven messages. The most recent one was from his mom asking if he had plans to come visit for his sister's birthday next month, but the rest were, of course, from Martin.

They started with *I'm so sorry. I never meant to hurt you. I was drunk and stupid* and *Don't go out tonight. Come home. Let's talk* but eventually morphed into *Will you PLEASE just talk to me?!!* and then finally *Fine! I'm going to Stallions. If you want to talk, you know where to find me.*

He was tempted to turn around and maybe have that talk, but then he noticed the amount of time between "Come home" and "I'm going to Stallions" was less than an hour, and he rolled his eyes and scowled. Kenny or one of the others had probably called or texted Martin during that hour... or maybe the hickey guy, what was his name? Chris?

It was all bullshit. Their entire relationship was bullshit.

"Bullshit!" he yelled to his empty car.

He even pounded the steering wheel a couple of times for good measure, which actually felt kind of good. Unfortunately, the cathartic rush didn't last long.

"Ow."

Flexing his bruised hands on the steering wheel, he went right back to obsessing about how blind he'd been, while simultaneously skittering away from any thoughts about their sex life. Under other circumstances, he might've congratulated himself on his ability to compartmentalize like that, but his self-esteem wasn't buying it.

Thankfully, he reached the entrance to Bev's community before he could drive himself completely insane. The development's warren-like streets and nearly identical houses demanded his full attention or he'd never find her place, particularly in the fading light.

He was barely out of his car before Bev rushed out the door, ushered him inside, and shoved a glass of wine into his hand. She dragged him to the kitchen and chattered away as she plied him with more wine and a plate of cheese and crackers while she pulled pots and pans out of cupboards that looked too small to house so many things.

Her husband, Isaac, arrived with the kids not long after, and he joined them in the kitchen. He and Bev kept up a steady stream of distracting conversation while they danced around each other preparing stuffed cabbage rolls and mashed potatoes, and the kids clattered noisily around the house, chasing the dog and generally getting underfoot.

It was chaotic, but the whole family scene was pretty adorable too, and Adrian found himself getting a little wistful as he watched. Luckily, Bev never let the conversation lag or his glass get empty enough for him to get morose. She was perfect, exactly what he needed, and he found himself wondering again why he didn't spend more time with her.

Oh yeah. Martin.

After dinner, they all sat on the back deck and watched the kids chase their golden retriever, Doofus, around the backyard, trying to get him to let go of the slobbery tennis ball that seemed permanently lodged in his mouth. The air was cool but not unpleasant. Isaac lit a fire in their copper fire bowl, and that, along with the sounds of crunching leaves and giggling children, was actually soothing… or it could've been the wine, though his buzz was nearly gone. While they talked and laughed, Bev and Isaac finished off the bottle, and Adrian sipped on the water he'd switched to halfway through the meal. But eventually the fire died down, his glass was empty, and the conversation petered out. It was time to go home and let this family get some sleep.

With regret, he said his good nights and headed for his car with Bev in tow.

"You're better off without him," Bev said quietly as she hugged him by his car.

"You're probably right."

"Aren't I always?"

At the apartment, a quick search through the bedroom closet showed Martin had taken their luggage and a small chunk of his enormous wardrobe, but not all. The note on the kitchen counter said, *Staying with friends. Call when you're ready to talk.*

But Adrian didn't want to talk. Martin had said enough the night before. Adrian was actually a little afraid of what else Martin might drop on him if given the chance. His fragile ego had enough cracks in it at the moment. Any more hits and it might shatter completely.

Sweatpants.

He crumpled the note and tossed it in the trash before grabbing the bottle of vodka they kept for Martin's "experimental cocktails" out of the cabinet. He slammed it on the counter and dug through the refrigerator until he found the cranberry juice. After filling a glass with ice, he took all three to the couch. He turned on the TV so the apartment's oppressive silence couldn't crush him, and then set about getting good and plastered. Since he'd never been much of a drinker, the process shouldn't take long, and the fact that he was getting drunk on a work night for the first time in his life didn't even enter into the equation.

Hours later, as he crouched on his knees, praying to the porcelain god, the old adage "wine before liquor, never been sicker" was on maddening replay in his head. The room spun, his skull pounded, and his stomach tried to twist itself into knots… but, looking on the bright side, at least those were the only words going round and round up there. He eventually passed out on the bed, achieving blessed oblivion without another second of introspection.

Mission accomplished, sort of.

CHAPTER FOUR

FOR THE first time in over two years, he actually called in sick the next day. It was probably the first time *ever* that he'd missed work for a reason other than a doctor's appointment, or being worried he might bring contagion into the office, but he just wasn't up to dealing with anyone, even Bev.

Except, he had to when she called his cell a couple of hours after he notified Mr. Perretti.

"Are you sure you're okay?" she asked as Adrian huddled farther beneath his blankets, shrinking away from the light streaming through his blinds.

He swallowed thickly and croaked, "Yeah. Just a bad night. I'll be in tomorrow." He tried a weak chuckle but wasn't sure he pulled it off. "You're the one always telling me I should use more of my leave. So here I am, taking a personal day."

"Okay. If that's all it is, I guess I'll see you tomorrow, then. Feel better, okay?"

Relieved she wasn't going to put up much of a fight and insist on coming to see him, he would've promised anything to get her off the phone. After hanging up, he curled into a ball and slept another couple of hours. He really did feel like death warmed over. He hadn't lied to Perretti about that, at least.

By the time one o'clock rolled around, he couldn't stay in bed any longer. He was awake now, and his thoughts wouldn't leave him alone. He stumbled to the kitchen and tossed out the coffee the machine had made that morning, dumping the grounds all over Martin's note in the trash can. After maneuvering around the small space like an arthritic ninety-year-old, so as not to jostle his aching head or be forced to make any sudden movements, he managed to prepare and keep down one whole piece of plain toast and one cup of fresh coffee. After that, however, he had no idea what to do with himself. He was feeling slightly more human, and it no longer hurt to be upright, but the oblivion he'd achieved the night before was only a fading memory.

For a brief moment, he glanced at the vodka bottle by the couch, contemplating a little hair of the dog, but the sudden cloying in his throat warned against it. He just wasn't much of a drinker, and he couldn't stay drunk forever anyway. After all, he had his incredibly boring and cheap life to get back to, sans his boyfriend… and other friends who apparently weren't.

With a piteous moan, he shuffled over and collapsed on the couch, burying his face in one of the artsy throw pillows Martin had convinced him he needed. Maybe a good day of wallowing in self-pity wasn't such a bad thing. He could try to get it out of his system, and then bounce back like little Miss Mary Sunshine, and everything would be roses again.

Or, he could be a grown-up and shake it off and cowboy up and whatever other idiom he could think of. Denial was something he was good at, obviously, since he'd lived in it for the entirety of his relationship with Martin… and possibly the entirety of his sex life.

In the end, option number one required less effort. He dragged his comforter to the couch, burrowed beneath it, and mainlined *Supernatural* on Netflix until his eyes bled, only getting up to eat, drink, and use the bathroom. He fell asleep again somewhere around episode fifteen of season one and thankfully slept through the night.

The next day he went to the office, as promised, and buried himself in his work, like nothing had happened. Bev poked her head through his door every hour or so, but when all he did was grunt at her, she'd back out again and disappear until the next time.

That night, after work, he plunked his butt on the couch with some Chinese takeout, and watched something he barely remembered on TV until it was time to go to bed and do it all over again.

Lather. Rinse. Repeat.

Martin didn't try to call again, so Adrian was free and clear to continue his little denial party throughout the rest of the workweek unmolested… despite the increasingly worried looks Bev kept giving him and her continually asking him if he was okay. The days passed in kind of a blur. He felt mostly numb and didn't do much of anything, but for some reason he was completely exhausted by the end of it.

When Friday night came around and he still hadn't heard from Martin, Adrian finally decided to break out of his cocoon just a little and start packing up Martin's things so he wouldn't have those reminders staring him in the face every time he opened a cabinet or a closet. He picked up boxes after work, and by seven o'clock, he had them all assembled in front of the TV—in order by size of course—and he was in the process of labeling them by what part of the home they went to—kitchen, bedroom, bathroom—when he froze with the Sharpie poised above a box flap.

What the hell am I doing?

He was a young, healthy gay man, barely a half hour from downtown Harrisburg, and he was spending his Friday night neatly organizing his ex-boyfriend's belongings into packing boxes.

He looked down at the Sharpie and then back up at the boxes.

He blinked.

Holy crap, I am boring.

Slowly backing away from the boxes, he set the Sharpie and packing tape on his coffee table, spun on his heel, and charged toward his bedroom.

He needed to get out.

In desperation, he flung open his closet and pulled out the pair of overpriced designer jeans Martin had insisted he buy, along with a blue-and-white striped polo that the salesclerk had said brought out the color of his eyes. After throwing them on, he grabbed his wallet, keys, and beige nylon jacket, slid into his loafers, and jogged down the stairs and out to his car.

Without thinking, he headed north to Harrisburg until he realized what a stupid idea that was. The last thing he needed was to run into Martin tonight, and it was pretty much guaranteed that Martin and his friends would be at one or all of the gay clubs/bars Harrisburg had to offer. There weren't that many.

Flipping a U-turn, Adrian headed back south. He vaguely remembered a pub in Lancaster they'd gone to once. Martin had spent the entire night making fun of the place, though Adrian hadn't seen anything wrong with it.

It took him a while, but he finally found it, and after circling the blocks nearby, he managed to snag a parking space. He had a moment of doubt, or two or three, as he locked his car and headed for the doors, but he didn't stop. Momentum and a crazed sort of desperation to prove something carried him all the way to the door and through it, and he was firmly ensconced on a barstool before he even stopped to breathe.

Though the place was small, it wasn't packed to the rafters yet, since it was still early on a Friday. He ordered a Guinness, because despite the somewhat modern touches to the tavern, it still had a pub feel, and that's what you did at a pub. You ordered Guinness, right?

He took a long pull from his glass the second the bartender plopped it down, and let the sound of laughter and conversation wash over him. He could do this. He hadn't been out by himself in a long time, and he wasn't exactly sure what he was trying to accomplish, but he could handle a night at a bar. He wasn't a complete failure at the scene. And even if he'd never exactly been a pro, he'd found a hookup or two in his time.

In fact, the more he thought about it, the more a hookup seemed precisely what the doctor ordered. He needed to get laid in the worst way, to get Martin's words out of his head.

Deliberately ignoring the fact that he hadn't sported wood once that entire week—except when he'd woken up with it one morning only to have it die shortly after in the shower—he downed what was left in his glass and signaled the bartender for another. He might not be a ten, but he wasn't a two either. He'd felt a few guys checking him out since he sat down. He should be able to find someone willing, even if he didn't get the pick of the litter, and then Martin and his *sweatpants* could go fuck themselves.

After his third glass, he was actually feeling pretty good, so when a nice-looking guy slid onto the stool next to him and smiled, Adrian smiled back.

Later, Adrian couldn't exactly remember if they'd shared any conversation, or if he'd even heard the guy's name. Everything was kind of hazy after his third beer. Somehow he ended up in a bathroom stall being groped by urgent hands, as he and whatever-his-name-was tried to lick each other's tonsils. He had his hands down the guy's pants, groping a nice-sized cock. The guy was panting and moaning words of encouragement. The whole scene should have been hot as hell, but Adrian just couldn't get into it. His dick informed him in no uncertain terms that it wasn't along for the ride.

Embarrassed and despondent, Adrian eventually had to admit defeat. Before the guy could realize what was going on and put the cap on his humiliation, Adrian dropped to his knees and blew him. He left the stall while the guy was still tucking himself in and didn't stop until he was standing outside on the street corner sucking in lungfuls of brisk autumn air and blinking away beer tears.

Before the guy could catch up to him, if he was even going to try, Adrian took off down the street at a brisk walk. He wandered around, peeking into store windows, trying really hard not to think about anything until he found another pub that had coffee and dessert on the menu. He hung out there until they closed, not making eye contact with anyone, and then took another nice long walk until he'd sobered enough to drive home.

If his goal had been to feel even shittier than before he went out, well, mission accomplished.

CHAPTER FIVE

SATURDAY MORNING dawned bleak and gray. It suited his mood to perfection. Adrian had thought he hit an all-time low spending the night hugging his toilet. Little had he known, it could get much, much worse. His attempt at fun had resulted in getting drunk on a few beers in a bar and blowing some stranger in the bathroom.

Woo-hoo.

He might have to burn the pants he wore last night after kneeling on that floor. He gave a full-body shudder as he shuffled to the bathroom.

What was I thinking?

He caught a look at his bloodshot, dull blue eyes and stringy, dirty blond hair in the mirror, winced, and quickly turned away.

He was thinking he didn't want to be the person Martin described, that's what. He was thinking he could prove Martin wrong, and then everything Martin said would be invalidated and his confidence wouldn't be flushed down the toilet.

The moving boxes glared at him in silent rebuke as he made his way past them for a cup of coffee, and again as he plopped down at his little table by the window. The table creaked under the weight of his elbows, and a piece of the peeling laminate from the top caught at his skin.

"I am not cheap. I'm frugal and earth conscious," he grumbled to the empty room. "I am not boring. I'm just not a partier."

That might have to become his daily mantra, because it wasn't helping much yet.

He needed to do something today, something spontaneous, only maybe a little closer to his tastes—a museum or a play or something. Harrisburg was a big town. He should be able to find something on a Saturday, something that didn't involve alcohol this time. He'd lose his mind if he stayed in his apartment. That was a certainty. And he could only bug Bev so many times before he wore out his welcome. If he got desperate enough, he could always go up to visit his folks in Rimersburg. Although, then he'd have to explain about Martin, and he definitely wasn't up for that.

What else could he do?

"If you were mine...."

The bass rumble from the man in the leather bar chose that moment to echo in his mind, and Adrian shivered in his T-shirt and flannel pajama bottoms.

"Pffft. As if," he said to his empty apartment.

Except his cock perked up for the first time in days, giving a little twitch, and he couldn't deny the goose bumps on his arms.

"If you were mine...."

"...a hot little power bottom like you...."

The words followed him to the kitchen as he cleaned and scrubbed away the remains of a week spent mostly moping. They followed him as he did laundry, and then as he began to remove Martin's belongings from the kitchen cabinets and living room shelves. He couldn't get them out of his head, and try as he might to deny it, to convince himself he wasn't that crazy, the seed of an idea began to germinate. By the time the sun set, he was standing in front of the mirror in his bathroom, talking to himself and trying not to hyperventilate.

"Are you really going to do this?"

He didn't bother answering. He turned on the shower, climbed in, and gave himself the scrubbing of a lifetime, making sure to spend extra time cleaning the areas sexy-power-bottom-Adrian hoped would be receiving plenty of attention in the near future.

This is crazy.

Avoiding his reflection in the mirror, he dried off with one of the fluffy designer towels Martin had picked out, which Adrian fully intended to keep. Then he dug through the plastic tub full of hair products Martin had tried and tossed aside—but Adrian couldn't bring himself to throw away—until he found something he thought might wrangle his dishwater blond mop into something stylish. He'd let it get a little longer than he liked, even before his sojourn in Mopeytown, and now the curls brushed his neck and had started flopping down on his forehead.

About a half hour later, he was reminded why he kept it short, since he had no idea what he was doing with all the goop and the hair dryer. Finally he gave up and declared it good enough. It would probably be dark in the bar.

Passing over his cheap body spray in favor of the collection of cologne bottles Martin had left behind, Adrian sniffed until he found one he liked, and applied it sparingly. Now, all he had to do was find something to wear.

His usual uniform of pressed slacks and a polo shirt or button-down was not going to send the right message… not the message he wanted to send.

Tonight he was not boring old Adrian Walnak.

He was hot. He was sexy.

He was out of his mind.

Shaking his head, he skimmed past the tiny corner of the closet Martin had left him until he reached what was left of Martin's clothes. Martin was shorter and a lot more slender than Adrian, but there might be a shirt he could wear. He finally decided on a black sateen button-down. Black might not be the new black, but Adrian didn't know what was, so he figured a classic would be his safest bet.

The shirt was tight enough to be a bit uncomfortable, but he'd seen Martin and his friends wear tighter, so he could suffer a little for fashion. Now all he had to do was find a pair of pants to go with it. There was no way anything Martin had would fit him, so he was forced to settle for a pair of worn jeans he thought made his ass look decent enough. He wanted to impress and maybe garner a little attention, not stand out like a sore thumb.

A quick glance in the mirror above the dresser and he decided he'd pass. The only real problem now was shoes. He had loafers, sneakers, and one pair of patent-leather dress shoes for special occasions. That was it. He needed to go shopping.

Of course, the tiny little voice inside his head that had been niggling at him, telling him he was being a fool, latched on to the fact that he was actually considering spending good money on something he would probably only wear once, and it cranked up the volume to eleven.

What was he doing? Who did he think he was? This was the dumbest idea he'd ever had in his life. Even if he made it all the way out there—a two-hour drive, by the way—the guy might not be there. In fact, it was highly probable he wouldn't be, and then what would Adrian do, spend another night getting drunk at a bar and blow some other guy in a bathroom only to slink home in disgrace?

He started to unbutton the shirt, fully intending to put it all away and forget he ever had this stupid idea. Except, out of the corner of his eye, he caught sight of Martin's moving boxes again, the ones *Adrian* had bought, arranged by size in a neat little row, sitting on his living room rug.

He couldn't *not* do this. And if the guy wasn't there, and no one else in the place gave him the same butterflies in his stomach, then he'd come home and take up skydiving or stock car racing or *something* to pretend he wasn't himself for however long it took to get his groove back.

Come on, Stella, let's do this.

He shoved his feet into a pair of loafers, grabbed his jacket, wallet, and keys on the way out, and left the apartment before he could change his mind again.

At the first shoe store he came to, he settled on a pair of black boots—not quite cowboy, not quite combat, and certainly not sturdy enough to hike in—in other words, completely frivolous. Tucking his loafers in the box, he wore the boots to the checkout. They were eighty dollars, and the little voice squawked as he handed over his debit card, but he didn't back down. If he never wore them again, he could always donate them and take the tax deduction. That was something at least.

Back in his car, he typed the bar's name into his GPS and headed for the highway. He was doing this. He was really doing it. He cranked up the eighties hair-band station on his satellite radio, rolled down the windows, and put his foot on the gas.

After a couple of miles, the autumn air got a little chilly, so he had to roll the windows back up, and he turned down the radio so he wouldn't lose his hearing, but even so, the little voice inside didn't make a peep until he pulled into the gravel lot in front of Deer Park—the very full gravel lot. Then maybe the little voice squeaked a little, but he shushed it.

The place was a lot busier this Saturday than it had been last time, although he probably should've expected it since it was close to ten instead of barely after six. Swallowing sudden queasiness, he parked next to a black shiny pickup truck and turned off the engine. It took him a few breaths to pull the keys out of the ignition and open the door, but he did it. His nipples hardened in protest at the brisk mountain air, but he took off his jacket anyway and tossed it in the car. All he had to do now was force his feet to take him the rest of the way. The bite in the air actually helped with that, propelling him forward before he turned into a Popsicle.

With determination, his new boots crunching satisfyingly on the gravel, he strode up to the porch and gripped the handle on the door. After one last deep breath, he dragged it open and stepped inside.

The pulsing music was a little overwhelming, and he was taken aback at the change in atmosphere. Instead of a few quiet, somewhat rough-looking parties clustered around the pool tables or hovering near the bar, the place was standing room only. The rainbow string lights were flashing to the beat of the music, and a disco ball spun above a seething crowd of dancers. The bar was nowhere near as large as Stallions, or any of the clubs he'd been to in Pittsburg or Philly, but it appeared to be the gay mecca in this little neck of the woods. He hadn't even known this many people lived around here.

He garnered a few looks as he struggled through the press of bodies to nab a recently vacated barstool, but he didn't return them, afraid to find out if they were good looks or bad ones. Jack was holding court at the far end, sporting another T-shirt with the sleeves cut off, and at the sight, Adrian finally smiled. At least something was slightly familiar. But his smile didn't last long as the sea of men ebbed and flowed around him and his confidence wavered.

Even if Mr. Tall Dark and Gorgeous were there, Adrian highly doubted the man would ever find him. That wasn't even taking into account the fact that the place was filled with much better options than Adrian.

Defensively, Adrian smoothed a hand down his shirt and lifted his chin. So what if he wasn't the best-looking guy in the place. He could grab somebody's attention. He didn't need Mr. Gorgeous's intense gaze and sexy voice. He could make do with a regular old hookup, as long as he found a bed this time instead of opting for the expediency of a bathroom while slobbering drunk. That was the reason he hadn't been able to get it up last time. He was sure of it… sort of.

"What can I get ya?"

The question, shouted at him over the music, almost made him fall off his barstool.

"Uh…."

"Hey! Welcome back. Didn't expect to see you again." Jack's smile was broad as he dropped a cocktail napkin on the bar, and Adrian returned it gratefully.

What would Martin say to his club bartenders?

"I decided to take you up on that offer of a drink," he shouted back with what he hoped was a flirty smile.

Jack's grin widened. "I wasn't the one offering to buy you the drink, if I remember correctly, but I'll get ya whatever you want now."

Adrian could feel his face flush, and he completely forgot what part he was supposed to be playing. "Yeah, uh, I guess I'll have a… uh… whisky and ginger ale?"

"Is that a question, or is that what you want?"

He could tell Jack was laughing at him a little bit, but it didn't seem mean, so he shook his head and smiled again. "It's what I want."

"Okay, then."

While Jack grabbed a bottle off the shelf behind the bar and moved to the ice bin and drink hoses, another man joined him to help with the crowd of waving arms at the far end. This man was huge, easily six and a half feet tall and just as broad as Jack, if not more so. While Adrian watched, the new guy slid a beefy arm, dusted with a healthy amount of silver hair, around Jack's back and then down to cop a handful of his behind. Jack didn't miss a beat filling Adrian's drink, even as he pushed his ass into the guy's grip before turning and striding back to where Adrian waited.

After one look at Adrian's face, Jack grinned broadly and winked. "That one's all mine, so don't get any ideas," he shouted laughingly as he handed over the drink. "He's also the sheriff, just FYI. That'll be five bucks."

Adrian tried to look as harmless as possible as he handed over the cash. Despite being a little scary, the big guy was handsome, in a papa bear kind of way, but that wasn't what Adrian was looking for.

Unfortunately, as he glanced nervously out into the sea of denim-and-leather-clad bodies, broken up here and there by glitter and bright colors, he had a bad feeling what he was looking for wasn't going to happen. The sheer desperation and bravado that had brought him this far was fading fast. He didn't belong here. He wasn't some hot little number who had guys falling all over themselves to ask him out. The competition in the bar tonight was stiff, and no way was anyone going to single him out.

He gripped his plastic cup tightly and drank half its contents in one gulp. He didn't want to get back in the car, though, not yet. That just sounded too pathetic, and his ass was still a little numb from the two-hour drive. He'd finish this drink and then switch to just ginger ale. Maybe he'd people-watch for an hour or so to sober up before he trudged his sorry ass back home.

He was halfway through his first plain ginger ale, letting the thump of the music and the buzz of dozens of conversations wash over him, when he felt a hand on his shoulder. Assuming it was someone trying to squeeze in to order from the bar, he shifted to the side to give them more room, and huddled a little more over his drink. Jack appeared in front of him a moment later, and Adrian nearly jumped out of his skin when the hand on his shoulder squeezed and a familiar voice shouted, "I'll have my usual and another for my friend here."

Sucking in a breath over the sudden tightness in his chest, Adrian licked his lips and forced his gaze upward until he met a pair of sexy hazel eyes. A dozen stupid things to say ran through his head like, "You're here!" or "Hi! Remember me? I'm the 'hot little power bottom' you'd never let come in here alone!" But thankfully he had enough restraint to keep that idiocy clamped tightly behind his lips. He'd left Adrian the Giant Dork at home… ostensibly.

Realizing he was simply staring with his mouth open, he grabbed his cup and took a drink to give him time to recover.

Shit! What would Martin say?

Honestly?

He'd probably say you're an idiot for using your ex-boyfriend as a model for flirting.

Drawing a blank, Adrian went for what he hoped was an open, come-hither smile, but what he was desperately afraid came off as a rictus instead. It couldn't have been too bad, because the proprietary hand on his shoulder slid lower to brand his back as the guy crowded closer.

"Here ya go! I'll put it on your tab."

"Thanks, Jack."

Jack's sudden reappearance nearly gave Adrian a heart attack, he was so focused on the man next to him, but if the guy noticed, he made no indication. He simply smiled and lifted his tumbler of dark amber liquid to his lips. Apparently Tall Dark and Gorgeous rated a real glass while the rest of the patrons made do with plastic.

Unable to tear his eyes away from the bob of the man's Adam's apple, Adrian clutched his cup and licked his lips.

"You gonna drink that?"

It was the humor in his deep voice that finally got through to him, and he felt himself flush all over. He downed the rest of his drink in one gulp, the ice cubes tumbling wetly against his nose, before reaching for the one the stranger had bought him.

"Thank you," Adrian said a little breathlessly, lifting the cup in salute.

The man leaned close, to be heard over the cacophony in the bar, and Adrian stopped breathing altogether. "I didn't think I'd see you again. Left the boyfriend at home this time, or is he still waiting outside?"

The warm breath on the shell of his ear sent a shiver through Adrian, and he flushed even hotter. The stranger smelled like leather and musk, with a hint of some sort of piney aftershave, and Adrian's mouth watered. Clutching his cup a little tighter, he had to swallow a couple of times before he could manage, "I don't know where the *ex*-boyfriend is. I'm here all on my lonesome this time."

"Oh really?"

The man drew back and gave Adrian another sexy smile. Adrian's skin was still tingling from the brush of the man's soft brown hair against his nose and cheek, and with the guy's scent still in his nostrils, all he could do was nod. He took a long swig from his drink to cover how flustered he was. An emotional wreck with low self-esteem was not sexy in any universe, he reminded himself.

Maybe this wasn't such a good idea.

The stranger started rubbing circles on his back, and all of Adrian's blood headed south. With his cock taking interest in life again, he forgot why he could have possibly thought this was a bad idea. He leaned back into that hand as it slid smoothly over his back, and tried to control his breathing.

"Yup, flying solo," he managed to get out with a grin that was only partially forced.

The guy's smile widened, and he lifted his own glass in salute before downing another sip, the Japanese wave tattoo on his forearm momentarily entrancing Adrian as it shifted over the muscles and veins.

"Then you won't mind if I buy you another drink?"

The words spoken close and warm into his ear again made Adrian's breath catch, but he retained enough brain cells to capture the guy's wrist as he raised it to get Jack's attention. Swallowing against the sudden frantic beating of his heart, he shook his head. Jack had forgotten and put whiskey in the one he had now. He needed to stop before he got plastered.

When the guy gave him a slight frown of disappointment, Adrian leaned close to explain. "I'll be useless if I have any more."

"Oh. Well, we wouldn't want that now, would we?"

The guy's sexy drawl almost drew a moan out of Adrian, but he stifled it. He was supposed to be playing the hot piece of ass, all confidence and boldness, not some gibbering amateur.

Having more courage of the liquid variety than anything else, Adrian sucked in a breath and yelled, "You want to get out of here?"

The guy looked nonplussed for half a breath before that sexy grin returned so quickly Adrian started to doubt what he'd seen. "Excellent idea. Let's go."

Before Adrian's body caught up to what his mouth had just suggested, the guy stepped away from the bar, grabbed Adrian by the hand, and all but dragged him through the crowd and out the door.

When the icy mountain air smacked him in the face, he regained some of his senses, and he asked, "Uh, shouldn't you pay your tab before just leaving like this?"

The guy smiled as he turned and crowded Adrian against the side of a truck in the gravel lot. "Jack knows I'm good for it."

Before Adrian could respond, the guy's thick leather-clad thigh was sliding between his legs and his intense gaze was boring down. Adrian's breath caught again as that thigh rubbed against the ache in his jeans. He clutched the man's belt and arched his hips in relief and joy that all appeared to be in working order again.

The moment the guy's soft, warm lips came down on his, Adrian gave up on acting cool and moaned into the kiss. He opened, and the man's tongue pressed inside, teasing and light but still fully in charge, and Adrian let go of the guy's belt and fisted his shirt to pull him closer still, demanding more. Taking his cue, the guy pressed his full length against Adrian, tangled his hands in Adrian's hair, and plundered his mouth until Adrian was breathless.

Panting into the heat between them, it took Adrian a moment to process that the stranger was talking to him, let alone make sense of the words.

"We should probably find somewhere a little warmer to do this."

"Wha…? Oh, yeah. I, uh, I'm not really from around here. It's a two-hour drive back for me, so, uh, your place?"

Adrian couldn't be sure in the semidarkness, but the guy's demeanor shifted. The heat in his eyes cooled just a touch as he seemed to study Adrian. Apparently Adrian's blank look in return as he tried to get the two brain cells left in his head to fire was good enough, because the guy smiled that sexy smile and stepped in close again.

"I know a place. There's a motel about ten minutes up the road," he whispered against Adrian's neck. He cupped Adrian's jaw in one of those big hands and slid the other around to grip his ass. One sucking kiss to the side of his neck, where the guy's stubble abraded his skin just so, and Adrian's last two brain cells waved good-bye to each other and floated away.

He nodded dumbly as the guy took his hand again and led him across the parking lot. "Come on. I'll drive, since you were worried you'd had too many." Halfway across the lot, he stopped suddenly enough that Adrian almost ran into him. "Do you have a jacket somewhere?"

Fumbling in his pocket for the keys, Adrian pointed with his free hand in the direction of his Honda.

"Good, go get it. I'll be back in a few seconds."

The guy was almost back to the bar before Adrian's brain caught up enough to ask, "Where are you going?"

"To get you a helmet."

"Oh. Okay."

Adrian stumbled in the direction of his car. He had the door open and was reaching across the passenger seat for his jacket when the guy's words finally sunk in.

"A helmet?"

He smacked his head on the frame of his car when he jerked himself back out of it. Hissing in pain, he clapped a hand to his head, rubbing the injured spot as he stared in burgeoning horror at the bar where the stranger had disappeared. He was still standing behind his open car door, rubbing his head, when the stranger reappeared, carrying something large and round.

When he spotted Adrian, the stranger strode quickly over, waving a green motorcycle helmet in the dim light from the bar windows. "Safety first. You ready?"

Adrian looked down at the windbreaker held loosely in his hand and then back up at the motorcycle helmet.

Was he ready?

Hell no, he wasn't ready.

But the thought of that long drive back to his empty apartment stopped him from saying the words, and he felt his head jerking up and down, more like a bobblehead than an actual nod. He hit the lock on his car, closed the door, and reached out to take the helmet in one shaking hand. The stranger didn't leave him time to take a fortifying breath before he enveloped Adrian's other hand in a warm, callused palm and began leading him across the gravel again. Despite his mind balking at what he knew was coming, Adrian found he kind of liked the hand-holding. The size and strength in the man's hand was comforting, even as he led Adrian to possible death and dismemberment.

In the dim light from a bulb mounted to a pole at the edge of the parking area, Adrian tugged on his windbreaker while the stranger unlocked a helmet from the back of a huge black-and-chrome motorcycle and fished a leather jacket out of a locked leather bag on the side. Trying to keep his heart rate within normal levels, Adrian cast a longing glance back at his safe and warm little Honda while Mr. Tall Dark and Gorgeous shrugged into his jacket, pulled on his helmet, and mounted the motorcycle. Adrian had thought the bike was big until the guy climbed onto it, but with his long, leather-clad legs and powerful frame, the man dwarfed the vehicle.

"Hop on," the guy said after walking the bike out of its parking space.

Adrian gulped and cast one last look at his car, but though the chill air and fear for his life were sobering him quickly, he still probably shouldn't drive anywhere, and his insurance rates would go through the roof if he let a stranger drive his car and something happened, not to mention giving your car keys to someone you barely knew was probably a bad idea in general.

Of course, riding off into the night on someone's motorcycle probably wasn't that bright either, but….

In for a penny….

With a slightly hysterical chuckle, he pulled his helmet on and climbed awkwardly behind the stranger. The guy looked back at Adrian with a smile.

"Ever been on a bike before?" he asked.

At Adrian's vehement headshake, the guy laughed. "Okay. Just hold on to me tight and lean in the direction I lean, and you'll be fine. I'll drive slow. You can put your hands in my jacket pockets if they get cold."

When he cranked the engine, Adrian had a moment of panic. "Wait!"

Mr. Sexy froze with his visor halfway down. "Yeah?"

"Uh, what's your name?"

The guy laughed. "Wyatt Prince. What's yours?"

"A-Adrian W-Walnak."

"Nice to meet you, Adrian," Wyatt replied wryly.

Wyatt flipped his visor the rest of the way down, and when the bike lurched forward, Adrian latched on to Wyatt's back like the thing from *Alien*. He felt rather than heard Wyatt's chuckle as they pulled out onto the road, and all Adrian could do was lower his visor, close his eyes, press his helmet-clad head to Wyatt's back, and wait for the ride to be over.

A frozen eternity of twisting mountain road later, Adrian felt the bike slow, and he opened his eyes just as Wyatt pulled into a small two-story motel. Though obviously a mom-and-pop kind of place, a little old and run-down, Adrian thought it looked like heaven. He didn't even want to consider that he'd have to get back on that bike at some point to return to his car. The possibility that Wyatt might leave him stranded here after they were done seemed almost preferable.

When Wyatt pulled into a spot next to the small building in front with "Office" on the door, Adrian slid off the bike on shaking legs.

"I'll be right back," Wyatt said after pulling off his helmet and setting it on the seat.

Adrian wasn't ready for speech yet, so he nodded, hoping his heart wasn't permanently lodged in his throat. He opted to walk the rest of the way when Wyatt returned with the key—an actual key, not a keycard. With a chuckle, Wyatt popped the kickstand up and walked the bike to a parking spot near the stairs to the second level. He then led the way up to number 203, unlocked the door, and stepped inside.

CHAPTER SIX

SHIVERING WITH cold, totally keyed up on adrenaline from his motorcycle ride of death, and fearing he would chicken out any second if he gave himself time to think, Adrian rushed Wyatt the moment the door closed. He tossed his helmet in the chair by the door, fisted Wyatt's jacket collar, and dragged Wyatt down for a desperate kiss. Unfortunately he kind of missed, because Wyatt was really tall, and Adrian closed his eyes too soon, and he ended up bashing his nose into Wyatt's upper lip and teeth.

"Ouch." Wyatt chuckled before sucking on the slight welling of blood from a split in his lip.

"Sorry," Adrian gasped, rubbing the bridge of his nose.

"No problem."

Wyatt appeared unfazed, so Adrian renewed his advance. This time their lips met without incident, and Adrian plunged his tongue into the wet heat of Wyatt's mouth. The man tasted of bourbon and a salty sweetness Adrian couldn't get enough of. Still running on pure bravado and shaking with adrenaline, he swung Wyatt around and tried to muscle him up against the door, like he'd seen in movies. But the reality of moving someone who, although seemingly willing, wasn't aware of your plan—and Adrian's slightly inebriated and jittery clumsiness—ended with Adrian tripping on his own feet, knocking his knee into the inside of Wyatt's, and then Wyatt bonking his head on the door when he lost his balance and fell against it.

"Oh God, I'm so sorry," Adrian managed as he untangled his limbs and got both of them mostly upright again.

Wyatt just gave him another chuckle as he rubbed his head for a second before fisting a hand in Adrian's windbreaker and dragging him forward. "No problem."

Wyatt took over the kiss this time, carefully drawing Adrian in as he leaned back against the door to put them closer in height. While their tongues tangled and breathless moans mingled, he felt Wyatt unzip his windbreaker and push it off his shoulders. Once free, Adrian did the same for Wyatt's leather jacket, dropping it on the floor. As Wyatt's big hands explored his back and sides, Adrian pulled Wyatt's black T-shirt out of his leather pants and pushed it up his chest, sliding the heels of his palms along the trail of dark hair that ran up the middle of his six-pack.

So fucking gorgeous.

"Ouch, ouch, ouch!" Wyatt hissed, jerking back.

Adrian stared down in horror at his elastic metal watchband now firmly caught in Wyatt's chest hair.

"Oh, God. Oh, God. I'm sorry. I'm sorry. Just let me…."

Adrian tried to move his hand, but Wyatt only hissed louder. Starting to panic, his hands shaking even worse, Adrian searched the room for help. He wasn't sure what he thought he'd find in a cheap hotel room, but he was past thinking clearly and on his way to wishing a hole would open up under his feet and swallow him up.

"Don't move." Wyatt's deep voice was startlingly calm, and Adrian froze. "Let me take care of it."

Adrian swallowed and reluctantly met Wyatt's gaze, but other than a slight pained pinch between his eyebrows, Wyatt was smiling, and his eyes sparkled with humor.

"Okay."

Holding as still as possible, Adrian watched while Wyatt stretched the watchband as far open as it would go, releasing his chest hair as Wyatt pulled it off Adrian's wrist and tossed it on the little table next to them.

"There we go. Crisis averted, and other than you needing to pull a few of my chest hairs out of the band, no harm done."

Wyatt's voice was just as warm and soothing as before, but Adrian was done. Three strikes were enough for him to get the message. Plus, his partial erection had evaporated along with what little faux confidence he'd had.

What did he think he was doing?

Wyatt's smile fell away, and his brows knitted in concern as Adrian moved away from him, but Adrian ignored him and kept going until he'd put as much space between them as the tiny room would allow.

With his back turned to Wyatt, Adrian slumped his shoulders and closed his eyes.

"I'm sorry," he said without turning around. "This isn't going to work."

"What?"

"This. Tonight. I think I should probably just head home."

"Why?"

The honest confusion in Wyatt's voice made Adrian turn and stare at him in disbelief.

"Why? Have you not been here the last five minutes? I mean, I've managed to bash you in the mouth, give you a concussion, and rip out half your chest hair in the time it takes most people to brush their teeth. Seriously, at the rate I'm going, you'll be in the hospital before we even get naked."

Wyatt chuckled, but that only made Adrian feel worse.

"I'm serious. I can't believe you didn't run after the first injury."

Adrian was shaking because he was on the verge of losing it in front of a virtual stranger. He could feel the pressure of pent-up emotions pressing against the back of his eyes, and he bit his lip to keep it from trembling like the rest of him. He watched warily as Wyatt pushed himself off the door and slowly approached.

"It's no big deal, Adrian, really. We got a little carried away. That's not a bad thing. If we slow down a little, I'm sure I can manage to get us naked without further injury. Trust me."

That sexy smirk was back, and his eyes were hot and filled with a confidence Adrian desperately wished for in himself, but it wasn't there.

"It's not just that... I—you don't understand. I don't know what you see when you look at me, but trust me, I'm not that guy. If I stay, you're only going to be disappointed, and I don't think I can handle that right now."

Wyatt stopped a few feet away from him and frowned. "I don't understand."

"I know."

Adrian blew out a breath and raked a hand through his hair, only then realizing what the helmet had done to his overproduced mop. He studiously ignored the mirror on top of the dresser across from the bed and curled in on himself a little more. "Look. It's been a shitty week. I got told some things about myself that hurt... a lot... and I just wanted to prove him wrong. I wanted to prove it to myself more than anything. Then I remembered that day at the bar. You said... you know, what you said to me, and I thought I could be that guy, just for one night. I thought I could pretend to be someone sexy and exciting. But fantasy can only take you so far. Tomorrow—or, hell, an hour from now—you'll know that for a fact, and I'm pretty sure I won't be able to handle your disappointment when you find out I'm not that guy."

With as much dignity as he could manage, Adrian sucked in a breath through the constriction in his throat, squared his shoulders, and stepped around Wyatt to retrieve his jacket from the floor and slide his watch back on—stray dark, wiry chest hairs and all.

"Hey, wait," Wyatt said gently as he came up behind Adrian.

"Look. I'm sorry. I don't mean to ruin your night. I'll pay for the room, and I'd appreciate a lift back to my car, if it's not too much to ask."

Adrian shivered for a different reason as a pair of big warm hands came to rest on his shoulders. "Just wait a second, okay? First off, what makes you so sure I'm going to be disappointed?"

Adrian bit his lip and shook his head. The dam inside him was on the verge of breaking, and he did *not* want to be anywhere anyone could see him when it did.

The pressure on his shoulders increased as Wyatt turned him around. Adrian couldn't lift his gaze to meet Wyatt's, so he spoke to Wyatt's chest.

"I'm not this guy. I don't go to bars and pick up strange sexy men for a hookup. Well, I mean, I *did*, but it isn't something I've done regularly… or ever, really. In a little while, you would've figured that out."

"Okay. So you don't do hookups often. Why does that guarantee I'm going to be disappointed? If I wanted a professional, I'd go hire one, wouldn't I?"

"It's not just that I'm not a professional." Adrian chuckled bitterly. "I'm *really* not a professional."

"Are you trying to tell me you're a virgin?"

The question shocked him so much, Adrian couldn't help but look up, and the expression on Wyatt's face startled a laugh out of him. "No! No, nothing like that."

After blowing out a breath, Wyatt gave him a sheepish smile, but the humor died with Wyatt's next words. "Then what?"

With a sigh of resignation, Adrian pulled away from him and stepped closer to the door. Without looking at Wyatt, he mumbled, "I'm a lousy lay, okay? You get it now?"

Adrian still didn't want to believe the words, but if his performance so far tonight was any indication, he certainly wouldn't be disproving them on this little outing. He just wanted to go home and lick his wounds in private, but then he felt Wyatt's hands return to his shoulders, urging him to turn around again.

When Adrian was facing him, Wyatt moved forward until Adrian's back was pressed against the door. He stepped into Adrian's space and cupped a hand under his chin until Adrian met his gentle hazel eyes.

"Who says?" Wyatt asked into the small space between them.

"My ex… and he should know."

Wyatt snorted derisively. "I doubt it."

Adrian didn't move as Wyatt stepped even closer and gave him a soft peck on the lips. "I firmly believe you get out of sex only what you're willing to put into it." He whispered this against Adrian's lips before brushing a kiss along Adrian's jaw. "And," he whispered hotly against Adrian's neck, "I can promise you, Adrian, the only possible way you could disappoint me tonight is if you left this room."

Adrian's breath caught as Wyatt sucked his earlobe into his hot mouth and nibbled it. When Wyatt slid his other hand around Adrian's back and cupped his ass, drawing him closer to all that heat and hardness, Adrian moaned. His cock began to fill again, and all the reasons why he shouldn't be doing this seemed on the verge of evaporating.

"Let me prove to you how wrong he is," Wyatt murmured with drugging sweetness as he combed his fingers through Adrian's hair and bent to capture his lips in another gentle kiss.

"You think you can?" Adrian asked dazedly, even as Wyatt swung him around and maneuvered him toward the bed.

Wyatt chuckled as he slid Adrian's jacket off his shoulders again. "Oh honey, I know I can."

And because Adrian wanted to believe him so badly, he made no move to stop Wyatt as he held Adrian's gaze and carefully removed Adrian's watch, setting it safely on the small wall-anchored nightstand by the bed.

"We'll just leave this right here, out of harm's way," Wyatt said with another smile.

Adrian didn't have time to flush in embarrassment, because Wyatt captured his mouth in a hot, wet kiss as he started on the buttons of Adrian's borrowed black sateen shirt.

Adrian surrendered to the inevitable. There was no way he'd be able to walk out on this gorgeous and surprisingly sweet man now. His dick would never forgive him. He sent up a silent prayer that if Wyatt was wrong, and he really was a lousy lay, at least Wyatt would be a good enough liar to spare Adrian's fragile little ego. Then he set to work on

Wyatt's belt buckle, careful not to pinch or pull or do any other kind of damage this time around.

Wyatt made a sexy rumbling sound when Adrian slid his hands inside the waistband of his leather pants and up under Wyatt's T-shirt to the warm, smooth skin beneath. Adrian had been looking to get laid, so he hadn't bothered with a T-shirt under the black sateen, and Wyatt let out another rumble of what Adrian hoped was appreciation as he pulled Adrian's shirt open.

"Very sexy," Wyatt murmured as he trailed his knuckles from Adrian's neck down to his navel, the slow drag setting Adrian's body on fire.

He liked slow. He could definitely get on board with slow.

While Adrian knew he wasn't the prime specimen of manflesh the man in front of him was, the look in Wyatt's eyes made him almost believe he could be. Wyatt's gaze was focused on him with an intensity and heat Adrian had never experienced before in a lover, and despite his fears, it made him feel like he could be that guy.

Surrendering to the fantasy, he tugged until Wyatt let go long enough for him to drag Wyatt's T-shirt over his head and toss it aside. He stepped close, pressing their chests together, rubbing his nipples against Wyatt's chest hair as he pushed his face into Wyatt's neck. Wyatt's scent was as intoxicating as before, and the salty-sweet taste of his skin was addicting. Gripping the hard muscles of Wyatt's back in both hands, Adrian rubbed and licked and sucked on the man's neck and collarbones. He kissed the hollow of his throat and traced the letters tattooed across Wyatt's skin with his tongue until he realized he was acting like a cat in heat while Wyatt simply cradled his head and rumbled sounds of encouragement.

Drawing back in embarrassment, Adrian panted, "Sorry. I got a little carried away."

Wyatt just gave him a lazy smile, his hazel gaze heavy-lidded but still intense. "Don't apologize. We have all night."

Adrian couldn't help the grimace that crossed his face, and he hung his head. "Yeah, but I'm sure me rubbing myself all over you wasn't exactly what you had in mind."

"What I had in mind was a hot night with a sexy man, nothing more specific than that." Wyatt stepped close again, and Adrian didn't try to move away. After another drugging kiss, Wyatt whispered, "But I'll let you in on a little secret about me. I get off on seeing my lovers get off. If my partner is enjoying himself, that's a *huge* turn-on for me." He took

Adrian's hand and pressed it to the hardness parting the zipper of his leather pants. "See?" Wyatt ground his erection into Adrian's palm. "Do what you enjoy, Adrian, and I promise you I'll be enjoying it right along with you. I'm in no hurry. You have my word."

Are you even real?

Keeping that thought to himself, along with the awed, puppy dog eyes he wanted to give the man, Adrian played it cool with a sexy smirk, getting into his role, now that he'd apparently been given permission to play. This was a once-in-a-lifetime opportunity here. He had a model-gorgeous, close to six-and-a-half-foot hunk not only allowing him but *encouraging* him to do as he wanted, a man who actually seemed to think Adrian wasn't a complete waste of time. Now all he had to do was not choke.

After giving the impressive erection beneath his hand another squeeze, Adrian took a quiet breath for courage and set to work unwrapping his gift like he knew what he was doing. He pulled the zipper down the rest of the way, parting the leather slowly. He slid his hands inside the waistband and spread his fingers to grab hold of Wyatt's hips and ass, squeezing a few healthy handfuls before pushing the leather down to his thighs.

Adrian licked his lips at the impressive bulge in Wyatt's black boxer briefs. The thin fabric left little to the imagination, and Adrian could feel the heat against his cheek as he bent to shove Wyatt's pants farther down.

"We're going to have to take my boots off before my pants will come off. You want to help me with that," Wyatt rumbled.

"Huh? Oh, yeah."

Adrian dropped to his knees like that's what he'd planned to do all along, but his fingers didn't seem to want to work right on the laces.

Double knots? Why did it have to be double knots?

The boots looked like a combination between combat and work boots. The laces were black and hard to see in the shadow Wyatt cast from the overhead light. Adrian didn't work well under pressure. The longer he took at this the more anxious he got.

Don't choke. Don't choke.

Then Wyatt's big warm hand rested on Adrian's head, and he threaded his fingers through Adrian's hair, petting and massaging his scalp, and Adrian relaxed. He pressed his cheek to Wyatt's erection and rubbed a little, breathing the man in, and Wyatt's pleased rumble gave him courage.

"Why don't you sit on the bed?" Adrian suggested.

"Excellent idea."

As awkward as Adrian shuffling around on his knees while Wyatt kind of waddled to get to the bed should've been, Wyatt seemed as unfazed as ever. His smile remained undimmed and his eyes still sparkled with heat and good humor. Adrian envied him that, but he wasn't going to waste time dwelling on it. He could finally see the laces well enough to get them undone, and he was only a few articles of clothing away from getting Wyatt naked.

On the bed, Wyatt propped himself on his elbows and watched Adrian strip off both boots and socks before he finally got the leather pants the rest of the way off.

Hallelujah.

"I kinda like being stripped like this. Makes me feel special," Wyatt drawled as Adrian climbed back to his feet. The man's smile was teasing, but his gaze was purely predatory, and Adrian's cock twitched, already straining the confines of his tight jeans.

"Come here. It's my turn," Wyatt commanded as he reached for Adrian's belt.

Before Adrian knew what was happening, Wyatt hauled him down onto the bed by his belt and then flipped him onto his back. He slid off the bed and made embarrassingly short work of Adrian's boots, socks, and jeans.

Now only in his underwear, Adrian scuttled to the center of the queen-size bed and lifted his arms as Wyatt draped himself on top of him. Adrian moaned and writhed against Wyatt. He wanted to touch the man everywhere at once. Every place on that gorgeous body begged to be handled. Since Wyatt had told him to do what he wanted, that's exactly what he did. He slid his palms along Wyatt's ribs, around his waist, and plunged them inside Wyatt's boxer briefs, gripping the smooth hard globes of his ass. He rubbed his calves along the backs of Wyatt's lightly furred legs and thrust his cock against the hard planes of Wyatt's belly, regretting the fact that his boxers were still in the way. And despite the fact that Wyatt probably thought he'd taken an octopus to bed, the man didn't appear to mind. He propped his elbows on either side of Adrian's head and continued to kiss Adrian breathless while Adrian writhed and grappled with his body.

Wyatt did take charge long enough to relieve them both of their underwear, since Adrian was too doped up on horniness to want to lose contact long enough to accomplish that. But naked was so much better. With no barrier between them, Adrian's cock found a happy valley between Wyatt's hip and groin as his hands explored the column of Wyatt's neck, broad shoulders, the inked designs covering his thick arms, and every other part of the man he could reach. The kissing went on and on until Adrian was pretty sure his face and neck would be beet red with stubble burn tomorrow, but he didn't care.

"Tell me what you want, Adrian." Wyatt's breathless demand brought Adrian back from his lust-induced fog.

"I, uh…."

"Tell me," Wyatt repeated in Adrian's ear as he ground his thick cock into Adrian's thigh. "You want to come on me like this? You want me to suck you? You want me to fuck you? Tell me."

All of those options seemed like pretty damned good ideas at that moment, but the memory of Wyatt calling him a sexy little power bottom that first night suddenly popped into his head and wouldn't be denied. Adrian wanted that. He wanted to be that guy—admired, desired, but still in control of his own pleasure.

"Fuck me," Adrian panted.

Wyatt drew back until Adrian met his gaze. "You sure?"

"Hell yeah. Fuck me."

The grin that spread across Wyatt's face would have melted stone, but Adrian only got to bask in it for a few seconds before Wyatt rolled off him and started fumbling with something on the floor. Wyatt lifted a wallet in the air a moment later and pulled a couple condoms and a few packets of lube from inside. He tossed them on the bed, dropped his wallet over the side, and then crawled over to Adrian and straddled his hips. With that grin still splitting his face, Wyatt tore open a packet of lube and squeezed some into his palm. He wrapped both their cocks in his big fist and began pumping.

Adrian was going to make some sort of wisecrack about Wyatt coming prepared, but all he managed was a gasped "Ngh" as his eyes rolled back in his head and he flexed his hips in rhythm with Wyatt's fist. In an embarrassingly short period of time, he could feel his orgasm building. He wanted to come badly, but not like this.

"I'm going to lose it if you keep that up," Adrian warned.

"You mean we might have to start all over again? That would be terrible."

Adrian managed a breathy chuckle that ended in a moan as Wyatt squeezed just that little bit more, but two of his brain cells were still capable of firing, and they cried, "Lube."

"Lube?"

Only then realizing he'd said the word out loud, Adrian put a hand over Wyatt's to stop him long enough to form some more words. "We have a limited amount, and it's been a while since I…."

He left the sentence hanging, hoping Wyatt could fill in the blank.

"Gotcha," Wyatt said as he released their cocks. He draped himself full-length on top of Adrian again, braced an elbow by his ear, and combed his nonlubed hand through Adrian's hair. He kissed Adrian deeply, giving him some time to cool down before he drew back again and grinned. "Well, waste not, want not."

Before Adrian knew what was happening, Wyatt flipped him over on his belly and pulled him up to his hands and knees. Expecting to hear the tearing of lube and condom packets any second, Adrian was surprised when Wyatt draped himself over Adrian's back and kissed and nibbled his neck before starting a slow slide down his spine. The sudden jolt of exhilaration at Wyatt manhandling him so easily morphed in to pure hedonistic languor as the hairs on Wyatt's chest teased Adrian's skin and the man's big hands caressed his flanks and his ass. He wanted to purr as Wyatt's lips and tongue painted a slow, wet path along his vertebrae, and he was nearly shaking by the time he felt the warm trickle of saliva down his crack.

Completely unashamed and glorying in the role he'd chosen to play, Adrian buried his face in his crossed arms on the mattress, spread his legs wider, and lifted his ass higher. Wyatt rewarded him with a light bite to his left asscheek and the slide of a warm, calloused thumb through the slick of saliva around his rim. The bite was followed by a sucking kiss over the mark while Wyatt's thumb massaged his opening teasingly. Though Adrian felt decadent and pampered, part of him couldn't quite believe he was doing this, allowing himself to be this open and vulnerable with a complete stranger. But that was before Wyatt replaced his thumb with his tongue. At that point, all bets were off, and Adrian surrendered. He could be aghast at himself tomorrow.

"Oh God," he moaned into his crossed arms as he pushed back against Wyatt's tongue.

Wyatt chuckled and the vibration forced another bead of precome from Adrian's throbbing cock. He didn't want Wyatt to stop, ever, but he really was going to come too soon if Wyatt didn't get on with the show.

"Fuck me," he croaked a little more harshly than he'd intended, arching his back to emphasize his point. Apparently, two-word sentences were all he was capable of at the moment.

Wyatt drew back with another breathless chuckle. "As you wish."

Wyatt's thumb was back at his entrance, rubbing and pushing in to the first knuckle even as Adrian heard another packet torn open and felt a squeeze of lube spread around and in his hole.

Thank God for multitaskers.

The crinkle of what Adrian hoped was the condom wrapper this time was followed by Wyatt switching to penetrating him with a finger. More lube followed, that finger slicking him deeper inside, and then finally Wyatt withdrew, and Adrian felt the blunt head of the man's sheathed cock, hot and slick at his entrance. Wyatt simply held his cockhead there, and Adrian got the hint. It was his turn to do a little work. That was only fair.

With a long exhale, Adrian pushed back until Wyatt's thick cockhead breached his rim. They both let out a relieved groan before Adrian continued to push until Wyatt's trimmed bush tickled Adrian's stretched and sensitive skin. With almost a purr, Wyatt draped himself over Adrian's back like a warm, fuzzy blanket as Adrian began to move, rolling his hips experimentally and changing his body's angle until Wyatt's cock rubbed on all the right places. Bracing a hand against the wall-mounted headboard, Adrian set a slow pace to start. Martin had always wanted to bottom, so Adrian hadn't been fucked since his previous boyfriend two years ago. His body needed a little time to remember, and, *gawd*, did that slow slide feel fantastic.

While Adrian concentrated on his rhythm, Wyatt kept himself busy doing other things. He tweaked and rolled Adrian's nipples. He petted and caressed Adrian's flanks. He kissed and nibbled and sucked everywhere he could reach along Adrian's neck and shoulders, all the while murmuring words of encouragement broken by groans of pleasure panted hotly against Adrian's skin.

They were both slick with sweat, and Adrian didn't even try to hold back the expletives pouring out of his mouth. His thighs ached and his dick throbbed with every drag across his prostate, but one of his thighs was threatening to cramp on him, so he couldn't keep this up much longer.

"Fuck me," Adrian demanded breathlessly, reaching for his cock.

As instructed, Wyatt took over. He braced one big hand on Adrian's shoulder, gripped Adrian's hip in the other, and started to thrust, while Adrian fisted his cock.

"Harder. I want to feel you," he grunted, and Wyatt took him at his word.

Adrian's bicep strained in protest as he braced it against the headboard for Wyatt's pounding. Their grunts and the slap of their bodies echoed off the sparsely decorated cream walls and popcorn ceiling, along with the creaking of the bed. Adrian cried out as his vision went white, and Wyatt rode him through his orgasm before clamping down hard on Adrian's shoulder and hip and moaning out his own release.

As soon as Wyatt pulled out, Adrian collapsed and kicked out his cramping leg. Wyatt dropped down beside him, his chest heaving and his limbs tangled with Adrian's, and Adrian chuckled between gasps. For once not caring how stupid he looked, he grinned like a fool, elated like he'd solved world hunger instead of just getting laid. He might gain a little perspective again after the orgasm high faded, but he was going to enjoy this feeling while it lasted. He hadn't fucked it up.

"Your ex is an idiot," Wyatt said a little while later. He climbed off the bed and headed for the bathroom.

"I'd like to think so," Adrian replied as he heard water splash in the sink.

He rolled toward the back of the room and watched in lazy appreciation as Wyatt strode out. The condom was gone, and the man was absolutely breathtaking as he sauntered across the ugly green mottled motel carpet, appearing completely at ease with his nudity.

Of course, what did he have to be ashamed of?

"You should," Wyatt said before he tossed Adrian a warm, damp washcloth.

While Adrian wiped down a little, Wyatt yawned broadly and climbed under the ugly motel bedspread. Adrian should've gone to the bathroom and done more than a cursory wipedown, but he was lazy with pleasure, his body still humming. His jaw cracked on a yawn, and he simply tossed the washcloth aside and climbed under the covers.

Wyatt moved to spoon him almost immediately, and Adrian fell asleep surrounded by warm muscle and bone, more content sleeping next to a stranger in a run-down roadside motel than he'd been in his own bed for a very long time.

Wyatt woke Adrian twice more in the night. The first time was to Wyatt's hand wrapping around his semihard dick, tugging teasingly on it and fondling his balls as Wyatt's other hand rubbed his belly and tweaked his nipples. Adrian moaned and arched against him, grinding Wyatt's hard cock against his ass. After a lot of teasing and touching, Wyatt rolled Adrian to face him, wrapped both their cocks in his fist, and jerked them until they came.

The second time, Adrian decided to take Wyatt's "waste not, want not" philosophy to heart. They still had one more condom and a packet of lube, not counting what Adrian had in his own wallet, and even though his ass was a little sore and would be worse tomorrow, Adrian managed to convince Wyatt that fucking him again was the best usage of them.

Though Wyatt showed a pleasing amount of concern for Adrian's welfare, he gave up and gave in without much of a fight. Adrian was on his back with his legs over Wyatt's shoulders in no time, panting out breathless demands as Wyatt pounded him into the mattress. He came with a cry and a burst of stars behind his eyelids, and Wyatt followed shortly thereafter with a low groan and a panted "Fuck that was good," before he pulled out and collapsed beside Adrian again.

This time, no matter how tired he was, Adrian couldn't get back under the covers without hosing off. Three rounds of sex had left his legs like jelly, but he was covered in lube, sweat, and come, and a washcloth was not going to cut it. He had to prop himself against the formed plastic wall of the shower while the spray beat down on him. He was slightly disappointed Wyatt didn't decide to climb in with him, but if he were being completely honest with himself, he didn't have anything left for fun in the shower. He wasn't in his twenties anymore. In fact, even in his twenties he couldn't remember having sex three times in a night.

Deliberately dragging his exhausted brain away from thoughts of his past exploits, or lack thereof, Adrian shut off the water, rubbed himself down with one of the two tiny, stiff white towels the motel provided, and stumbled back to the bed.

Wyatt was snoring lightly when Adrian got there. He'd straightened out the mess they'd made of the blankets and sheets, and with a sigh of contentment, Adrian sank gratefully onto the slightly hard, lumpy mattress and bleached sheets. His lips curved when Wyatt wrapped his arms around him and pulled Adrian against his chest again. He didn't think Wyatt was even aware he'd done it.

CHAPTER SEVEN

MORNING DAWNED bright and clear, if the shaft of light penetrating the gap between the blinds and the wall was any indication. Wyatt cringed away from it, pulling the blanket higher to block it out. It had been a very long time since he'd stayed up most of the night fucking, and his body was reminding him he wasn't twenty-two anymore. Hell, he wasn't even thirty-two anymore.

Unfortunately he needed coffee, and since there didn't appear to be any hiding under his pillow, he was going to have to get up… that and he needed to take a leak. With regret, he stretched out some of his tired muscles and carefully drew the blanket away from his face. If he got up slowly enough, maybe he wouldn't wake Adrian, and he could climb back into the warm cocoon afterward. Except Adrian was already awake when Wyatt's eyes cleared enough to get a good look at him in the dim light. Adrian lay still as a stone, staring up at the popcorn ceiling like it held the answers to life. Wyatt might have thought he was dead if not for the steady rise and fall of his chest and the occasional blink.

"Hey." His voice was gruff with sleep, and he cleared his throat.

"Hey."

"Whatcha doing?"

"Staring at the ceiling."

Wyatt smiled. Adrian's self-deprecating and dry sense of humor was something Wyatt wished he had time to get used to.

"Is something wrong?"

"Why would you say that?"

Since Adrian hadn't stopped drilling holes in the ceiling with his eyes, and his voice sounded like it might crack at any second, the answer was pretty obvious. He decided to wait Adrian out. It didn't take long before Adrian glanced in his direction and smiled sheepishly.

"Sorry. I guess I'm having a moment. You don't need me to unload on you."

With a shrug, Wyatt stretched and propped himself on an elbow. His bathroom break could wait a few more minutes.

"I'm the one who asked, remember?"

Adrian smiled that sweet, embarrassed smile of his that did funny things to Wyatt's insides.

"Last night was really good."

Wyatt couldn't help the cocky grin that split his face. Last night had been really good. But Adrian wasn't smiling anymore.

"Uh. I'd say thank you, but you don't seem all that happy about it."

"No. I mean, yes. I am. Happy about it, that is. But you don't understand. It was really, *really* good, like the-best-sex-I've-ever-had-in-my-life good. You deserve a medal, really."

Wyatt almost laughed, but the distress in Adrian's tone smothered the urge. "And that's a bad thing?"

Adrian groaned and fixed his gaze on the ceiling again. "It is when I'm thirty-two years old and I didn't realize sex could be like that until just last night…. I mean, truth be told, I never understood what all the fuss was about. It felt good, but so did jerking off, you know?" Adrian grimaced as he searched Wyatt's face for a moment before turning away again. "Actually, you probably don't know. You were probably phenomenal in the sack from day one. But me, I'm feeling like I've been doing it wrong all these years, that my ex was right, and I really did suck at it. And if he was right about that, he was probably right about everything else he said, and I'm—"

Wyatt stopped him with a kiss. Adrian sounded like he was about to hyperventilate, and that was not how he wanted their lovely night together to end. He'd never left a lover unhappy, and he certainly didn't intend to break that streak with sweet Adrian.

At first Adrian tensed beneath his kiss. Wyatt slid across the small space left between them, pressed his thigh between Adrian's, and draped himself halfway across Adrian's chest. He sucked and nibbled on Adrian's lips until the man melted beneath him and the tension left his body.

He drew back, tugging gently on Adrian's swollen bottom lip before letting it go and gazing into Adrian's slightly glazed blue eyes. "I don't know what you did before, but I speak from experience when I say you were fantastic last night."

"You did most of the work."

Adrian's slightly breathless rejoinder was accompanied by a flush to his cheeks that had nothing to do with sex, and Wyatt shook his head. "That's not true. I distinctly remember us having a discussion before we really got started. I told you what I like from a partner, and you delivered. That's what's called doing it right." He smiled affectionately at Adrian and brushed a lock of dark blond hair off his forehead. "We obviously don't know each other that well, but I usually have a pretty good read on a person after I've been naked with them." He grinned and waggled his eyebrows until Adrian laughed. "And I'm pretty sure if that ex of yours had told you what he wanted, you would've given it to him. Am I right?"

At Adrian's begrudging nod, he continued, "And I don't know about you, but I believe if I don't tell a lover what I want, that's my fault, not his." He slid the rest of the way on top of Adrian. Straddling Adrian's hips, he gripped Adrian's wrists and drew them up until he had them pinned to the pillow above his head. "As I told you last night," he whispered against Adrian's lips between plucking kisses, "I like to please my partner." Another kiss. "I get off when they do." He kissed along Adrian's jaw and down to his neck, his lips dragging across the light stubble he could barely see glinting in the small shaft of light from behind the curtains. "If they want to be tied up, or held down, rubbed in oil while scented candles and soft ocean sounds fill the air, pampered in a bubble bath, or pounded into the mattress until they scream my name, I'm pretty much up for anything. All they have to do is tell me… and that's what I like."

Wyatt found where he'd left a slight hickey last night and sucked on it again until Adrian gasped and shifted beneath him. When he lifted his gaze to Adrian's, he found the man watching him with so much longing and heat, his cock throbbed painfully, ordering him to forget his exhaustion and any lingering aches and pains and repeat last night, hour for hour. But he managed to rein in his libido with a little dose of reality. He had obligations elsewhere, he still had a full bladder, and he didn't want to prolong their parting long enough for things to get awkward. With a steadying breath, he released Adrian's wrists, sat back on his heels, and tried to remember where his argument had left off.

"I'm gonna try to be more generous here than I think your asshole ex deserves, but it could be your ex just assumed you couldn't give him what he wanted, or maybe what you like and what he likes aren't the same thing. But that's on him for not being up-front about it and blaming you for it. And as for the rest of your sexual experiences, maybe—" He stopped himself before he could say *maybe you just hadn't found the right guy yet*, as that would've opened himself up to a conversation he did not want to have. "—maybe you haven't enjoyed it as much because you've been too busy worrying about what your lovers want."

"Maybe."

The heat slowly faded from Adrian's eyes the more Wyatt spoke, and Wyatt was sorry to see it go. Studiously ignoring Adrian's partial erection, nestled close to his own against Adrian's belly, Wyatt shifted off him and swung his legs over the side of the bed.

"Be back in a few," he said as casually as he could muster.

He could feel Adrian's gaze on him as he walked to the bathroom, but he didn't turn around. Closing the door behind him, Wyatt rested against the cold metal door until his erection flagged enough to let him take a leak. Afterward he hopped in the shower for a quick rinse and dried off with one of the two skimpy white towels on the bar. He was still scrubbing it through his damp hair when he stepped back into the main room. Adrian was already dressed and sitting at the small round table at the front of the room, with his hands wrapped around a steaming paper cup.

"I left some in the pot for you," Adrian said quietly, pointing to the ridiculously small coffeepot on the dresser by the television.

The smile he gave Wyatt was sheepish, and he didn't meet Wyatt's gaze.

"Thanks," he replied gruffly.

He hated this part. He'd met someone sexy and interesting, someone he could probably connect with more than just superficially, and because of the mess his life was, he'd have to walk away.

After pulling on his clothes, he made use of the other paper cup by the coffee machine and sipped at the bitter brew while the silence in the room became oppressive.

"Look, I—"

"I'm sorry, but I—"

They both started at the same time and ended up sharing a chuckle.

"You go ahead," Wyatt said.

"I just wanted to apologize for getting all weird on you this morning, that's all. I know that's not what you signed up for."

"I don't mind. I appreciated the compliment, not only on my skills in bed, but that you felt comfortable enough to talk to me."

Adrian smiled, and Wyatt let out a relieved breath as the heaviness dissipated from the room. He would have liked to spend a little more time nursing that smile back to full health, but he was running late as it was.

"Look, I'm sorry I can't hang out any longer, but I promised to help a friend with a project today, and I'm already late. If I'm going to take you back to your car, we're going to need to leave soon."

"Oh… yeah sure, no problem. Just let me get my shoes and we can go."

While Adrian pulled on and laced his boots, Wyatt did the same, and then there was nothing left but to collect their jackets and helmets and head out the door.

"I can go check us out if you want," Adrian offered when they reached Wyatt's bike, but Wyatt shook his head.

"I'll do it. You can wait here."

"But the least I can do is pay my half of the room. I don't have much cash on me, but I can have him put half on my card."

"It's probably best if we don't. This area is pretty accepting, as these places go, but I think the old guy behind the counter might feel a little uncomfortable if you go in there offering to split a single room with me." To dispel the awkwardness money talk always created, Wyatt grabbed the front of Adrian's windbreaker and dragged him in for a kiss. "I paid up front, anyway, so all I have to do is drop off the key."

"Oh. Okay."

He smirked at the dazed smile Adrian gave him and sauntered off to the office. The motel was old enough it had actual keys instead of key cards, and Wyatt handed it over to the old guy behind the counter. He'd had to pay extra and in advance because he didn't have a credit card.

The ride back to Deer Park went a lot faster than Wyatt would've liked. Adrian clung to him like a monkey, exactly like he had the night before, and as soon as Adrian stepped off the bike, the cool, early autumn mountain air rushed in, chilling his back. Given the thickness of his leather jacket, Wyatt knew it was more a symbolic chill than an actual one, and he sighed in regret.

Adrian stepped up next to him, pulled off his helmet, and held it up. "Do I give this to you or leave it with someone?"

Lifting his visor, Wyatt said, "They're closed up now, but you can leave it around the side of the building, and I'll let Jack know where it is."

"Okay."

Wyatt waited until he came back, and Adrian bit his lip and searched Wyatt's face. After a moment, Adrian cleared his throat. "Listen, I meant what I said. I really had a good time last night, and… well… I, uh, thought maybe we could try to do it again sometime? If you gave me your cell, I could maybe call you, and we could, you know… maybe meet here or something."

"I'm sorry. I don't have a cell. I—"

The speed with which Adrian's expression went from nervous but hopeful to completely closed off and stony took Wyatt's breath away, silencing whatever else he was going to say.

"Oh, yeah. Okay. I guess I'll see you around or something, then… maybe."

Adrian spun on his heel and headed for his small sedan at a jog.

"Shit."

After cutting his engine and hopping off his bike, Wyatt set his helmet on the ground and hurried to catch up to him. As he approached the side of Adrian's car, Adrian dropped his keys and swore loudly.

"Adrian, wait. Hold on there, okay?"

"Aren't you already late for something?" Adrian asked tersely as he bent and picked up his keys. His jaw was clenched tightly enough Wyatt could see it pop, and his hand shook so much he couldn't seem to get his key in the lock.

With a sigh, Wyatt enfolded Adrian's hand in his own and guided the key into the lock, but before Adrian could open the door, Wyatt stepped in close, backing Adrian up against the side of the car.

"You didn't let me finish," Wyatt said quietly.

Adrian's eyes were defiant as he lifted his gaze to meet Wyatt's. "What is there to say? I got it. You don't have to spell it out for me."

"Yeah, I think I do. I wasn't lying, Adrian. I really don't have a cell phone."

Wyatt expected Adrian's frown of disbelief. He'd seen it from enough other people he'd met. He probably should've invested in another burner phone, but he hadn't really needed one since he'd gotten rid of his last.

"I wasn't trying to blow you off, okay?"

Adrian bit his lip and nodded, and Wyatt really wanted to nibble on that spot too. With a deep exhale, Wyatt cupped Adrian's neck and gave it a gentle squeeze. "Look, Adrian, I enjoyed last night very much. It wasn't just you, and I would definitely like to repeat it, but I have to tell you, I'm not in a place where I can offer you much more than that. Due to personal circumstances, I'm not free to be anything more to *anyone* right now. I want to be up front about that from the start. Do you understand?"

Adrian was killing him with the lip biting, but Wyatt was able to tear his gaze away from Adrian's mouth long enough to see him nod. "Okay. You're not married, are you?"

"No."

"Significant other? Boyfriend?"

"No."

"Okay."

Taking a chance, Wyatt smoothed his knuckles down Adrian's lightly stubbled cheek and did something he was probably going to regret. "How about we meet at that motel, two weeks from now, Saturday night?"

Adrian's wide blue eyes searched his face. "Really?"

"Yeah. If you're free, I'll get the same room, number 203, say eight o'clock? I'll bring the pizza, you bring the beer, and we can stay in all night."

Adrian closed his eyes and let out a shuddering breath. When he opened them again, he held Wyatt's gaze and smiled shyly. "I'd like that."

"Okay, then. Good. We'll plan on that. Since you said you aren't from around here, and just in case something happens, why don't you give me your cell? If for some reason I can't make it, I promise you I will call before you drive all the way out here, okay? You have my word."

"Okay."

Wyatt reluctantly stepped back as Adrian shifted to the side and opened his car door. He stretched across the seats and pulled a pen and notepad from his glove compartment. After scribbling down his number, he tore the page out and handed it to Wyatt.

"That's me," he said before worrying his bottom lip again.

If he stayed any longer, Wyatt was going to end up on top of Adrian in the backseat of Adrian's car, so he took another couple of steps back and smiled. "Two weeks. Eight o'clock, Saturday night, room 203."

"What if they don't have that room available?"

Adrian's smile was teasing now, and Wyatt couldn't stop his grin. "It will be."

"Okay, then."

"Okay."

Turning before they started giving each other googly eyes, Wyatt picked his helmet off the ground, pulled it on, and climbed back on his bike. His grin and the giddy feeling lasted right up until he passed through the gate and onto the gravel road that led to Everly. As the first of the spires came into view, his grin died completely, and he realized what a sad commentary on his life it was that a two-week commitment was the best he had to offer anyone.

Damn, that's depressing.

CHAPTER EIGHT

"MY, MY, don't you look chipper for a Monday."

Adrian jumped and clutched a hand to his chest. He hadn't heard her come in. As her words sank in, past the frantic beating of his heart, he could feel a blush creeping up his cheeks, and he began nervously reshuffling papers on his desk.

"Do I?"

Beverly snorted. "Since I caught you staring at that accounts receivable spreadsheet on your screen like Brad Pitt was staring back at you, I'm gonna say yeah, you do. I'm also gonna say you either won a Caribbean cruise over the weekend or you got laid."

"Bev!"

"Adrian!"

She even mimicked his feigned gasp of moral outrage, and he couldn't keep a straight face after that. He laughed and flushed an even deeper shade of red, but he neither confirmed nor denied.

At least he thought he didn't.

"You did get laid. Good for you!" With a quick glance behind her to make sure no one else had come into their offices, she stepped all the way inside and closed his door. "Please, tell me it wasn't Martin."

He grimaced. "I wouldn't be this chipper if it had been Martin."

"Oh my. Meee-*ow*."

"Sorry," he apologized automatically. "That wasn't very nice of me, was it?"

"I think you deserve a little cattiness after what he did to you. So… tell me, tell me."

"Tell you what?"

She pinned him with her patented narrow-eyed mommy stare. "Details!"

Adrian's eyebrows shot up. They'd never actually had that kind of friendship before—friendly work banter maybe, but juicy bits? Adrian thought about it for a few seconds and then gave a purely internal shrug. It wasn't as if he had many people to confide in anymore, and he supposed after dumping all of his drama on her last week, she deserved some positive news too.

"You sure you want details?" he asked, just in case.

She rolled her eyes behind her glasses. "You don't have to go into intimate detail, but you can at least tell me the who, when, where."

She took a seat at one of the two cheap wood chairs in front of his desk, propped her elbows on her knees, and rested her chin on her clasped hands. Adrian wondered for a moment if he could die from blushing.

"I was still kind of messed up from the fight with Martin, despite all the nice things you said," he began.

"They weren't just nice, Adrian. They were true."

"I know. I just… there were things Martin said that I didn't share with you, embarrassing things, and I just couldn't shake them, so I decided to prove him wrong."

A worried frown creased her brow. "Uh-oh."

"Don't worry. I didn't do anything too crazy…. Or maybe I did, kind of." Getting drunk two hours from home and climbing on the back of a motorcycle with a stranger while leaving his car behind probably hadn't been the safest thing he'd ever done, particularly since no one knew where he was. But it had all turned out better than okay, and he had no intentions of doing that again, so he was going to let himself off with a judgment of temporary insanity.

Beverly's worried frown only got worse, so Adrian decided not to share that part. She didn't need to know everything.

He cleared his throat. "Anyway, I went for a drive Sunday and ended up at a gay bar a couple of hours from here called Deer Park. It's kind of rustic meets rainbow, very butch with leather daddies and all that, but clubby on the weekends apparently."

Her eyebrows shot up, and she giggled. "Why, Adrian, I had no idea you were into that kind of thing. And here I was asking my friends if they knew any nice white-collar men I could set you up with."

Adrian choked on the sip of tepid coffee he'd taken. After a coughing fit and scrambling for the pile of take-out napkins he'd collected in the drawer of his desk, he glared at Bev while she grinned back at him. "Dear God, no… on both counts." When she pouted at him, Adrian cleared his throat and tried for a more moderate tone. "I mean, don't worry about me, please. I can find my own dates… and no, I'm not into the leather kink, and I don't want a daddy. I have a father, and he's almost a four-hour drive away, just where I like him to be."

"Fine, fine. Back to the story," she said, waving a dismissive hand.

He had a bad feeling she wasn't going to give up on the whole matchmaking thing, but he let it go. Nothing could ruin his happy today.

"Okay. So I met a guy at the club. He's absolutely gorgeous. I mean, like, cover-of-a-magazine gorgeous—dark hair, hazel eyes, five-o'clock shadow, tattoos all over, sculpted lips…." Adrian's mouth started watering just thinking about them, and he tugged the collar of his shirt higher, making sure it hadn't slid down to reveal the hickey Wyatt had left. Next time he'd make sure to ask Wyatt to keep any marks lower, or he'd need to wear a turtleneck to work.

Next time.

"Adrian?"

"Hmmm?"

"Someone's besotted." Beverly's laugh broke him out of the spell, and he grimaced.

"Besotted? Give me a break. Who even uses that word?"

"English minor," she shot back. "And you're not going to distract me that easily. Tell me, tell me, before one of the bosses shows up and I have to pretend I'm working."

"Fine. I met this guy, Wyatt, and we went to a motel for the night, and it was fabulous and wonderful, and we're going to meet again in a couple of weeks."

"That so great! I'm so glad. I hated seeing you beat down by what that asshole said to you." She gave him an encouraging smile and stood to go, but she stopped with her hand on the doorknob and turned back to him. "Just, you know, you might want to go slow with this one. There's that whole rebound-relationship thing to consider."

"I know. I'll be careful. And thanks for being there for me last week, Bev. You're a good egg."

"I know." She flipped her hair over her shoulder dramatically, but her short pageboy haircut diminished the effect, and her grand exit was ruined when she almost ran into their boss on the other side of the door. "Oh! Mr. Perretti, good morning, sir."

"Good morning, Mrs. Tullman, Mr. Walnak. How were your weekends?"

Adrian stood up and returned the man's affable smile with what he hoped was a reasonable facsimile. Jim Perretti was always nice, a good boss who left him and Bev mostly to themselves, but for some reason Adrian was always nervous whenever the man was anywhere near him.

"It was very good, sir," Beverly replied first. "My youngest's soccer team won their third game of the season."

"Wonderful, wonderful." Perretti's expectant gaze swung to Adrian, and Adrian scrambled to find some sort of wholesome bullshit to feed the man.

Damn Bev and her endless archive of perfect family anecdotes. "Oh yes, and I got banged longways, sideways, and crossways by a hot stranger in a cheap motel" isn't exactly going to cut it.

Bev wasn't helping. Over their boss's shoulder, she smiled benignly at him with one eyebrow raised, and Adrian would've glared at her if Perretti wasn't watching and waiting.

"I, uh, I'm afraid my weekend wasn't as exciting. Laundry and a good book," he lied.

Perretti only nodded. "Nothing wrong with that. I like a quiet night myself from time to time, if only the family would leave me alone long enough to get it." He chuckled, and Adrian's shoulders slumped in relief. One of these days, he wasn't going to get nervous around this man. He just wasn't sure how many years it was going to take.

Thankfully, it looked like the awkward, Monday morning small talk portion was over, and Perretti was ready to get down to business.

"Anyway, I won't keep you two for long. I just wanted to check on the quarterly reports to make sure everything was going okay."

"Yes, sir. We're compiling them now. They'll be in your in-box at the end of the week, on time and in order, same as always."

"Good, good," he replied somewhat absently, and then he cleared his throat. "Only that last part is the other thing I came here to talk to you about. It seems Mr. Pacciano is instituting a new policy with regards to our office documents, and I wanted to relay the news in person first. From now on, he doesn't want us using e-mail for any important documentation."

"Sir?"

Beverly looked as confused as Adrian felt, so at least he wasn't alone.

"You'll get a memorandum fully explaining the policy sometime this afternoon, but I figured I should come down myself and talk you through the basics. Effective immediately, your reports to me should be uploaded to CDs and brought to my office directly."

"Is there something wrong we should know about?" Beverly asked.

Perretti hesitated a beat, and Adrian noticed a bead of sweat along his hairline, but he smiled and shook his head. "No. I'm sure it's nothing. I think the big boss has just been watching too many news programs. He's paranoid the Chinese are going to hack our system or something. He'll probably change his mind again in a couple of weeks, but it's best to humor him for the time being."

"Yes, sir," Adrian said, trying to hide his skepticism.

It wasn't as if they were in a position to argue. It seemed silly to waste time with disks. Even a thumb drive would be better than that, but at least he wasn't asking them to waste paper on printing the reports out, and disks could be recycled.

Perretti gave them each another smile. "Okay, then, back to work. Oh, and we'll be sending a tech support guy in sometime later this week or next to update your security and whatever other magic those guys are supposed to perform, so don't be surprised when he shows up… and you might want to do any backups you've missed before he gets here. Call me if you have any questions once the memo arrives."

He gave them a cheery wave before the elevator door closed, and Adrian and Beverly were alone again.

"That was weird."

Beverly nodded. "Something must have happened. Nobody makes policy changes like that out of the blue. I mean, I honestly thought the big boss never even saw our reports, let alone read them. I thought he just sat behind his desk and counted his piles of money while smoking a cigar and laughing at us schmucks in the trenches." She smiled absently at Adrian's chuckle, then worried her lower lip. "Maybe Alicia knows something. I might just have to swing by sales this afternoon and see if she's got the dirt on what happened. I think she's sleeping with one of the VPs."

"How do you know these things?"

She rolled her eyes at him. "I talk to people, Adrian. Maybe you should try it sometime."

"I talk to people."

"Uh-huh. Sweetie, 'You forgot to send in your expense report' and 'I need your sales receipts by Friday' is not talking to people."

He threw up his hands in defeat. "Okay, okay, so I'm not an extrovert. That's what I have you for, isn't it?"

She laughed and shook her head. "If you're counting on me for that, you're in trouble. I talk to people, but I'm as much of an introvert as you are. I just have more practice at faking sociability because I have kids and I have to. Alicia's kid is on my Briley's soccer team, that's all, and she loves to gossip. She's a true extrovert—probably why she's in sales." With a shrug and another smile, she headed to her office. "I'll talk to Alicia after lunch, but I think we should get cranking if we're going to have the report done in time to walk it to Perretti's office, instead of staying up all night and shooting it to him in an e-mail from your couch, like you did first quarter."

Adrian rolled his eyes. "That wasn't my fault," he called to her retreating back. "He was the one who didn't get the numbers to us until late. He's just lucky I didn't have anything better to do on a Friday night."

She poked her head out of her door and grinned at him. "Then you should definitely get a move on, since you obviously have someone better to do now."

She winked at him before closing her door, and Adrian shook his head. He had a feeling he'd given her the wrong impression about him and Wyatt, but he wasn't going to work too hard to correct that. She didn't need to know Wyatt was only a hookup, and a long-distance hookup at that. That was *if* Wyatt even showed up at the motel in two weeks and didn't blow him off sometime in the interim. But he was not going to think about that. He was also not going to get his hopes up either. He was going to do his job and pack up Martin's things and live his life as he had before… and he was not going to obsess about a gorgeous man who rocked his world and had offered to do it again in two weeks.

Nope. Not going to obsess. Not one little bit.

Over the next few hours, he did manage to get some work done, but only just barely. Beverly finally dragged him away to lunch at noon, since he hadn't remembered to pack anything that morning. She tried to pump him for more information about Wyatt over their fried rice and egg rolls, but when it became obvious Adrian didn't know much of anything, she threw up her hands.

"What did you guys talk about, if you didn't learn any of this?"

The look on Adrian's blushing face must have spoken volumes, because her cheeks flushed too. "Oh. Oh! Yeah. Gotcha. Silly me."

Beverly shoved a plastic forkful of fried rice into her mouth, and after a short, awkward silence, she started talking about her kids. She kept up her monologue through the check and their walk back to their building, and Adrian listened, grateful they weren't talking about his sex life anymore. The whole topic in general had him pretty flustered and uncertain, so, as before, avoidance and denial seemed the safest bet.

Unfortunately, back in his office, Adrian spotted the expected memo in his In basket the moment he stepped through the door, and his stomach twisted. He did not like change, and on top of the mess his personal life was, he needed his work to be as boring and predictable as always. Sudden policy changes were not part of that scenario. Picking it up like he was afraid it would bite him, he scanned it and then scanned it again.

Bev was standing in his doorway, holding her copy, a minute later. "What the hell?"

"Effective immediately, all company-owned computers and business documents will remain on the premises, unless given explicit permission by management," Adrian read from the paragraph he'd scanned twice now to make sure he hadn't misunderstood. "What's going on?"

"Wish I knew," Bev replied. "I mean, it's not as if we take work home all the time, but Perretti has never had a problem with us working overtime at home or giving me a work-at-home day when one of my kids was sick or something. It's just weird."

"Yeah, it is." Adrian chewed his lip. "You think the big boss is off his medication or something? I mean, we work for a construction company, for God's sakes. It's not like we're trafficking in state secrets."

"I don't get it either, but shit like this makes me nervous. You think we should be dusting off our résumés?"

Adrian walked around his desk and dropped into his chair. "I guess it couldn't hurt. I mean, it's not like I have much to add to it since I got the job here, but it might be worth digging it out again and polishing it up."

"Yeah. I'm gonna go up to sales now and see what Alicia knows. They have the best coffee in the building up there, anyway… and muffins."

With a quick wave, she was out the door and headed for the elevator, leaving him to scan the memo one more time.

Essentially, management wanted no company information leaving the building or easily accessible from an outside source. E-mails were to contain no sensitive information, and, as Perretti had said before, documents were to be hand delivered. Adrian tried to convince himself it was just some stupid paranoia of Mr. Pacciano's. The guy was a character by all accounts, though he rarely deigned to communicate directly with office grunts like him and Beverly, so any information of that kind was always secondhand. But Adrian's workday had now officially burst the euphoric little bubble he'd been in since Saturday night, leaving a tense and slightly queasy feeling in his gut, no matter what excuses he tried to come up with.

CHAPTER NINE

SATURDAY AFTERNOON, two weeks later, Adrian packed his overnight bag with nervous anticipation and a profound sense of relief. In all the time he'd been working for Pacciano Bros, he'd never been so glad for his weekend off, and only part of that had to do with his plans. It had taken almost all of those two weeks for the furor over the memo to die down. Adrian had been largely sheltered from it, tucked away as the accounting offices were from the other departments, but Beverly had told him the building was buzzing like a kicked hornet's nest. Apparently, Adrian wasn't the only one who didn't like his staid and predictable work environment messed with.

Perretti had only come down once or twice in that time, but Bev had heard through the grapevine that he and the other department managers had their hands full smoothing ruffled feathers. Everyone wanted to know what was going on, and they weren't buying whatever the bosses were selling.

Alicia's vice president, one of the Pacciano cousins, wasn't sharing either, if he knew anything, so Adrian and Bev were still in the dark like everyone else. He couldn't wait to get out of town and forget about it all for a while. He just hoped Wyatt was true to his word and actually showed up for their rendezvous. Otherwise, he was going to feel like a first-rate asshole for falling for a perfect stranger's line of bull on top of the tension he was carrying from work.

With one last deep, fortifying breath, he grabbed his overnight bag and the cooler bag he'd packed with two kinds of beer, some snacks, good coffee for the morning, and several ice packs, and headed to his car. He tossed the two bags in the backseat, shut the door, and lifted his face to the clear blue sky. The sun was warm, cutting the slightly chilly autumn air even though it was dropping quickly toward the horizon.

Smiling and waving at a neighbor as she loaded her kids into her minivan, he pulled off his jacket and was about to open the front door and toss it onto the passenger seat, when the neighbor called to him.

"Hey! Adrian, right?"

Surprised, he turned and smiled at the young woman. They'd met once or twice at the mailboxes, but that was about the extent of their communication.

"Hey, uh…."

Shit.

"Amanda," she provided with a smile, her blue eyes crinkling as she brushed her blonde-highlighted auburn hair out of her face.

"Hey, Amanda. How are you?"

"I'm good. I'm good. Um, listen, I can see you're on your way out, so I don't want to keep you. I just wondered if you knew who owns that car over there."

Adrian followed her nod to the one tiny stretch of road across the street from their complex that didn't have No Parking or Standing signs plastered all over it. The only car parked there was a nondescript, dark four-door sedan. Its only distinguishing feature was the fact that all the windows were tinted enough he couldn't see inside. He'd seen a few cars in the lot with tinted windows before, but they'd all had silly racing stripes, aftermarket spoilers, and special mufflers that seemed designed to do the exact opposite of their intended purpose—nothing like this plain, kind of ominous-looking car.

After a few seconds, he realized he was staring at a parked car that was doing absolutely nothing but sitting there, and he shook his head.

"Sorry. I have no idea. Why?"

She frowned and shrugged. "It's nothing, really. I just figured I'd ask since you were here. My boyfriend likes to keep his company van where he can see it from the apartment, and since the community doesn't allow commercial vehicles in the lot overnight, he's been using that spot over there. Only that car started parking there, and I wondered if anyone knew whose it was. I'd willingly give them my extra pass to use in the lot, if they wanted it. But I have to figure out whose it is first." She glanced over her shoulder, checking on her kids in the minivan before she turned back to him and shrugged again. "I guess I could leave a note on it or something, but I hate giving out my number without knowing who I'm giving it to, you know?"

"Yeah. Sorry I couldn't help, but if I hear anything, I'll let you know."

"Thanks." With a smile and a wave, she walked back over to her van to finish strapping her two kids into their car seats.

He gave one more suspicious glance toward the car across the street before rolling his eyes. These last two weeks at work were making him paranoid. Maybe he needed to cut back on the coffee… or the number of episodes of *CSI* he watched.

After tossing his jacket onto the passenger seat, he climbed in and pulled out of the parking lot, studiously ignoring the stupid, harmless sedan as he passed it. He put on his sunglasses, cranked up the seventies station on his satellite radio for something upbeat, put on the cruise control, and headed out on the highway.

Singing along to the songs he knew at the top of his lungs, he probably looked like a huge dork as he drove into the sunset, but he didn't care.

This dork is getting laid.

At least he hoped he was.

A little over two hours later, he pulled into a space beneath one of the two overhead lights in the motel's parking lot and cut his engine. Grabbing his jacket, he stepped out into the chill mountain air and scanned the lot while the red neon Vacancy sign flashed at the edge of his vision. His earlier optimism faded when he didn't see Wyatt's motorcycle, but he shoved his disappointment down. Wyatt might be running late, or maybe he'd driven another vehicle.

His throat tightened a little despite the myriad of perfectly logical reasons why Wyatt's motorcycle wasn't there, but he climbed the stairs to the second floor anyway. The window was dark, but he took a breath and knocked on the door of room 203. When no one answered, his heart fell a little more. Feeling like the fool he probably was, he knocked a little louder, just in case, praying he didn't wake some redneck who'd pummel him into tiny pieces for disturbing his sleep. He was just about to head back to his car in defeat when a light switched on inside, just visible around the blackout curtains and blinds. He heard the chain being drawn back a moment later, and then Wyatt stood in the open door, haloed in the light from the bedside lamp.

And the angels sang.

Adrian's heart did a one-eighty from the crushing depths of rejection to a happy dance in his chest when Wyatt gave him that gorgeous, sexy smile.

"Hey there," Wyatt said.

"Hey."

That was the best Adrian could come up with at the moment. Wyatt was heavy-lidded and a little rumpled, like he'd just rolled out of bed, and *bed* and *Wyatt* was about as far as his brain got before it started to shut down. He stood there stupidly until Wyatt's eyes began to twinkle with amusement.

His gaze traveled lazily down Adrian's body and back up again before he said, "Is that all you brought with you?"

"What? Oh! No, I'm sorry… uh, my stuff's in the car. I just didn't see your motorcycle, so I wasn't sure if I should bring it up yet."

"It's getting a little cold for the bike, and it needs some work anyway. I borrowed a friend's truck for tonight. It's the red one down there."

Wyatt pointed to a rusted vintage Ford pickup truck. In the weak lighting, what little paint Adrian could see was chipped and dull with age, to the point that he'd hardly have called the color red, but he supposed that was as good a description as any. Wyatt seemed to have a penchant for driving alarmingly risky vehicles. You couldn't have paid Adrian to take an old heap like that on these mountain roads.

"Do you need any help with your stuff?" Wyatt asked, snapping Adrian's wandering attention back where it belonged.

Adrian glanced down at Wyatt's bare feet, poking out from the ragged hems of his faded jeans, and shook his head. "I got it. I'll be right back."

Forcing himself to walk at a dignified pace, despite the sudden rapid thumping in his chest, he retrieved his bag and the cooler bag and climbed back up to where Wyatt waited in the doorway. Wyatt took the cooler from Adrian's shoulder and stepped to the side so Adrian could come in.

"I ordered the pizza to be delivered at about a quarter after," Wyatt said as he set the cooler on the small table by the window. "I figured you'd probably be the punctual type."

Adrian winced as he shut the door behind him. "That obvious, huh?"

Wyatt sidled up to him, took the zipper pull of Adrian's jacket between his thumb and forefinger and slowly drew it down. "Not obvious, no. I'd say maybe I was just hoping."

Adrian forgot to breathe when Wyatt lifted his heated gaze. His entire body flushed, and he was pretty sure he'd never heard anything as sexy as Wyatt's voice accompanied by the slow parting of the nylon zipper teeth on his windbreaker.

What were we talking about?

He had no clue. Two weeks of nerves and doubts and pent-up desire were hitting him all at once. At this point, he was so desperately happy Wyatt was taking charge and seemed completely oblivious to Adrian's awkwardness, he would've probably agreed to anything, as long as Wyatt didn't stop.

His jacket slipped to the floor, quickly forgotten as Wyatt stepped closer. The warm scents of soap, Wyatt's piney cologne, and musk enveloped him, making Adrian's head spin. Despite the warmth of his own flushed cheeks, he could feel the heat pouring off Wyatt's body, and without thinking, he buried his face in the hollow of Wyatt's shoulder and inhaled deeply. The softness of Wyatt's worn T-shirt against his face reminded Adrian of burrowing in a pile of warm laundry, fresh from the dryer, when he was a little kid. He could spend hours just wrapped up in this man.

A rumble vibrated through Wyatt's chest as he slid a hand into Adrian's hair and another around his side, drawing him even closer. Adrian clutched at Wyatt's back, gripping the hard muscle there. He rocked his hips a little against Wyatt's thigh as Wyatt's hand slid lower, grabbing his ass through his jeans and squeezing. Adrian didn't know what it was about this man that made him want to roll around in him like a cat in catnip, but he did have enough mental capacity left to realize his current actions weren't exactly going to win him any sex god trophies with a man as gorgeous as Wyatt.

The man had been more than understanding their first time around, a fact that still made Adrian cringe every time he thought about how awkward and pathetic he'd been. He fully intended to step up his game this time, or he might not get a third chance.

No one was that patient.

Reluctantly easing his monkey grip on Wyatt's body, he laid a few teasing kisses on Wyatt's neck, tasting the salt of his skin.

This was good too—more than good.

The man was a feast for the senses, and Adrian could still fill himself up while doing everything in his power to make a good showing. He wasn't a complete novice at this stuff. He knew how to get a guy off, no matter what Martin said. He'd spent the last two weeks thinking of things he should've done better. All he had to do now was remember what they were—despite the fact that most of the blood was leaving his brain.

Wyatt made another rumbling sound as Adrian sucked a red mark onto his collarbone and began unbuckling his belt. He unzipped Wyatt's jeans and dug his fingers inside the waistband, freeing Wyatt's T-shirt and tugging it up until he could get his hands on skin. Smooth and warm, Wyatt's taut belly called to him, and Adrian dropped to his knees to brush his lips across it before trailing light kisses down his treasure trail. He pressed his face against the erection straining the confines of Wyatt's black boxer briefs, and Wyatt moaned. With a pleased smile, Adrian nuzzled the base of Wyatt's cock, mouthing the cotton as he gripped the soft worn denim in his hands and tugged Wyatt's jeans farther down his thighs.

He could do this. He could be the hot sex god Wyatt deserved. He could make a man as gorgeous as this melt and beg. He could—

A hard knock on the motel room door nearly had Adrian bashing his forehead into Wyatt's most sensitive area when he jolted. Instead, in an attempt to avoid that calamity, Adrian ended up falling backward onto his ass.

"Shit," Wyatt said with a strained chuckle. "I'm guessing that's the pizza. Talk about bad timing."

The knocking came again, and Wyatt yelled, "Be right there."

Adrian had been doing so well too. At least he thought he had.

While he scrambled to his feet, blushing furiously, Wyatt pulled up his jeans and zipped them with a grimace. Adrian winced in sympathy. Forcing that monster back into his jeans was undoubtedly a very unpleasant experience.

Adrian plopped his ass onto the edge of the bed as Wyatt grabbed his wallet and opened the door. The deliveryman was an older guy, maybe in his sixties, longish salt-and-pepper hair under a blue baseball cap. The guy didn't even spare a glance for Adrian or anything beyond Wyatt. Adrian supposed he should have been grateful for that. At least Wyatt was the only one who'd see his embarrassment.

After the money exchanged hands, Wyatt closed the door and put the deadbolt and chain back on. He set the pizza box on top of the cooler bag and hurried over to where Adrian sat.

"So, where were we?"

Adrian had been thinking the mood was lost, but it seemed that was only on his part. The grin Wyatt gave him and the obvious bulge in the man's jeans had not dwindled in the least. Too bad the whole sex god fantasy Adrian had going on had begun to crumble under a dose of reality.

"You sure you don't want to eat it while it's hot?"

"I definitely want you to eat it while it's still hot."

The smirk and leer that accompanied that line were too much for Adrian, and he snorted. He clamped a hand over his mouth in embarrassment at the sound that came out of him, but Wyatt just chuckled. His eyes were still sparkling with mirth as he bent down, cupped Adrian's chin in a large warm palm, and kissed him deeply. Adrian's eyes drifted closed, and he melted as Wyatt's tongue explored his mouth.

"What can I get you?" Wyatt whispered against his lips before trailing a few kisses down his neck.

"Are we doing delivery boy porn now?" Adrian asked breathlessly.

Wyatt laughed against his skin before he drew back and smiled down into Adrian's eyes. "Whatever you want, remember?"

Adrian swallowed. "But what do you want?"

Hunching down to talk to Adrian like that must have been awkward, because Wyatt dropped to his knees between Adrian's legs and braced his palms on the mattress on either side of him. "I told you last time. I want to see you lose it. I want to hear you moan, and feel you shake… to make you pant, and, if possible, black out from coming so hard."

Jeebus, the man has a way with words.

The deep rumble of his voice was like a physical thing, touching Adrian in all the right places. The sad truth was Wyatt wouldn't have to do much more than talk to see Adrian lose it. But Wyatt wasn't done.

"Tell me how to do that, Adrian," Wyatt murmured against Adrian's lips. He bent and nipped at the muscle connecting Adrian's shoulder and neck. "Tell me how to make you scream with pleasure. Tell me what you want."

They'd barely gotten started, and Adrian was already breathing like they'd run a marathon. Whatever brilliant plans of seduction he'd come up with over the last two weeks completely decamped, leaving only mush behind—warm, horny mush. So he ended up vocalizing the only stray thought he could manage.

"I just want to touch you," he croaked.

Wyatt pulled back until he could hold Adrian's gaze. "Yeah?" His hazel eyes were crinkled at the corners, and his grin was broad.

Adrian could only nod, and Wyatt's grin widened. He stood up, pulled his T-shirt off, and tossed it to the side, exposing that well-muscled, lightly furred, and tattooed torso that haunted Adrian's dreams. He cringed inwardly at the somewhat embarrassing realization that Wyatt had trimmed his chest hair to a safer length, but he didn't take his eyes off the gorgeous specimen in front of him for a second.

Wyatt seemed to enjoy putting on this little show, because he took his time unzipping his jeans and shimmying them down his hips. He rubbed himself a bit through his underwear, his eyes riveted on Adrian as he did it, his grin seductive. After stepping out of his jeans and kicking them to the side, he closed the small space between them, slid his thumbs inside the waistband of his black boxer briefs, and peeled them down, one slow inch at a time, not stopping until they puddled at his feet.

Gloriously nude and seemingly unconcerned with that fact—because he had good reason to be proud—Wyatt spread his arms wide. "Touch me anywhere you want."

This wasn't exactly how Adrian had planned it, but he wasn't a moron. Reaching out, he slid his palms up Wyatt's devil horns and around his hips, tugging him the last few inches forward. Wyatt's cock was at the perfect height, and Adrian leaned in and brushed his lips up the shaft, reveling in the silkiness of the skin and the smooth ridges of the veins as he moved over them. Wyatt gave a little shiver, and Adrian smiled against his shaft. Wyatt wasn't the only one who could take pleasure in his lover's reactions. He gripped the base of Wyatt's cock and rubbed the head across his lips. Wyatt cupped Adrian's skull, threading his fingers through his hair and gently massaging his scalp.

Encouraged, Adrian opened his lips and suckled Wyatt's crown. Then he swallowed as much of Wyatt's cock as he could without gagging and drew back up again, savoring the stretch of his lips, the salty tang of Wyatt's skin, and the smooth, slippery glide of it against his tongue. He hadn't had a lover this big in… pretty much ever, actually. He was going to have to work at this.

Wyatt carded his fingers through Adrian's hair. "You're thinking too hard," Wyatt said huskily.

"Huh?"

"I said you're thinking too hard. This isn't a test. Just do what feels good." His smile was gentle and warm despite the flush in his cheeks and the darkness of his eyes.

"I want to make you feel good too."

"Believe me. You are. But I'm not in a hurry. We have all night, don't we?"

"Yeah."

"So let's take all night."

"The pizza's going to get cold."

He chuckled. "There's no such thing as bad pizza, cold or otherwise."

After another caress of Adrian's scalp, Wyatt released his grip, stepped around him, and crawled to the center of the mattress. Stretched out on his back, in all his glory, he propped one arm behind his head and crooked a finger at Adrian. "Come here."

Adrian kicked off his loafers—not as cool as the boots but much easier to remove—and lay down beside him. Cupping the back of Adrian's head, Wyatt drew him in for a long slow kiss. "I told you, don't worry about me," Wyatt murmured.

"My parents didn't teach me to be selfish."

"It's not selfish if it's what I'm asking for. I'm going to get off. You don't have to worry about that."

"I want it to be good for you, really good. You kinda rocked my world last time. I just want to return the favor… get a little of my pride back maybe." Adrian snapped his mouth shut after that leaked out. What was he saying? He wasn't even drunk. "I—I'm sorry. I shouldn't have—"

Cheeks flaming in mortification, Adrian drew back a little, but Wyatt didn't let him get far.

"Don't apologize. You don't have anything to be sorry for. I wouldn't be here if you hadn't kinda rocked my world too. I like the way you look at me. I like the way you touch me. I like the sounds you make when I touch you…." He chuckled. "And I *really* liked the way you rode me like your very own prize bull. That was pretty damned hot."

Choking on a laugh, Adrian sputtered, "How do you say stuff like that?"

"Simple, I open my mouth. Would you prefer 'sex kitten' instead of 'prize bull'? I can be a sex kitten, no problem."

Adrian didn't think his face could possibly get any redder, but he was grinning like a fool at the same time. "Should I get you a nametag with 'sex kitten' on it?"

Wyatt grinned and glanced pointedly down at his very naked body. "Nah. Nowhere to pin it."

Glancing down at himself must have made Wyatt realize how *not* naked Adrian was, because he started tugging at Adrian's clothes then, with a mock frown on his face, and Adrian laughingly obliged him. It took some awkward contorting, but Adrian was naked and lying on top of Wyatt in short order. Feeling frenzied all of a sudden, Adrian ground his cock against Wyatt's as he kissed and stroked any part of the man he could reach.

Wyatt's hands weren't idle either. He gripped Adrian's ass in one firm hand, holding him close, while the other roamed the planes of Adrian's back and shoulders.

Still not quite believing Wyatt was just letting him rub all over him and rut against him like this, Adrian was on the verge of orgasm in a matter of minutes. He tried to stave it off by holding still and concentrating on kissing the life out of Wyatt's gorgeous lips, but Wyatt gripped his ass harder and ground his hips up into Adrian and tipped him over the edge.

"Fuck!" Adrian cried as he sat back on Wyatt's thighs, straddled his hips, and grabbed his dick, pumping furiously. With another cry, he shot ribbons of white all over Wyatt's cock and belly.

Chest heaving and thighs quivering, he wrung the last of his orgasm out in a glistening puddle on Wyatt's abdomen, gaze riveted to the spot until Wyatt groaned. Glancing up, he found Wyatt's eyes fixed on the same spot as he gripped his own cock and pumped it hard and fast. It only took a few seconds before Wyatt's orgasm spilled out and mixed with Adrian's on his stomach. The muscles in Wyatt's neck, thick forearm, and bicep corded and strained under their inked designs as he curled in on himself, and Adrian was pretty sure he'd never seen anything so beautiful.

As Adrian stared, Wyatt collapsed back on the mattress with a breathless chuckle. "Now that was hot."

It was poetry… or at least he *is.*

Before that could show on Adrian's face, he closed his eyes and flopped onto the mattress next to Wyatt. He stretched out with a groan and a breathless chuckle of his own. He felt good, giddy all the way down to his toes, and all from a little frottage.

Who'd a thunk it?

He would have been embarrassed, except when he opened his eyes again, Wyatt was watching him with a lazy, sated smile on his face. The evidence of their orgasms still coated his cock and belly, but he didn't seem overly concerned with it.

"I'll get you a washcloth," Adrian said, struggling to sit up. He swung his legs over the side of the bed and shuffled quickly to the bathroom. After cleaning himself with one washcloth, he dampened another and carried it back to the bed.

"Thanks," Wyatt said. "That only stays hot until it starts to get cold and sticky."

Wyatt tossed the washcloth aside and rolled off the mattress. He grabbed the pizza box and dug a couple of beer bottles out of Adrian's cooler bag, while Adrian marveled again at his complete lack of self-consciousness. If only he could be that confident, that at ease with another person in the room. He'd honestly been considering going in search of his boxers shortly before Wyatt bounced off the bed. Now he felt kind of silly. They were going to have sex again. That was pretty much guaranteed. And the room was plenty warm enough, so why would he bother putting any clothes back on?

After opening and handing Adrian a bottle, Wyatt tossed the pizza box and some paper napkins on the bed between them and crawled up to rest his back against the headboard. Adrian watched Wyatt's throat muscles work as he took a long pull from his beer. The silence could have easily been awkward if Wyatt hadn't been so relaxed. Adrian decided to mirror his attitude and stretched out on the bed. He sipped at his own beer and dug out a slice of pizza. It was still warm and tasted incredible. That probably had more to do with the fact that he was starving all of a sudden, but the pizza was surprisingly good for delivery out in the boonies.

Wyatt must have been starved as well, because he was on his third slice before Adrian was halfway through his second. His appetite was actually kind of sexy.

Who was he kidding? Everything about the man was sexy, from his quiet confidence to his ready smile. Adrian could probably wax poetic about the man's feet or the way he brushed his teeth, given enough time.

Besotted much?

He tensed a little then as that niggle of self-doubt at the back of his mind reared its ugly head again. Why on earth was a man like this even bothering with him? The question had been nagging him like crazy, despite his best efforts to ignore it. He didn't have the balls to ask, though. It would be too humiliating, and he was a little afraid of what the answer might be. If Martin had taught him anything, it was that there was such a thing as too much honesty.

He emptied his beer and quickly got up to grab another.

"Would you like one?" he asked, remembering his manners.

"Yeah. Thanks."

Twisting off the cap, he handed it over before climbing back on his side of the bed. The lack of conversation was starting to get to him. Wyatt seemed perfectly fine, if his slouched position and contented smile were to be believed, but Adrian was getting edgy.

Why can't I be that cool?

"I can hear the gears clacking around in your head, Adrian. Something you want to talk about?"

Adrian started guiltily and returned his wandering gaze to Wyatt's now slightly concerned face.

"Sorry."

"Nothing to be sorry about. If you got something on your mind, you can tell me."

Adrian laughed, trying and failing to sound nonchalant. "It's nothing. Just being stupid, I guess."

"I highly doubt that." Wyatt set the pizza box on the floor and scooted closer to him. "Stupid is definitely not a word that comes to mind when I look at you."

"What does come to mind?" When Wyatt lifted his eyebrows, Adrian flushed and stuttered, "I mean. I guess I can't help but wonder… uh, that is, I don't really get…."

He needed to stop now, shut his mouth, and laugh it off. This was the reason he could not be that cool, because he was a giant dork. If Martin was to be believed, he was a giant, boring, cheap, lousy-laying dork. He chugged his second beer, swung his legs over the side of the bed again, and grabbed his jeans, suddenly supremely uncomfortable that he was naked.

He was grappling with his pants, trying to free his boxers from them, when Wyatt stopped him with a gentle drag of knuckles down Adrian's spine and a single, softly spoken word. "Hey."

When Adrian just sat there, hunched over and unmoving, Wyatt asked, "What's wrong?"

I'm being a basket case? A bundle of issues I didn't even know I had until a few weeks ago? I'm out of my league here and I know it?

None of these were going to win him any brownie points, but he had to say something. Temporarily abandoning his fight to free his underwear, Adrian sighed and said, "Can I ask you a question without you thinking I'm a complete loser?"

He was glad he'd asked that before looking over his shoulder, because he never would have gotten the question out after. Wyatt was stretched on his side behind him, looking like a gift from the gods, except for his concerned expression, and Adrian wanted to talk about his *feelings*. What the hell was wrong with him? But his self-confidence was flagging, and as that seemed to precede other parts of him flagging right along with it, the last thing he needed was a failure to perform at a key moment. That would put the nail in the coffin of his self-confidence for sure.

"I'm almost positive there is nothing you could do or say that would make me think you were a loser, so I can answer that question with a yes, absolutely," Wyatt replied.

Oh.

Okay, here goes.

"That first night at Deer Park, why did you come over and talk to me?"

Wyatt looked confused. "Uh, same reason any guy would, I guess."

"But why me?"

He leaned back into the pillows and smiled. "I thought you were the sexiest thing in the place."

"Seriously?"

He rolled his eyes. "Yeah, *seriously*. I liked what I saw, and the closer I got, the more I liked. It's no big mystery."

Adrian still didn't quite understand what it was Wyatt saw that no one else seemed to, but he wasn't going to admit it. If Wyatt was delusional, Adrian would be a fool to disabuse him of it. But, now that the subject had come up.... "What about what you said to me? That whole 'power bottom' thing. Why did you say that?"

Wyatt's lips quirked a little. "Struck a nerve, did I?" When Adrian frowned at him, Wyatt's smile faded. "I don't know. I don't always have a filter on my mouth. You looked so good sitting there in your pressed khakis, with the perfect crease down the front, and that polo shirt under your jacket that looked like someone had ironed it too. You were so tidy, so clean. I had a sudden need to get you a little rumpled, a little dirty." He gave Adrian a playful, speculative glance. "You know it's usually the quiet ones who turn out to be the wildest in bed."

Wyatt's sexy smile returned, and with it Adrian's libido. The way Wyatt was looking at him made Adrian's pulse thrum in his neck and his mouth suddenly go dry. That kind of heat couldn't be faked, right? And even if it could, why would anyone bother?

Clearing his throat, Adrian managed to croak out, "And you just assumed I was a bottom?"

With a shrug, Wyatt's eyelids drooped, and he licked his lips. "I thought maybe you'd like to get fucked, yeah. It wasn't an insult." He scooted closer, drew himself up on his knees behind Adrian, and dug his fingers into Adrian's hair, tilting his head to the side and kissing his nape. "I prefer to top, sure, but no matter who's doing what to whom, I like a demanding lover, someone who tells me how to please him."

Wyatt kissed and nibbled some more on Adrian's neck and shoulders, and Adrian shivered. He was forgetting why exactly this conversation had seemed so important a minute ago.

"Can I ask you a question now, Adrian?" Wyatt murmured against his skin.

"Mmmm?"

"Why did you come back to Deer Park? What made you come all this way?"

Adrian laughed breathlessly as goose bumps sprang up all over him. "Uh, have you seen yourself? I mean, look at you. You're gorgeous."

That earned him a chuckle. "I'm glad you think so," Wyatt rumbled before nibbling on his earlobe.

"I think you'd have a hard time finding anyone who didn't think so. You probably get picked up all the time." That came out a little more bitterly than Adrian had intended, despite the breathy quality of his voice.

Wyatt must have heard the sharpness, though, because he stopped his oral assault on Adrian and wrapped his arms around Adrian's shoulders, hugging him from behind. Resting his chin on Adrian's shoulder, he said, "I've had my fair share, I guess. I won't lie. Except I'm usually the one who does the picking up, not the other way around. But you, Adrian, you drove two hours, all the way back here to the middle of nowhere, on the off chance I might be at Deer Park on that same night—when I'm sure there are plenty of guys hotter than me closer to home. Why was that?"

Flustered, Adrian defended, "Well, it wasn't that far, and you obviously knew the bartender, and I came up on a Saturday, just like before. It wasn't a big stretch to think you might be there."

"It's still a long way to go for a hookup you probably could've gotten at home."

Adrian hated when gorgeous people were smart too. It seemed unfair somehow. "You sure you want to delve that deeply into my psyche?" he joked.

Wyatt squeezed him a little tighter, buried his face in Adrian's hair, and held on for a few beats, saying nothing. The embrace lasted long enough Adrian was on the verge of asking if Wyatt was okay, when

Wyatt released him suddenly and stretched out on the mattress again. His teasing smile seemed at odds with the look in his eyes, but Adrian couldn't tell what that look was.

"Dr. Freud is in, if you want…. You don't have to tell me, if you don't."

Wyatt was giving him an out, but he couldn't take it. He'd started this. It wouldn't be fair for him to be the only one on the receiving end of an ego stroking. Wyatt had been nothing but kind and supportive to someone he barely knew. The least Adrian could do was be honest in return.

"No one ever said anything like that to me before. I mean, if you haven't guessed, I'm not usually the kind of guy other guys walk right up and whisper sexy nothings to. Honestly? You made me feel more desired, more special, in a couple of sentences, than I think anyone ever has… even the guy who supposedly cared enough about me to move in with me. You made me feel sexy. I liked it. I wanted to be that guy." Wishing he'd had a few more beers before this conversation, Adrian ducked his head and shrugged. "Of course, I'm sure that's not exactly what you were shooting for. I mean, like you said, you pick up guys all the time. It was just a really good line, and it worked… obviously."

He forced a laugh, hoping Wyatt would laugh too, but no such luck. Unable to face him, Adrian stood up to get that beer, or three, he'd been longing for. Wyatt was off the bed and standing in front of him before he got the bottle open. He forgot how tall Wyatt was until the man was standing next to him and he had to tip his head back to look him in the eyes. Wyatt's eyes this time were wide with sincerity as he gripped Adrian's shoulders, his habitual grin absent.

"Adrian, it wasn't just a line…. I mean, yes, obviously, I wanted to pick you up, but I wasn't just slinging bullshit. We don't exactly know each other well, but I hope by now you've figured out that I'm not that guy. Even if I don't always think before I open my mouth, I say what I mean, and I mean what I say. I was honest with you. You have my word on that. I'm flattered what I said got to you enough for you to come all the way back out here. I'm grateful too…. If you let me, I'll show you just how grateful."

His teasing smile crept back as he waggled his eyebrows, and Adrian pushed his doubts back into the box they'd escaped from. What kind of idiot looked a gift horse in the mouth, especially when he'd promised himself he wouldn't?

He set his beer on the table next to the cooler bag and stepped toward Wyatt's body. As Wyatt's growing erection pressed into his belly, Adrian tipped his head back to receive Wyatt's kiss. It was a little embarrassing but thrilling in an odd way that he had to stand up on tiptoes to wrap his arms around Wyatt's neck, but he made up for the tiny hit to his masculine pride by taking over the kiss and ravaging his mouth.

Wyatt wanted him, right now. Why he did, and whether he would tomorrow, couldn't matter. Adrian was not going to let his neuroses get in the way of being well and truly fucked. That would be just plain stupid.

Wyatt half carried, half dragged Adrian back to the bed and collapsed on top of him. If a decidedly unmanly nervous giggle escaped him at that point, he would never admit to it publicly. When Adrian wrapped his legs around Wyatt's waist, Wyatt growled and pumped his hips. They kissed and grappled on the bed until they were a sweaty tangle of panting breaths and moans of encouragement. When Adrian felt like he couldn't take it anymore, he rolled over onto his side and ground his ass back against Wyatt's cock. He wanted to be fucked *now*.

Wyatt let out a pained groan. "Hold on, baby. I gotta get the stuff."

Oh yeah, condoms and lube. Those are important.

Wyatt rolled away and reached for his pants, but Adrian stopped him. "Wait. I got it."

He'd come fully prepared this time.

His aching cock giving him speed, he jumped off the bed and hurried awkwardly back to the cooler bag where he'd tossed the full box of condoms and brand-new bottle of lube he'd picked up at the same time as the groceries. He winced a little as he dug them out of the bottom of the bag, sandwiched between two freezer packs. They were icy… not his best idea ever, but he'd wanted more than a couple little packets of lube, especially after how sore he'd been the last time. Wyatt was a lot to handle for someone who hadn't bottomed much over the last few years.

He handed the supplies over to Wyatt with a grimace. "I'd appreciate a little warm-up."

Wyatt chuckled. "Of course."

Adrian watched him open the condom box and tear off a packet. Tossing the box and extras behind him, Wyatt tucked the packet under his hip, flinching a little at the chill. With his teeth, he peeled the plastic seal off the lube and squirted some into his palm, closing his fingers over it. Adrian quickly scrambled back into position on his side, arching his back in invitation, and Wyatt spooned against him. Wyatt's shorn chest hair tickled Adrian's back, and Adrian wiggled, luxuriating in the feeling, at least until Wyatt wrapped his slicked fist around Adrian's cock and gave it a few pumps. After that, Adrian became singularly focused on what was happening below his waist.

Taking Wyatt's earlier words about being a demanding lover to heart, Adrian shoved his ass back again without shame. On cue, Wyatt let go of Adrian's cock and his slick fingers found Adrian's crack. He began to tease Adrian's crease and rim, and Adrian decided to get even further into his role as impatience got the better of him.

"More," he panted. "Give it to me."

Without a word, Wyatt bit the back of Adrian's neck as his finger pushed inside. Wyatt's blunt teeth on his skin sent a shiver down Adrian's spine, and he moaned and rolled his hips, trying to force Wyatt's finger deeper, but Wyatt withdrew only a few seconds later. Adrian was about to growl over his shoulder when he heard the lube cap pop again, and he huffed out a breath. He'd been the one to insist on the warming of the lube. And really, icy lube did not sound fun at this juncture. He'd just have to find some patience somewhere.

He moaned in relief when Wyatt pressed two fingers inside him again. The lube was still a little on the cool side, but he didn't care. He reached down and lifted his leg up and out.

Screw the foreplay.

He could be a little sore tomorrow.

"I'm good. I want you, *now*."

Wyatt's fingers disappeared again, and Adrian heard the tearing of the foil packet. Then Wyatt's sheathed cock was at his entrance, and Adrian let out a satisfied groan as Wyatt stretched and filled him in one long, slow glide. Wyatt's arm replaced Adrian's, lifting his leg higher while he locked the other arm around Adrian's chest. Wyatt began to fuck him, slow and steady, and Adrian grabbed his cock and took up the same pace as he pushed back into each thrust. He was hot and aching, flushed and sweaty. Part of him wanted to demand Wyatt go harder and deeper, but another part wanted this slow, deep fucking to last forever.

Wyatt buried his face against Adrian's neck and shoulder, whispering and moaning against Adrian's skin as he clutched at Adrian's chest. Adrian didn't have enough brain cells left to decipher the words, if there were any. He was a puddle of happy, horny want, and he totally forgot he was supposed to be topping from the bottom… at least until his balls began to ache and the need to come became all-consuming.

"Harder," he ground out.

He braced his free arm on the headboard above his head, shoved his ass back into each thrust, and worked his cock fast, as Wyatt obligingly tightened his grip and slammed into him. The bed rocked alarmingly, squeaking and banging against the wall. Adrian's calf muscle started to cramp in the leg that was currently up in the air, but he ignored it as best he could as his toes curled and he clenched all over in orgasm. He ground his ass back against Wyatt and growled around clenched teeth as he came all over his belly and hand, and Wyatt's grip tightened enough to bruise as he pistoned a few more times and froze.

Adrian barely heard Wyatt's moan of completion over the pounding in his ears as he tried to catch his breath. He would've liked to have thrown out a smooth compliment, clap his hands, or even an Austin Powers "Yeah, baby!" But now that the euphoria was fading, what came out of his mouth was more like "Ow, ow, ow!" as he rolled out of Wyatt's grip and straightened his leg.

"What's wrong?" Wyatt asked, hovering over him worriedly.

Adrian grimaced up at him as he flexed his toes. "Leg cramp."

Wyatt's warm, rough hands immediately began massaging his thigh. "Here?"

"No… lower… calf," he gritted out.

Wyatt knuckled and squeezed the offending muscle and after a brief increase in pain, the cramping eased. Adrian blew out a relieved breath, ending on a moan as Wyatt rubbed the muscles just right.

The man had magic hands. There was no other possible explanation.

"That was embarrassing," Adrian groaned as his face flamed. "Thanks."

With another warm smile, Wyatt eased up on the massage and stretched out next to him again. "No problem. It happens to the best of us."

Somehow Adrian could not picture Wyatt doing anything so awkward and uncool, but he accepted the words in the spirit they were meant. Apparently, Wyatt didn't mind that Adrian was a complete dork. In fact, if what he'd said earlier was to be believed, he might even find Adrian's dorkiness attractive.

Isn't that just too good to be true.

After getting rid of the condom, Wyatt wiped himself on the cloth he'd used earlier and rolled off the bed. He snagged another beer out of the cooler and pointed to the one Adrian had set aside. "Want yours?"

At Adrian's nod, he brought both bottles back with him and stretched out on the bed again. Adrian scooted up against the headboard, after taking the washcloth Wyatt had left on the bed and wiping himself off as well. He tossed it aside and relaxed into the pile of pillows behind him, taking a long pull from his beer when Wyatt handed it over.

They'd only been there a couple of hours at the most, and they'd gone two rounds already. Adrian would've been more impressed with himself if he weren't struggling to stay awake. But he was not going to pass out first. Nope. He definitely was not. His pride had already taken enough hits for the evening.

Stifling a yawn behind his bottle, Adrian blinked rapidly and opened his eyes wide. He thought about giving himself a few slaps on the face, but he figured he'd look a little insane doing it. Luckily Wyatt yawned shortly thereafter and slid lower on the mattress.

"Great sex, good pizza, and good beer, what more could a man ask for… except maybe a good nap?" The last words were spoken on a yawn, and Adrian smiled.

Oh, thank God.

It was a small, probably petty victory, but he'd take it.

"Sounds like an excellent idea," Adrian murmured, as if he hadn't already been about to pass out.

He hated wasting a perfectly good beer, but he really couldn't keep his eyes open long enough to finish it. He took another long pull and set it aside before climbing under the covers. When Wyatt spooned him, Adrian happily nestled back against him, drew Wyatt's arm across his chest, and held it there. He fell asleep before his brain could remind him that this was only supposed to be a temporary arrangement.

CHAPTER TEN

WHEN WYATT woke a few hours later, he was disappointed to find his arms empty. It took him a moment to remember why that was. Frowning, he searched the darkness of the room for any sign of Adrian and was surprised at his relief when he spotted the man in the chair by the door, eating cold pizza by the light of his cell phone.

"Hey," he croaked.

Adrian started before giving him a tentative smile.

"Hungry?" Wyatt asked needlessly, to break what suddenly seemed like an awkward silence.

"Yeah. A little."

"You could've turned on a light. I wouldn't have minded."

"I didn't want to wake you."

Wyatt propped himself up on his elbows and turned on the lamp next to the bed, blinking in the light. Adrian's voice sounded tense, and Wyatt sat up a little straighter as he wiped the sleep out of his eyes.

"Is something wrong?"

"No, not really," Adrian replied quietly, giving him a bland look. When Wyatt cocked an eyebrow at him and waited, Adrian eventually smiled and rolled his eyes. "Okay, not wrong, exactly. I guess I was just sitting here thinking about how I know almost nothing about you… you know, for someone who I'm being so, uh, *intimate* with. I mean, after the conversations we've had, you know things about me that almost no one else does, and yet I know little more than your last name."

You don't even know that much.

If Wyatt hadn't started to tense, he would've found Adrian's blush endearing. But there was a reason he usually only did one-night stands, where exchange of personal information was limited. He really didn't like to lie. But, God, how he'd missed having the chance to get to know a lover, to learn his body and all the things that made him whimper and moan and beg. A single night just wasn't enough time for what he really wanted.

"What do you want to know?" he asked, feigning an ease he didn't feel. He folded his arms behind his head and stretched, liking the way Adrian's eyes grew hooded as he watched.

Distraction could work wonders, even if a tiny part of him hoped Adrian wouldn't fall for it.

"Uh." Adrian shook his head and cleared his throat. "I don't know. I guess I want to know the normal stuff, like where you live, what you do for a living. We kinda skipped right to the deep stuff... or at least I did, dumping my neuroses all over you."

Adrian ended with a pained laugh that made Wyatt want to drag him back to bed and kiss him until he could laugh for real. Instead Wyatt smiled and said, "You didn't dump anything on me. Like I said, I was flattered. Besides, small talk is highly overrated in my opinion."

Wyatt considered leaving it at that and steering the conversation away from himself again, but stopped. It wasn't as if Adrian was asking for his family history or anything. He didn't have to be that paranoid. Too much secrecy and he might actually succeed in convincing Adrian the drive wasn't worth it for what he had to offer.

"As to your questions, I'm staying with a friend about a half hour from here, because I'm kind of between jobs at the moment."

There. Not exactly flattering, but not an out-and-out lie either.

Adrian's eyes widened. "Oh, jeez. I'm so sorry. I didn't know. And here I let you pay for my drinks and this room... twice now. I wish you'd said something."

"Hey, don't worry about it. I'm not destitute or anything. I'm doing fine, really."

The way Adrian chewed on his lower lip was adorable except for the fact that he looked so skeptical. Wyatt had enough pride he couldn't take that look directed at him. "Really, Adrian, it's fine. I tend to move around a lot. That's all. I'm not hurting for cash or anything. I just decided to come back home for a while, and I haven't made up my mind where I'm going next, so I'm staying with a friend while I figure it out."

"Home?"

Shit.

"Yeah, sort of. I grew up around here. Every once in a while, I get the urge to wander back."

"You have family here?"

Covering a grimace, Wyatt shook his head. "Not anymore. My dad and his second wife moved away a long time ago. The mountains just feel like home, I guess."

Only when he noticed how soft and sympathetic Adrian's gaze had become did Wyatt realize how wistful he sounded. He needed to get a grip. He took a swig of his tepid and somewhat flat beer from earlier and then cleared his throat. Sharing time was over.

"What about you?" he asked.

"Me?"

"Yeah, what do you do, Adrian Walnak?"

Adrian flushed a little but squared his shoulders and lifted his chin. "I'm an accountant." Adrian must have misinterpreted Wyatt's smile because he rolled his eyes. "Yeah, I know, not exactly exciting. It pays the bills."

"Nothing wrong with that, unless you don't like your job."

"No. I like it."

"Then why apologize?"

"I wasn't... exactly apologizing. I just... well, it's not exactly the sexiest profession."

Wyatt smirked and flexed his hips under the sheet, drawing Adrian's attention to his already half-hard cock. "I wouldn't necessarily say that."

That startled a real laugh out of Adrian, and he looked at Wyatt like he was just a little crazy. "Seriously?"

To drive his point home and to hopefully add a little wattage to the smile Adrian was giving him, Wyatt reached down and rubbed his cock through the sheet, leaving his hand there to better outline it beneath the fabric. "Seriously. You wear glasses when you're working?"

Adrian blinked at him before shrugging. "Sometimes. I have a pair to cut down the glare and help with eye fatigue when I've been staring too long at the monitor."

"You keep them with you?"

"I usually leave them in my desk. I don't need them very often."

"Too bad. Maybe next time."

It took a second or two before Adrian seemed to figure out what Wyatt was getting at. When he did, he got the sexiest grin on his face before licking his lips.

"Yeah? You want to see me in my glasses?"

Wyatt rubbed his dick some more as he nodded. For some reason, Adrian had gotten dressed in his undershirt and boxers when he got up, but that just made Wyatt even hotter, thinking about getting him back out of them. Something about the pristine white shirt and the crisp cotton plaid made him ache to twist his hands in the fabric, to leave wrinkles behind. He was tempted to tear them off just to hear the cloth rip, but he figured he'd leave that for another time, when Adrian knew him a little better.

And there was no way he was going to look too closely at that thought right now, not with Adrian crossing the room toward him.

Despite the cute little button on the front, Adrian's boxers gaped when he straddled Wyatt's hips, revealing tantalizing peeks of Adrian's growing erection and soft balls. Wyatt reached forward and molded that crisp cotton around Adrian's cock, squeezing and stroking. Adrian's eyes closed and he moaned, grinding his hips before he bent down and pressed their mouths together.

Adrian was ready to play, and Wyatt was more than happy to oblige. He hadn't actually been trying to deflect this time, but he wasn't going to complain about the result either.

Living in the moment was never easier.

THE NEXT time Wyatt woke, Adrian was still wrapped tightly in his arms, but Wyatt's happy smile only lasted until he was awake enough for reality to set in. As carefully as he could manage, he extricated himself from the human pretzel they'd formed and stumbled to the bathroom as Adrian made a few grumbling noises and snuggled deeper under the blankets.

After taking care of business, Wyatt splashed some water on his face and scrubbed the sleep out of his eyes with a scratchy, overbleached hand towel.

"You gotta keep it together, man," he whispered to his reflection in the mirror above the sink. Bracing his hands on the ugly Formica counter, he scowled down at the cute, tidy little travel case Adrian had left by the sink. Wyatt had no doubt, if he opened it up, everything a man could possibly need would be in matching bottles, neatly aligned in their appropriate compartments. Wyatt hadn't even bothered to pack a toothbrush.

He scowled because he wanted to smile so badly.

Coming home in the first place had probably been a mistake. Furlough was putting ideas in his head—not that they hadn't already been there, whispering in the background—but his oldest and dearest friend was giving them validation, volume. And Adrian….

He closed his eyes, tipped his head back, and stretched, folding his arms behind his head and arching his spine. The stiffness of his muscles and the popping and creaking of his joints reminded him just how tired he was—tired of motel rooms, tired of new towns and new jobs. But whenever he thought of stopping, of building a life somewhere, that gut-deep fear came roaring back too, the urge to run.

"God, I'm a mess," he muttered, glaring at the ugly popcorn ceiling before dropping his arms to his sides again and blowing out a breath.

When he stepped back into the room, the lights were already on, the little coffeepot was hissing and burbling, and Adrian was propped up on the bed in his boxers.

"My turn," Adrian said with a small smile.

He hopped off the bed and headed toward the bathroom, but stopped when he reached Wyatt, and gave him a quick peck on the lips. "Good morning."

He sounded happy, content, and that should have been a good thing, except it made Wyatt want to curl up with him in bed again and never leave.

He had to put some distance between them, and there was no time like the present.

He needed a shower, badly, but he could wait until he was back at Furlough's. Grimacing, he pulled on yesterday's clothes as he heard the toilet flush and then the shower cut on. For about two seconds, he considered taking the coward's way out and yelling his good-byes through the door while Adrian was in the shower, but he tossed that idea aside. He wasn't a dick. He didn't want to be a dick, ever. Just because any hint of making a real connection with another human being sent little swirls of panic through his gut didn't mean he couldn't man up enough to be a good guy.

The coffeemaker stopped hissing and spitting, and he turned to it in relief, something beyond his own thoughts to keep him occupied while he waited for Adrian to finish in the bathroom. He couldn't help but smile when he got a good look at the spread Adrian had left. Sitting next to the generic, crappy little plastic machine was a fancy bag of gourmet coffee, a small bottle of some froufrou-flavored creamer, a pint carton of half-and-half, an assortment of sweeteners, two travel mugs, and two pastries on napkins.

God, he's fucking adorable.

With a rueful shake of his head, he poured himself a cup, black with a little sugar, and plopped on the edge of the bed. Luckily, Adrian's shower was quick, so Wyatt didn't have too much time to wallow in might-have-beens. That only ever ended in him getting pissed off at things he really couldn't do anything about, and pissed off was not how he wanted to live his life.

Taking a cleansing breath, he plastered a smile on his face that quickly turned into a real one when Adrian came out of the bathroom in just a towel, sparkly clean, with his dark blond hair combed in tidy little waves.

"Thanks for the coffee," he said, only leering a little bit.

Adrian's answering smile didn't last long as he took in the fact that Wyatt was dressed in all but his boots and jacket. He shrugged as he headed over to his leather overnight bag. "No problem. I hate the stuff hotels usually provide, and there's never enough cream and sugar, so I figured I'd just pick up some extra." He didn't look at Wyatt as he busied himself pulling neatly folded clothes out of his bag.

His voice sounded a little strained, and he seemed to be taking an inordinate amount of care in getting his clothes out, but maybe that was just Wyatt's guilt talking. Adrian wasn't the fuck-and-run type. Wyatt had known that from the start, but he'd been up front with Adrian, so he shouldn't feel guilty.

Really, he shouldn't.

"I should—"

"Do you have time for—"

They both started and stopped, and Wyatt chuckled. "Go ahead."

"Okay. I just wondered if you had time to go to breakfast.... I mean, if you wanted to... before I head back. After all, I think I owe you at least that after picking up the tab for me this far."

Fucking adorable.

After a purely internal sigh, Wyatt shook his head. "You don't owe me anything. I told you. It's my pleasure. I can't today, though. I'm sorry."

He wasn't lying, not exactly.

Adrian continued to fuss with his clothes on the dresser, picking at lint Wyatt couldn't see. He didn't raise his head as he said, "Okay. That's fine. Maybe next time, then."

When he did turn to meet Wyatt's gaze after an awkward silence, his expression was guarded. "I guess I'll see you again in two weeks?"

He should say no. He should pack his gear and leave town before wishing and Furlough got the better of his defenses and common sense.

"How about we make it one week instead, next Saturday?"

He could hang around for another week at least. He hadn't decided where he was going next anyway. One more night together wouldn't make that much difference, right?

The smile Wyatt received almost made him forget why this was a bad idea. But, just to be safe, he made sure their good-byes had more heat than tenderness. He'd just have to make sure to keep it all about the sex next time, and neither one of them would get hurt when he had to leave… and Furlough could keep his grumbling and speculative glances to himself.

CHAPTER ELEVEN

FOR WHAT seemed like the hundredth time that week, Adrian blushed red to the tips of his ears as Beverly grinned at him over lunch.

"Come on Adrian. I'm an old married woman now, a mom. Details, I need details. How else can I live vicariously through you and your little slutcapades?"

"Slutcapades? Really?"

He threw a curly fry at her, and she caught it and ate it.

"Details!"

Adrian wasn't quite sure when it happened, but his friendship with Bev had gotten a lot more intimate over the last few weeks. Maybe it was because he finally had something exciting to share or because the atmosphere at the office was still a little tense, with Perretti hovering and checking in more often than he ever had in the past. In an attempt to distract them both, Adrian had shared more than he'd intended, and that only seemed to encourage her to poke at him for more.

"I don't know. It feels a little weird talking about this," he hedged, not for the first time.

She rolled her eyes. "I said I'm *a* mom, not *your* mom. Come on. Don't be a prude."

He snorted and took a bite of his burger to give his blush a chance to fade. If he were honest, this was what he needed. He needed to treat his time with Wyatt as something he could gossip and laugh about, instead of something to keep hidden and precious. He wasn't in some starry-eyed, romantic, secret love affair. He was meeting a virtual stranger every couple of weeks for no-strings-attached sex. They'd laid the ground rules up front. He just needed to relax and enjoy it for what it was.

The little voice in the back of his head informed him of the unlikelihood of success with that plan on a regular basis, but Adrian just as regularly ignored it.

"Adrian? Hello?"

"Sorry. Just thinking."

"I bet."

He threw another fry at her. "Mind out of the gutter, please."

"Why would I do that?" She sobered a little. "Hey, Adrian, I don't want to burst your bubble or anything, but you don't think this guy's like married or anything, right? Like the reason he's hooking up with you at a hotel is because he has a wife and kids at home?"

Why is it people always say they don't want to burst your bubble, and then do exactly that?

His last bite of his burger didn't go down very well, and his throat felt raw by the time he finished swallowing. "I don't think so."

"I'm sorry. I just think you're a really great guy, and I don't want to see you get hurt again, particularly right after that asshole Martin."

"Yeah, I know. But Wyatt said he wouldn't lie to me, and I guess I either have to believe him or I have to stop seeing him. I mean, what am I going to do, follow him home? I think he'd notice that, since there's like only one road out of the motel, and I go in the opposite direction from him to get home. Not that I've thought about it or anything. I'm not a stalker."

"Uh-huh." The knowing smile was all it took for Adrian to start blushing again, and he scowled at her.

"Besides," he continued, "this is supposed to be casual. I'm not going to interrogate the man every time I see him. He doesn't have to share his life story with me if he doesn't want to, not when we're just fuck buddies."

"Are you good with that? Just a little sex, no relationship?"

He groaned, shoved his plate aside, and put his head down on the table. "Of course I'm not. Who am I kidding? The man is every gay boy's wet dream—tall, dark, gorgeous, great in bed, but just a little mysterious and a hint of danger with the leather and those incredible tattoos. At least, he's *this* gay boy's wet dream. How could I not want more?" He lifted his head and pouted into Bev's understanding face. "That someone like *that* would even look at someone like me twice…. Shit like that doesn't happen. I should be on my knees thanking whatever fairy godmother swooped down and bashed him on the head with her wand. Instead all I can think about is what if he lived here and we could go to a restaurant or cuddle on my couch and watch movies together."

"Have you asked him for something more?"

"He told me before we started that this was all he could give."

"But that was weeks ago, right? Maybe he's changed his mind."

"What, because my sparkling personality and mad skills in bed made him suddenly realize he couldn't live without me?"

Her sweet, sympathetic expression morphed into one of frowning disapproval. "That's Martin talking… and self-deprecation is not sexy, by the way. I happen to like the guy you're putting down."

"I know. I know. I just… my hopeful little heart doesn't need any encouragement at this point. I'm afraid if I ask for more, I'll lose what I already have. Just being with him makes me feel so much better about myself. He never has one negative thing to say to me, not one. And maybe that would change if we spent more time together. I don't know."

"You're a mess," she teased.

"Yeah."

After a quick glance at his watch, he sighed and straightened in his seat. Lunch hour was almost over. It was time to stop whining and get back to work, so he could go home and obsess a little more before he packed up and headed out for his oh-so-casual hookup the next day.

"Come on. It's time to go do what they pay us for."

Unfortunately the second half of his Friday dragged on interminably. His reports were done for the week, and Perretti had already come to get them, instead of waiting for them to be delivered. E-mail had been fairly quiet since the memo, so he was becoming desperate for anything to help him pass the time.

In the end, he finally resigned himself to tackling the arduous task of cataloguing and boxing up some of the old files in his cabinet. The drawers were getting a little tight, and he'd been putting it off for a while. Now was as good a time as any, especially if it made the hands on the clock start moving again.

"Dear God, it's come to this?" Beverly said from his doorway a couple of hours later.

He was sitting in a pile of files, checking dates and making sure everything was labeled properly before stuffing any papers from two years ago or older into a storage box.

"Yup. I had to do something, or I was going to climb the walls. At least you have vendor checks to print and send off," he grumbled.

"Oh yeah, they're a load of laughs. Well, chin up. It's almost five o'clock, and then we're out of here."

"True." Adrian stood up and stretched some of the kinks out of his back from sitting hunched over for so long. He dusted off his knees and then put the lid on the box and lifted it to his desk. "I'll go slow carrying this down to the dungeon, and hopefully by the time I get back, time will have miraculously sped up, and I can leave."

"You know, you could've just taken some of that vacation time you never use and left hours ago." She laughed when he looked at her like he couldn't understand what language she was speaking. "Yeah, okay, I forgot who I was talking to. Whatever, just go. Go, boxboy, down to the dungeon with you. If you're not back by five, I'll send a search party to make sure you haven't been buried by an avalanche of ancient paperwork."

She wasn't exactly kidding. The "dungeon," as they called it, was nearly a whole basement floor of shelved paperwork. Pacciano Bros was doing well, but there had to be decades' worth of papers down there, considering what his and Beverly's office had produced in the years since he'd started working for them.

He'd suggested to Perretti on numerous occasions that they should hire a shredding company to come in and get rid of the bulk of it, before it became a fire hazard, but he'd mostly been brushed off on the subject and had given up. It wasn't his mess, and as long as the sprinklers and fire alarms worked, he supposed they'd be just fine if the worst did happen. His and Bev's offices were only a short drop to the ground outside, if they needed to jump out a window. The VPs and big bosses were the ones who had to worry, all the way up on the top floor.

With box in hand, he headed for the elevator and took it down to the dungeon. He had to prop the box on his hip to punch in the code for the lock. Why they needed a lock for all these dusty files, he'd never know, but he was just the numbers grunt. It wasn't his place to ask.

Once through the door, he hit the light switch and froze in the doorway, not sure he believed his eyes. The room was empty. The rows of metal shelves held nothing but the outlines of boxes in the dust. He took a few more steps in, set the box he carried on the first shelf he came to, and spun around.

Huh. Weird.

Maybe Perretti or upper management had finally listened to him and cleaned the place up. They must have done it over a weekend. But even if they had, there still should have been at least some boxes left from the last few years. He'd carried one down for Bev only six months ago or so, and he was pretty sure businesses had to keep personnel files forever.

He went straight to Bev's office when he got back upstairs, and propped himself in her doorway. "Hey, Bev?"

"Yeah?"

"Did Perretti mention anything to you about clearing out the dungeon?"

She looked up from her screen and squinted at him from behind her glasses. "No. Why?"

"Because it's empty. I mean *really* empty. Everything's gone."

"Seriously?"

"Yeah."

"Weird."

"That's what I thought. I think he's actually still here. He hasn't come down yet to say good-bye for the weekend, so I'm going to go up and ask him about it. Wanna come?"

She grimaced and shook her head. "I have to get these done and sent out so I can go home. Let me know how it goes up on the executive management floor. Maybe they'll let you use their gold toilet while you're up there."

Ever since she'd found out that the senior managers all had their own floor, instead of being down with their departments, she'd been a little testy on the subject. He'd thought it odd too, but it didn't bother him as much as it did Bev. With Perretti up there, he wouldn't be breathing down their necks, and they'd have the peace and quiet, and freedom, to do their jobs.

Liza, Perretti's secretary, wasn't at her desk when he got off the elevator, so he went straight to the man's door and knocked.

"Yes?"

Adrian opened the door a crack and peeked in. "Hi, sir. I just wanted to check in before I left for the weekend…. Are you okay?"

Perretti looked flushed, and he had beads of sweat on his forehead, though the temperature in the office was perfectly comfortable.

"Of course, of course. Come in, Adrian," Perretti answered as he quickly collected the papers on his desk and shoved the whole untidy stack into his briefcase. "What can I do for you?"

Adrian lifted his eyebrows a little at the whole scene in general. This was doing nothing to help his recent job-related anxiety. "It's almost time for Bev and I to cut out for the weekend, but I just went down to the dun—uh, the *records* room—to drop off a box of files, and it was cleared out."

Perretti froze and gave Adrian a slow blink before he smiled wide and waved a dismissive hand. "Oh yeah. I forgot to mention that. We decided to hire a company to digitize some of that old stuff. Like you said before, it's a fire hazard having all that paper down there. We should have done it a long time ago." As he spoke in an oddly loud voice, he came around the desk and put an arm on Adrian's shoulders and began steering him toward the door. "One of the big guys finally approved the funding for it, so I decided to jump on it before he changed his mind. They said we'd have the digitized files back in a couple of months. But if you need anything, I can always call them up and have them ship whatever it is back. No worries."

"Uh, okay."

Perretti herded him out the door and back to the elevators. "Tell Beverly I hope you both have a nice weekend, okay? And I'll see you Monday."

Adrian stepped into the elevator and pushed the button for his floor in a daze. He returned Perretti's single good-bye wave as the doors closed and then froze with his hand still in the air and stared at his blurry reflection in the steel door for a good few seconds.

What the hell?

"Hey. How'd it go?" Bev asked as he wandered into her office a minute later.

"I don't actually know."

"Okay?"

"He was weird. He said they'd paid a company to digitize the records and shipped them off."

"That's great. So he finally listened to you. That's a good thing, right?"

"Yeah. It is. It's just he was acting kind of weird. He was sweating, and he put his arm around my shoulders."

Beverly straightened from getting her purse out of her desk and stared at him. "Really? Like he actually touched you other than a handshake?"

"That's what I'm saying. He never does stuff like that. You know, I was finally starting to calm down after that memo thing, but this is freaking me out all over again."

She grabbed her coat and pulled it on as she nodded. "I've been working on my résumé nonstop and doing job searches. I like this job and all, and I'd miss working with you like crazy, but I got kids to feed."

"Yeah. I did a little brushing up on my résumé too," he said as he took her cue and headed for his office to grab his jacket and shoulder bag.

"At least you have your savings," she said as she followed him to his doorway. "You should be okay for a while if things do go to shit."

"I did that more for my parents… well, my mom really, since my dad's too proud to ever take any money from me or my sister, even if they really needed it. The man would rather starve and go without heat than take a penny from anyone. Even his own children."

"Such a good son," she said with a smile, patting him on the back as he joined her and they walked together toward the stairs. "I can only hope my kids will look after Isaac and me like that someday—in fact, I'm counting on it."

He laughed and she gave him a smirk. "Yeah, right," he said. "Like you don't have a concrete investment plan and more than healthy 401(k) for both you and Isaac."

"A girl can't be too careful."

"True. Hopefully this will all blow over in a week or two, and there will be a reasonable explanation for everything, and we won't have to worry about it," he said lightly.

"Look at you, being all optimistic," she said, laughing as she punched his arm. "You need to get laid more often. It definitely agrees with you."

And just like that, his blush was back in full force, and he scowled at her as they joined the rest of the office workforce heading for the parking lot. "Go get in your car, crazy woman." He pulled her in for a brief hug before giving her a gentle shove toward her car.

"Have a good weekend," she practically sang to him, her smile wide and knowing. "Lunch on Monday is on me, but only as long as you provide the entertainment."

He rolled his eyes at her, but he was smiling as he headed for his car. Perretti's odd behavior still worried him, but he absolutely refused to let it spoil his weekend. He hadn't lost his job yet, and Bev was right—he did have plenty of cushion to see him through even if he did, though he hated to touch that money unless absolutely necessary.

Hoping to chase away the unease that had pooled in his gut, he cranked up his radio and headed home. He only had about twenty-four hours to pack an overnight bag and go to the grocery store before he headed out for his naughty weekend assignation.

How on earth would he squeeze everything in?

THE NEXT day, as Adrian surveyed the tablecloth, place settings, cloth napkins, and candles he'd set out on the tiny table in the motel room, he thought he might have gone too far. He'd made it a point to leave a couple of hours early, after what Wyatt had told him about not having a job. He was going to pay for the room this time. It was only fair. But then he'd spied a cute little autumn-themed tablecloth in the seasonal section of the grocery store, and some gold-ringed autumn plates, and some scented candles… and what seemed like a good idea at the time had snowballed into something just a little over-the-top for fuck buddies.

They weren't having Thanksgiving dinner, for Chrissakes.

Trying not to have a minor anxiety attack over it, Adrian decided he could scale it back a bit. Moving to the window, he started wrestling with the blackout drapes and sheers to see if he could open the window and air out the heavy scent of pumpkin spice. But he barely got past the tangle of fabric when Wyatt passed by the window and knocked on the door.

Well, shit. He's early.

"Heyyy," Adrian said, trying not to blush and plastering a big smile across his face that was only partly forced. "I didn't expect you for another hour at least."

Wyatt looked gorgeous as usual, in a tight pair of worn jeans, black T-shirt, and his leather jacket and boots. In honor of their conversation last week, Adrian had gone for a neatly pressed polo shirt and khakis, which he now smoothed sweaty palms down as Wyatt took in the room with raised eyebrows and a grin.

"This all for me?"

With a shrug, he said, "Oh, well, you know. I just saw this stuff at the grocery store and thought the place could use a little something." Taking another quick glance at the table, Adrian grimaced. Yeah. The bottle of Pinot, the brie and crackers, dried apricots and dates, and the sliced soppressata had been a step or two beyond way too far. He should never have been allowed in the grocery store to shop for a hookup on his own. What was he thinking?

Turning back to Wyatt, Adrian opened his mouth to try to play it down some more, but all he managed was a surprised grunt as Wyatt dragged him close and kissed him hard. He didn't get a chance to say much of anything over the next hour, other than "God yes" and "more" and "harder" after Wyatt lifted him and practically threw him on the bed. Clothes flew in every direction, and it was all Adrian could do to keep up. Wyatt was everywhere, wrapped around him, down between his legs, draped over his back, his tongue and hands and cock working miracles.

Adrian didn't have time to think, just react to the hottest, most frantic sexual experience of his life.

When it was over, all he could do was stare at the ceiling and gasp for breath. Apparently he needed to use the treadmill in the corner of his bedroom as something other than a clothes hanger… or ask if maybe Wyatt could make house calls. He chuckled, and Wyatt was suddenly hovering over him, grinning that sexy grin of his.

"Something funny?"

"I was just picturing you in Lycra and a muscle shirt yelling at me to finish four more reps."

"Ooookay."

"I think I need to get in better shape if we're going to do that some more."

"You liked that, huh?" His grin widened as he slid a palm down Adrian's sweaty chest and left it resting, warm and big, splayed across Adrian's belly. "Well, we'll have to see what we can do about that."

He leaned down and kissed Adrian tenderly, a slow slide of lips with a gentle tug on Adrian's lower lip as he drew back. "Thanks for getting the room, by the way, though you didn't have to."

"It was only fair. You got it the last two times."

Wyatt's smile dimmed a little. "You don't have to worry about the money, though. It's no big deal. Like I said, I'm doing fine, even if I'm not working right now. I'm good."

"So what do you do when you are working?" Adrian asked, deliberately changing the subject.

Wyatt settled back a little, propped on his elbow facing Adrian. "A little bit of everything, I guess. I've been a mechanic, a bouncer, a bartender, a tattoo artist. I've worked construction a few times, worked building security once or twice."

All jobs that are easy to leave in one place and pick up in another, Wyatt didn't have to say. Instead of dwelling on it, though, Adrian forced an encouraging smile. He wanted to hear as much as Wyatt was willing to tell him. "Did you do any of your tattoos?"

Wyatt sat up and held out his left arm. "Some of these. The Japanese wave pattern and the tribal star. Most of the rest I got from friends, since it's not so easy to ink yourself. I got a lot during my apprenticeship period with this funny old guy named Theo in Chattanooga. I stayed there a year just to have the time with him. He was great, taught me a lot, though he worked me like a dog."

Almost desperate to keep Wyatt sharing, Adrian asked, "What about this one?" pointing to the letters "L. I. H." in black script just below Wyatt's collarbones.

Wyatt's playful smile died quickly enough to make Adrian wince. Apparently he'd chosen poorly.

Wyatt withdrew and swung his legs over the side of the bed with a casual, full-body stretch that didn't look casual at all. "That's for my grandfather," he replied quietly, just when Adrian had assumed he wouldn't answer. He didn't turn around as he continued. "It stands for loyalty, integrity, and honor. He always said they were the most important things for a man to learn in this world. I put them there to remind me."

You're killin' me.

Could the man be any more perfect? Of course he could. He could declare his undying love and promise never to leave Adrian's side.

Before Adrian could get too wrapped up in fantasyland or ask anything else incredibly personal, Wyatt stood up and headed for the table. "I'm starved," he said. "You mind if I dig in?"

"Oh, sure, go ahead," Adrian replied hurriedly as he pulled on his boxers and moved to join him.

Wyatt was still gloriously, confidently nude, but Adrian felt weird about sitting at the table without any clothes on, and who knew what was in the upholstery of the crappy hotel chairs around it.

"I feel kind of bad just ordering pizza after you got all this," Wyatt said around a bit of dried apricot.

"Don't be. I got a little carried away." He pulled two beers out of the cooler bag on the floor in the corner and handed one over to Wyatt. He could feel the blush spreading across his cheeks again as the scent of artificial pumpkin spice started to get a little overpowering.

"I like it. It's sweet."

Blushing even harder now, Adrian stuffed food in his mouth before he said anything he might regret, like gushing all over Wyatt like he was the boy band to Adrian's twelve-year-old girl.

They both stayed relatively silent while they ate what Adrian had brought and then plowed their way through the pizza Wyatt had delivered. Apparently, once Wyatt had refueled, he was ready to go again, because he dragged Adrian into the small bathroom for the best shower of Adrian's life and then took Adrian from behind against the bathroom counter while he held Adrian's gaze in the mirror.

Given the fact that Adrian had never really considered himself a full-on bottom—or a top for that matter—he was certainly enjoying the role he'd chosen to the hilt. He didn't even have to try to be bossy anymore. It just sort of came out, though he'd never been particularly vocal before. Of course, apparently he'd never had great sex before either, so yeah.

Sweaty again and jelly-legged, Adrian flopped onto the bed with a moan of pure hedonistic exhaustion, and Wyatt joined him a moment later, laughing quietly. As before, Wyatt wrapped Adrian tightly in his arms and drew him back against his chest, cuddled close in a way Adrian could so easily get used to.

CHAPTER TWELVE

WYATT WOKE with Adrian still snoring softly in his arms. Burying his face in Adrian's dark blond hair, Wyatt closed his eyes and inhaled deeply, squeezing Adrian tighter.

How long had it been since he'd had a lover he could curl up with like this? He couldn't even remember.

Maybe Furlough was right. Maybe he was just jumping at shadows. Ever since the day he'd packed a bag and run for his life, he'd promised himself that one day he'd be able to come home. One day his real life, the life he was meant to have—the legacy he was meant to take on—would begin. But it was always *one day*, some distant magical time when he would know beyond a shadow of a doubt that it was safe to come home. There would be some sort of sign from the heavens giving him the all clear.

Except maybe there wouldn't be any kind of sign. Maybe he'd just have to take it on faith that the danger had passed.

He shifted uneasily on the mattress and clutched Adrian a little tighter. Could he do it? Could he stick around and see where this thing with Adrian might lead?

He wasn't an idiot. They'd made a connection, however tenuous. If he stayed, maybe….

"Uh, Wyatt, I can't breathe," Adrian gasped out, and Wyatt jerked and released the death grip he had on the man.

"Sorry. Sorry."

Adrian rolled onto his back and looked up at him with concern. "Everything okay?"

Wyatt melted. That right there was what he needed, someone who cared enough to ask, someone there when he got home after a long day, someone in his arms when he woke up in the morning. Stifling a sigh of regret, he shook his head. "I'm fine."

Feeling surprisingly vulnerable and exposed, he rolled off the bed and headed for the bathroom to give himself a minute to get his shit together. He was hardly going to be Adrian's fantasy bad boy if he started weeping in front of him… and he liked being Adrian's fantasy. He liked it a lot.

After taking care of business and a quick splash of water on his face, Wyatt propped himself in the bathroom doorway and watched as Adrian puttered around the crappy little coffeepot. If they kept meeting like this, Wyatt wouldn't be surprised if Adrian brought a real coffeepot from home to go with his fancy coffee and nice mugs. The thought made him smile.

"You want to get some breakfast this morning before you go home?" Wyatt asked before he could reconsider.

Adrian froze with the bag of coffee in his hand. He gazed at Wyatt with such a mixture of disbelief and guarded hope, Wyatt's chest tightened.

"Really? I mean, you have time this weekend?"

While he hadn't exactly lied the other weekend, Wyatt still felt a stab of guilt. "Yeah. There's a diner up the road a bit. We could hit it on your way."

"Okay. Sure. That would be great."

The speed with which Adrian showered and packed up, as if he were afraid Wyatt might change his mind, made Wyatt's chest tighten even more, or maybe that was just nerves. If he'd had a spare breath, he would've laughed at himself. They'd gotten together three times now and spent the night exploring every intimate inch of each other's bodies, and the prospect of going out to eat had him nervous as a virgin on prom night. How fucked-up was that?

His stomach clenched as he helped Adrian carry his various bags down to his car. "It's just a few miles up the road."

"Yeah, I pass it on the way in."

"Good. Then I guess I'll meet you there."

Ignoring the temptation to give Adrian a peck on the lips like they were boyfriends, Wyatt stuffed his hands in his jacket pockets and headed for his bike. Furlough had needed his truck, and the weather had decided to stay nice for the weekend, so he'd been glad to get another ride in before he had to either put it away for the season or be forced to head south.

At the diner, they sat across the Formica-topped table from each other in a red vinyl-upholstered booth. An awkward silence descended, and Wyatt's usual calm seemed to have deserted him.

This was a bad idea. They didn't have anything in common. Their lives were as different as different could be. How he ever thought they could—

"You know, it's totally unfair," Adrian said, staring longingly at the plates of pancakes, eggs, and sausage and biscuits Wyatt had heaped in front of him. "I'd gain twenty pounds eating half that much."

In relief more than anything, Wyatt grinned and settled back against the vinyl, stretching his legs under the table until they bumped Adrian's. "I think we burned enough calories last night that you could manage it."

Adrian choked on the spoonful of oatmeal he'd just put in his mouth. Blushing, he scanned the Sunday brunch crowd around them and then bugged his eyes out at Wyatt.

"What?" Wyatt's grin widened. "If anyone heard that, they deserve what they get for eavesdropping." Taking pity on Adrian's flaming cheeks, he leaned across the table before he said, "And as for the food, you should order whatever you want, Adrian. You have nothing to worry about." He gave Adrian a once-over with heavy-lidded eyes and licked his lips to drive home his point.

If anything, Adrian's blush only darkened, but he was smiling, and that was all Wyatt really cared about. "You're adorable. You know that?"

The words just slipped out, but Wyatt had no intention of taking them back, especially after Adrian said, "Yeah?" with that hint of tremulous hope Wyatt had seen earlier.

Obviously Wyatt hadn't managed to repair the damage that asshole of an ex had done to Adrian's self-esteem quite as much as he'd hoped.

He sat back in his chair and pursed his lips. "Hasn't anyone ever told you that before? I can't believe that."

Adrian grimaced and chuckled. "Not unless you count my mom."

"Seriously?"

Adrian shrugged. "Seriously."

"See, now that, I just don't understand."

"You have no idea how much I appreciate that."

"Huh?"

With a laugh, Adrian said, "The fact that you truly don't understand why anyone hasn't said those things to me makes it all the sweeter, really. You have no idea how rare it is to be with someone who goes out of his way to say such nice things, *all* the time."

Wyatt frowned. "But I'm not going out of my way. I mean, what does it cost to pay someone a compliment? Nothing. If you can make someone's day a little brighter just by letting them know what you like about them, why the hell not?" He pointed his fork at Adrian. "I think you need to hang out with better people… except maybe your mom. She sounds nice."

Adrian's answering smile made Wyatt squirm in his seat. Adrian seemed both amused and touched as he set to finishing off his bowl of oatmeal. Unable to stand watching him a moment longer, Wyatt shoved his half-eaten stack of pancakes across the table and tossed a couple of pieces of bacon on top.

"Oatmeal is not real breakfast," he said gruffly.

Adrian grinned at him as he picked up a slice of bacon, dragged it through the syrup on the plate, and bit into it with a groan. The sound he made and the syrup glistening on his lips made Wyatt seriously consider checking back in to their motel room as he shifted his hips to give his cock more room in his jeans. The man was sexy without even trying… and he had no idea.

Struggling with physical and emotional discomfort, Wyatt dropped his gaze back to his plate and finished off his biscuits and gravy with renewed intensity. He needed to think. Waking all cuddled up with Adrian, warm and happy, had messed with his head, turned his brains to soft gooey mush. He needed some distance before he made any decisions.

"So are you free next Saturday, or do we need to go back to two weeks again?" Adrian asked into the silence that fell as they cleaned their plates.

"I'm good for next Saturday," he replied after a slight pause. It was only another week in town. He could commit to that much.

"Oh good. Me too."

Adrian's reply was a little breathless, but his smile was pure happiness, and Wyatt found himself answering it with one of his own. He'd do a lot to keep that smile there.

He almost let Adrian get away without a good-bye kiss, but on sudden impulse, he dragged the man around the side of the diner for a brief, but very hot, wordless farewell that left him aching and just a little giddy.

Watching Adrian drive away took some of the spring out of his step, but Wyatt still felt pretty damned good as he hopped on his bike. He hummed to himself the entire ride home, and this time when Everly came into view, he didn't flinch away. He squared his shoulders, parked the bike right out front, by the empty fountain, and climbed off.

Staring up at the imposing structure that had once been home, he hesitated as a wash of conflicting emotions assailed him. Good and bad memories competed for his attention, and he had to work hard to shove the bad ones down.

He'd just about dredged up the courage to mount the steps when the barking, scrabbling whirlwind that was Furlough's pack came bursting over the hill, barreling straight at him, and he braced himself against their charge. After a couple of months on the property, the dogs knew him now, but that didn't stop the sudden, instinctual fear from pumping adrenaline into his system. Nothing like the sight of the flashing teeth and claws of four enormous German shepherds to remind a man how ill-equipped a hairless ape was to defend himself on his own. Then the dogs were bouncing around him, all sloppy tongues and wagging tails, and he let out the breath he hadn't known he was holding.

"Hey, boys. Where's Daddy?"

"Alpha, Bravo, Charlie, Delta, *fuss!*"

Furlough came limping over the hill with his shotgun over his shoulder. Obeying his command, the dogs immediately ran to his side, gazing up at him as if he hung the moon. "Oh, it's you," Furlough said gruffly. "What are you doing up here?"

"Nice to see you too, old man." Wyatt laughed. "And to answer your question, I thought I might just take a look inside, check things out."

Furlough's bushy eyebrows shot to his close-cropped white hairline as Wyatt tried to feign nonchalance.

"You going to let me in, or what?" Wyatt threw at him crankily as Furlough continued to stare at him in silence.

The smile Furlough gave him as he limped up the stone steps and pulled out his giant key ring was smug. He was enjoying this way too much, and Wyatt was tempted to turn around and head back to the cottage, just to wipe that smile off his face, but he didn't.

The enormous, intricately carved oak doors swung open easily on well-oiled hinges, but Wyatt expected nothing less with Furlough as the caretaker. The old man loved this place, probably even more than Wyatt did, especially since he didn't have the taint of betrayal casting a pall over it.

Despite the fact that Furlough kept the place in pristine condition, the air was heavy with disuse and old ghosts as the tread of their boots echoed around the marble entry and up the double staircases. Though it was what everyone oohed and aahed over, the grand entrance had always seemed a bit cold to him. It was his least favorite section of the house, with its icy, gray-veined white marble floors and columns and gaudy crystal chandelier. He much preferred the dark wood floors and thick Persian rugs in the sitting rooms, the library, and his grandfather's office.

Goose bumps rose on his arms, and Wyatt shrugged deeper into his jacket. Despite the protection of his driving gloves, he tucked his hands in his pockets as the vast cavern of a room reminded him of the day he'd woken up to an empty house, with only a short, quickly scrawled note from his father left on the marble-topped table to the right of the front doors. Resisting the urge to glance back at that table now, he scanned the rest of the hall as if he didn't know every nook and cranny by heart.

Furlough remained a silent, solid presence behind him while the dogs stood guard on the steps outside. With effort, Wyatt shook off the bad memories, squared his shoulders, and headed for the east wing. Dust motes swirled in the shafts of sunlight spilling through the massive floor-to-ceiling drapes as he hurried through room after room until he reached the relative comfort of his grandfather's office.

His father had taken it over when the old man had passed away, but Wyatt would always remember it as his grandfather's room. The dark wood built-in bookcases lining most of the walls were still packed with all the books Wyatt remembered. The crystal decanters still sat on a side table by the door, though they no longer held the deep amber bourbon his grandfather had preferred. The room was hushed, waiting… waiting for Wyatt to take over the reins, to fill it with a family again.

"You look good in here," Furlough murmured from the doorway. "You want me to start a fire?"

Wyatt lifted a hand toward the carved marble fireplace on the wall across from the desk, and he was tempted, if only for the memories it would conjure. He'd spent a lot of time on the rug in front of that fireplace, a little boy playing with his toys, secure in the knowledge that he was loved and had a place in the world. But the fireplace was empty, as was the ornate iron rack beside it. He shook his head. He'd fill it himself if he really wanted to. For now, though, he'd gone as far down memory lane as he could. He needed some fresh air, and some good hard labor to clear his head.

If there was anything Furlough was good at, it was providing hard work.

"Come on, old man. Don't we have some trails to clear or some fence to check?"

Stepping around Furlough, Wyatt made his way back outside in a hurry and filled his lungs with crisp mountain air to dispel any ghosts from the past still clinging to him. Without waiting for Furlough to lock up, he hopped on his bike and rode it down to the cottage.

He'd be back inside the house again, sooner rather than later, if he knew Furlough. The man was like a terrier. Now that Wyatt had opened that door, Furlough wouldn't let up until Wyatt either caved in and agreed to stay or ran again.

Gratefully he stepped inside the warm comfort of Furlough's little cottage and climbed the stairs to his guest bedroom. As he slumped on the bed to untie his boots so he could change into his work clothes, he thought staying might be an option this time, and he allowed himself a hesitant smile.

CHAPTER THIRTEEN

ADRIAN DANCED in his seat and sang loudly to the radio all the way home from his weekend assignation. His more logical side did try to point out that a little breakfast and the promise of another hookup next Saturday didn't actually constitute a date, and no change in the status of their relationship had been discussed, but obviously his heart wasn't buying it. Something had changed. Wyatt had opened up a bit more, had invited *him* to breakfast this time, and maybe next time Adrian could push it a little further.

He could do slow and steady like a champ.

The rest of his Sunday flew by as he did laundry and all the other little errands he'd neglected the day before. Still a little giddy Sunday night, he'd even gone out for a run, though chilly as it was, he'd be pulling out that treadmill before too long if he wanted to make this a regular thing.

Monday morning he was still feeling good, energized. He greeted Beverly in the parking lot with a huge smile and kissed her on the cheek when she handed over the take-out coffee she'd picked up for him on her way in.

"Someone is chipper this morning," she said with a laugh and a pretty blush.

Adrian smiled around the rim of his cup. "You might say that."

"Had a good weekend, I take it?"

"I had a great weekend."

When Adrian only grinned wider around his cup, she narrowed her eyes at him and made a swipe for his coffee. "Come on. Tell. Or I'm taking that back, and you can get your own coffee."

Laughing as he danced out of her reach, he was just about to give in and spill when he spotted Perretti headed in their direction. Motioning for Bev to look behind her, Adrian sobered quickly before he stepped forward to shake the man's hand.

"Good morning, sir. How was your weekend?"

Perretti gave them both a smile. "It was good. How about you two? Do anything fun this weekend?"

Bev wasn't helping at all as she smirked around her cup and tipped her hand to Adrian, giving him the floor. He stumbled out some sort of noncommittal reply before Bev finally took pity on him and chimed in with her wholesome family tales of soccer games and leaf-raking shenanigans.

"Excellent," Perretti said when she'd finished. "It's a busy time of year for all of us. Well, don't let me keep you. I just thought I'd say hi before I went upstairs."

As the glass doors closed behind Perretti, Adrian turned to Bev and saw her wearing the same look of confusion that was probably on his face.

"Well, that was weird." Bev was the first to speak out loud. "It's still in the a.m. on a *Monday*, even. I mean, shouldn't he be in bed recovering from his Sunday golf game and happy hour at the country club or something?"

"He's been weird for weeks now," Adrian agreed as they started walking toward the doors. Once inside, he paused in the lobby and worried his lower lip. "On the other hand, maybe we're just being paranoid again. I mean, maybe he's turning over a new leaf, or he's just as concerned about losing his job as we are, so no more moseying in at the crack of noon on Mondays."

Bev's lips twisted unattractively as she headed for the stairs. "Yeah right. Like the good ol' boys' network upstairs would ever give up one of their own. He's in tight with the Big Boss. It's us peons who get the shaft when times get tight, not guys like him." She laughed as Adrian scanned their vicinity to make sure no one heard. She'd disappeared into the stairwell by the time he turned back, and he hurried to catch up to her. At the top of the stairs, she grinned and held open the door to their floor. Punching him lightly on the arm as he passed, she said, "But look at you being Mr. Glass Half-Full. The sex is doing wonders for your outlook. Now I *really* want to meet this guy."

Adrian blew a raspberry over his shoulder as he kept walking toward his office. "Don't you have work to do?"

She sighed loudly and headed for her door. "Fine. But you can't hide forever. At lunchtime, you're mine, Mister."

IF HE'D hoped Bev would be the voice of reason, he'd hoped in vain. She was just as giddy as he was when he told her about his weekend—sans the juicier bits, despite her continual pout. He still considered himself a gentleman, and gentlemen didn't kiss and tell—or do *whatever* and tell.

By quitting time Tuesday, he did manage to rein in some of his schoolgirl giddiness, with the help of a painfully stilted phone conversation with Martin regarding the rest of his stuff. It had felt like talking to a stranger, but Martin had somehow managed to con him into dropping some of his boxes of clothes off that night after work, and still with no clear plan for the reallocation of the rest of the stuff. After hanging up, Adrian couldn't quite figure out how Martin had done it.

Bev had been disgusted with him when he told her. Being the champion for his rights that she was, she'd told him to dump the crap by the curb and tell Martin he could pick it up or the trash man would, but Adrian wasn't quite ready for that level of assholery. He honestly didn't feel much of anything other than mild annoyance at the inconvenience of finding parking downtown and helping Kenny haul the boxes up to his apartment, where Martin was apparently couch surfing… or bed surfing. Adrian frankly didn't care which.

He was a little surprised at that, but proud too. As he climbed back into his car and headed home, he thought maybe Wyatt's calm was beginning to rub off on him. Of course, thinking of Wyatt rubbing off on him made his brain go in an entirely different direction and his drive home a little uncomfortable. But a lonely dinner on his couch helped dispel that quite handily.

Unfortunately for his peace of mind, or fortunately—he couldn't decide which—Wyatt chose that night to call him for the first time.

He was just settling into bed with a new book when his phone rang on the nightstand. He didn't recognize the number, and ordinarily would've let it go to voice mail, but it was after ten o'clock, so it could possibly be important.

"Hello?"

"Adrian? It's Wyatt."

Adrian's heart did a little flip until he remembered why Wyatt had taken his number in the first place. "You're not canceling, are you?"

Did that sound as pathetic as I think?

He couldn't take it back now.

"No. I just, uh…." Wyatt cleared his throat, and Adrian had the crazy thought that the man sounded nervous. "I was wondering if you had any interest in maybe staying a little longer next time and going on a hike with me on Sunday before you head home."

Adrian's mouth fell open as his heart rate kicked up.

"Adrian?"

"Yes! Uh, yes, that sounds like fun. I'd love to. You want me to pack a lunch or something?"

"You mean like a picnic?"

Adrian could almost hear Wyatt's sexy grin in his voice, replacing whatever nervous tinge he thought he'd heard before. The sound and the image it conjured settled Adrian's frantic heartbeat into just a little tingling of butterflies in his stomach. "Yeah."

"You have a basket and one of those checkered tablecloths?" Wyatt drawled.

Luckily Adrian's blush could not be seen over the phone. How could the man make asking about a tablecloth sound like porn?

He did in fact have the whole picnic basket setup. He'd bought it for his and Martin's ill-fated outing.

Had it only been a month since that fiasco?

"Yeah. I do," he admitted.

Wyatt's deep chuckle had Adrian's cock twitching. "Good. Are you going to bring your glasses this time too?"

Adrian's flush spread down his chest, and he couldn't stop smiling. "If you want me to."

"I do."

"Okay."

"I'll see you on Saturday, then."

"You will."

"Good night, Adrian."

Adrian was fully hard by the time he pushed End on his phone. Wyatt's last words, spoken all deep and sexy, replayed over and over as Adrian shoved his hand down his pajama pants. He stroked himself off imagining Wyatt's hands on him and all the incredible, hot, and creative things Wyatt did to him and would be doing to him, in only a few short days. He passed out with a smile on his face and dreamed of Wyatt at his side at one of Bev and Isaac's barbecues.

…and if he and Wyatt happened to be wearing matching rings as they drank beer and laughed, his subconscious could be forgiven just this once.

After that night, though, he could not make the besotted schoolgirl in his head behave for the life of him. He tried. He really did. He went over and over their first conversation where Wyatt said sex was all he had to give. He lectured himself on being a grown man who should have grown-up expectations and not read too much into a little infatuation.

He wasn't gone enough that he was making room in his closets for the man or anything. He hadn't ridden that far on the crazy train. But he hadn't tried to fill the empty space left from packing up Martin's things either. That wasn't the same as making room, though.

It wasn't.

And if, just maybe, he fantasized about cooking dinner for Wyatt in his apartment, cuddling on the couch watching a movie, or going to Sunday brunch at The Sturges Speakeasy and kissing Wyatt in front of Martin and friends, it was all just a fun fantasy. He wouldn't actually do the whole rubbing-their-noses-in-it restaurant thing... probably.

By the time five o'clock rolled around on Friday, Adrian was so ready to be gone, he didn't even bat an eyelash when he spotted Perretti, his face red and glistening and suit rumpled, shuffling across the parking lot and continuously glancing over his shoulder like the devil was chasing him.

Bev's eyes bugged out a little, and she gave Adrian the side-eye, but Adrian didn't even want to think about it right now.

"Don't worry. We'll figure it out," he said, because he knew how worried she was. He got his head out of the clouds long enough to give her a hug. "Monday, screw the paperwork, you and I will take a couple hours and work on our résumés and maybe put together a couple of LinkedIn profiles... put the feelers out. You know, even if the worst happens and we lose our jobs here and can't get another right away, tax season is right around the corner. We'll be able to find something to tide us over at least until April 15. Right?"

She nodded as some of the lines around her eyes and above the bridge of her nose softened. "The sex must really be good for you. I can't think of any other reason why you aren't freaking out as much as I am right now."

He laughed and gave her another hug. "It's going to be okay. Sometimes it's good to just be a peon. We apparently don't have to deal with whatever Perretti does. I swear he's lost what little hair he had left in the last few weeks."

"I just wish we knew what the hell was going on. I mean, they've told us almost nothing, like we're too blind to notice things have gotten weird. If they're just planning on selling the place, that's no big deal. We might still have jobs… or if it's an IRS audit, I'm good with that. We've done our jobs. Perretti has no reason to freak. He knows we're good. They should at least tell us so we know what to do to get ready for whatever it is."

Adrian shook his head. There wasn't much he could say. He knew as much as she did, and they'd been going over the same ground off and on for weeks. All he could do was not panic until they heard something.

"It's going to be okay. We're the dream team, right?"

His best pep talk voice earned him a weak smile, an eye roll, and a shove in the direction of his car. "Go. Go get laid. Have your naughty sex weekend for the both of us while I'm carting my kids to soccer finals and football games."

She gave him the out, and he took it with a smile and wave. "Monday."

CHAPTER FOURTEEN

DELTA SHADOWED Wyatt all the way to the gate as he drove Furlough's beat-up old truck down the drive. The rest of the dogs were up with their master, but Delta had taken a shine to him in the last couple of months. It was probably the extra scratches and illicit cuddling he gave the beast when Furlough wasn't around. The man ran his dogs like a military unit, and Wyatt was probably undoing years of training, but he couldn't help it. He hadn't stayed put anywhere long enough to own a dog since he'd moved away from home, and he missed it. His grandpa had always had dogs around, had even given Wyatt a puppy of his own, a springer spaniel he'd named Rags, once upon a time.

Those were the memories he tried to focus on these days as Furlough found more and more reasons for Wyatt to spend time in the castle—patching the roof, checking for termite damage, inspecting the pipes. And as the thought of staying took root in his mind, Wyatt had even considered taking Adrian hiking on some of his family's property, instead of the state park he'd originally planned. He definitely wasn't ready to bring Adrian to the castle, not yet anyway, but a hike on the property outside the fence would be more private than a public park.

Smiling at Delta in his rearview mirror, he paused at the gates to make sure the dog didn't do something crazy like try to follow him out, but he should have known better. As soon as the gate clanked closed behind him, Delta turned and trotted back up the hill, and Wyatt pulled out onto the road and headed for the motel and Adrian.

When he spotted Adrian's car in the dim lights of the motel parking lot, he smiled. This would be the second time Adrian had gotten there before him, and he knew why. Adrian wanted to pay because he thought he was helping. He brought that table setting and candles and coffee because he wanted to pamper. He was so abso-fucking-lutely adorable, and sweet, and sincere, Wyatt was having a hard time remembering why he hadn't already snapped him up for something more than sex.

Dragging his hand over his jaw to try to wipe the stupid grin off his face, Wyatt gave himself a brief check in the rearview mirror to make sure he didn't have anything stuck in his teeth or any clumps of hair sticking up at odd angles. Satisfied, he reached for the door handle but froze as the light from a passing car illuminated the wide gravel parking area across the road from the motel. He blinked, and blinked again, but no matter how hard he tried, he couldn't deny what he'd seen in that brief flash of light. Among the dark looming shapes of a couple of eighteen-wheelers and a moving van sat a plain, dark, four-door sedan.

Ordinarily, Wyatt probably wouldn't have noticed it. Although it seemed a little strange for someone to park a sedan in what was obviously a truck parking area, when there were still plenty of slots open at the motel, it was the silhouettes outlined in the high beams of the passing car that made his heart leap into his throat and his stomach turn cold.

Wyatt's gaze stayed riveted on the car as he struggled to breathe, but no one got out of it. In the headlights from another passing vehicle, he saw them again, two figures, just sitting, watching the hotel from across the street. Clenching his jaw, Wyatt dragged his gaze away from them and up to the light leaking through the blinds in room 203.

Fuck!

He couldn't get out of the car or they'd spot him. Maybe they already knew Furlough's truck. Maybe they didn't.

Struggling against the familiar panic, he spared one last regret-filled glance for room 203 and cranked the ignition. Backing out of the spot, he gripped the steering wheel hard enough to make his knuckles pop. If they had seen him, he could lead them away from Adrian. Furlough's truck wasn't exactly built for speed, but it was four-wheel drive. He might be able to lose them somewhere… maybe.

His mind was racing. How could they possibly know about the motel?

He'd come home, so that would certainly explain how they'd found him. Although it seemed somewhat crazy that they'd still have a watch on the estate after all these years. Maybe someone in town had been paid to keep an eye out for him, or they'd just told someone who knew someone who knew someone… and so on until the wrong people got wind. But he'd been looking for signs. Even if he'd started to let his guard down over the last few years, he shouldn't have missed a tail.

Frantically searching his rearview until the motel passed out of sight, he never saw the car pull out. Maybe they'd been looking for his bike and didn't know about Furlough's truck. Some of his panic ebbed as he scanned the darkness behind him, but not all. Those men had been watching the motel, waiting. He'd been a fool to think he could come home to stay, that fifteen years was enough time for men like that to let go of a grudge. He needed to run again, and not just for his own protection, but for Furlough and now Adrian too.

Adrian.

Wyatt swerved into Deer Park's parking lot in a spray of gravel and jumped out of the truck. Jogging past the rows of parked cars, he pushed his way through the loiterers smoking outside and the press of bodies inside, heading straight for the bar. The thumping club music and flashing lights in full Saturday night swing made him cringe. What had seemed like a beautiful diversion, and ripe hunting ground, now felt ominous and grating.

Sucking in air, he tried to calm down. He needed to get a grip before he had his first full-on panic attack in over ten years.

"Jack!" he yelled above the music, waving at the bartender from the spot he'd wedged himself into at the end of the bar.

The scowl the kid in the seat he'd squeezed in next to morphed into fish lips and open appraisal as his gaze raked Wyatt from head to toe, but Wyatt didn't have time to be nice or interested. When he turned back to the bar, Jack was there, beaming at him. "Hey there, stranger! You haven't been in for a while. You want your usual?"

"No, Jack." Wyatt swallowed and straightened his shoulders. "I just need to use your phone. Can I?"

Jack's smile faded as a frown appeared between his brows, but despite the early hour, Deer Park was hopping, and he had at least a half-dozen people waving for service, even with his partner, Ian, manning the other end. Despite his obvious concern, Jack pulled the ugly yellow phone from behind the counter before smiling an apology and heading for his next customer.

Wyatt dragged the phone into the hallway with the bathrooms, as far as the cord would take him. The music was still loud, but there wasn't much he could do about that. Regretting the fact that he hadn't gotten around to buying a new pay-as-you-go phone—regretting a lot of things actually—Wyatt dialed and waited.

Adrian picked up after the first ring, and Wyatt's heart squeezed a little.

"Hello?"

"Hey, Adrian. It's me, Wyatt."

"Hey! Where are you?"

It about killed him, but he had to do it. Like ripping off a bandage, he'd make it quick, if not painless.

"I can't come tonight. I'm sorry."

"What? I mean, I thought you said…. Why?"

Wyatt clapped a hand to his forehead and began rubbing his temples. The hurt and confusion in Adrian's voice was killing him. He couldn't think about anything but getting back to his bike and bolting. "I'm so sorry, but I just can't."

"But… but I came all this way. You said you'd give me more notice than that. You promised. I packed the picnic for tomorrow and everything."

Go ahead. Twist the knife. I deserve it.

"I know. I know. God. It was a last-minute thing. I didn't plan it. Maybe, maybe if you check out now, he'll give you a refund."

It sounded stupid, but Wyatt was too keyed up to come up with some other plausible reason to get Adrian out of that motel and safely on his way home.

After a pause, Adrian stuttered, "Uh, okay. I guess I could check… but… I mean, if you just can't come tonight, I can still meet you tomorrow for that hike. We could still do that, right?"

Wyatt closed his eyes and gritted his teeth. He needed to finish this now. "I'm sorry, Adrian, I can't. I'm, uh, going to have to go away for a while. I don't know when I'll be back."

"You… *what*? But I don't understand. I thought…."

"I'm sorry, Adrian. I have to go…. You're a great guy. Don't let anyone tell you differently, okay?" This most inane of inane declarations was met with the silence it deserved, and Wyatt groaned inwardly. "Good-bye, Adrian."

After hanging up, he wanted to spend a good hour banging his forehead against the wood-paneled hallway, but fear got his legs moving. He put the phone back on the bar, catching Jack's eyes and mouthing a "thank you" before heading for the doors. He didn't miss the frown Jack threw at him, but the place was too busy for any kind of conversation. Maybe he'd send the man a postcard on his way south. As good-byes went, it was pretty shitty, but better than what he'd just done to Adrian.

Outside, he scanned the parking lot for the dark sedan, but he didn't see it, or anyone sitting in their vehicles who weren't busy doing something that steamed up the windows. Even so, he skulked in the shadows, skirting the perimeter of the lot before climbing in Furlough's truck from the passenger side and sliding across the bench seat.

As he pulled out, he still didn't see anyone following him, but once his paranoia and flight response had kicked in, it took a long time to turn it off again. He drove the long way around, doubling back to the estate from the opposite direction he usually took. At the gate, he scanned the blackness in all directions as he keyed in the code and waited impatiently for the gates to open. The tires spun out in the cold, muddy gravel as he floored it up the hill, but he backed off the accelerator as he approached Furlough's cottage. Furlough would skin him alive, leaving nothing for the men searching for him, if he heard Wyatt gouging trenches in his carefully maintained road.

After pulling in, he raced inside and up the stairs, ignoring Furlough's "Hey. What are you doing back?" shouted from the living room, over the television and barking dogs.

In his room, he grabbed everything out of the dresser and closet. He would've loved to just stuff it all in bags so he could be on his way, but his bike only had so much room for storage, and he had to pack everything neatly if he didn't want to leave most of it behind. He could probably buy new when he got where he was going, but he had some old favorites he didn't want to give up.

"What the hell do you think you're doing?" Furlough growled from the doorway.

Without looking up, Wyatt answered, "Packing."

He'd hoped to save this conversation for when he was already headed out the door, but one quick, guilty glance at the brick of a man standing in his path, frowning, with his arms crossed over his chest, and Wyatt knew he wasn't going to be that lucky.

"Why are you packing?" Furlough asked with exaggerated patience.

Wyatt sighed and picked up another shirt. Folding it as quickly as he could, he said, "They found me. They're here. I have to go."

"Where?" Furlough growled.

"They were waiting for me at the hotel, two men in a car."

"Two men in a car? That's it? That's what you saw?"

"Yes."

"And on that intel, you're just going to pack up all your stuff and run?"

Wyatt rounded on the old man and threw his hands in the air. "What should I do, just wait around, hoping I'm wrong, until they come for me, and risk them hurting you or… or someone else in the process?"

"I can take care of myself."

"Of course you can. I never said you couldn't. That's still not a risk I'm willing to take."

Forgoing the extra trip to get his saddlebags, Wyatt used the bedsheet as a makeshift sack and slung it over his shoulder. He made as if to push past Furlough, but the old man put a hand on his chest that didn't give an inch. "No."

"No?"

"No. I'm not going to let you do it again. I should've stopped you the first time." Furlough took a step forward, and then another, backing Wyatt into the room, despite the fact that Wyatt had a good eight inches on him. "For fifteen years, I've regretted letting you go. This is your home. This is your legacy. You and me, we'll fight for it together."

"Don't be ridiculous! It's just a house. It's not worth—"

"Your grandfather entrusted it to you, his life's work, his father's and his father's father's…. It's more than just a house. It's your life."

"I'm trying to protect my life! And yours and Adrian's! The house and its legacy will still be here in another ten, twenty, a *hundred* years."

"But you won't be, and neither will I."

Wyatt saw more than anger in Furlough's faded blue eyes, now that they were close enough to be shouting in each other's faces. He saw sadness too, and that more than anything made him stop and take a breath. He set his clothes back on the bed and used both hands to scrub his cheeks before he let them drop. "I know, Furlough, and I'm sorry. Look, I won't be gone as long this time."

"You won't be gone at all," Furlough growled. "If it is really them, it's time we showed these bastards you're done running."

With a helpless chuckle, Wyatt rolled his eyes. "This isn't *Rambo*, old man… or the OK Corral."

"And this ain't the movies or the Wild West," Furlough countered angrily. "We have a perfectly proficient sheriff's department, and thanks to the trust, we have a state-of-the-art security system… plus my crack team here," he said, pointing to the four dogs crowded nervously in the hall, watching Wyatt and Furlough go at it. "No one gets on this mountain without me knowing it, and all we have to do is hold out until Ian and his deputies get here."

With a deep sigh, Wyatt let go of his anger. It wasn't doing any of them any good, and it wasn't even directed at Furlough. In a move that caught the old man completely off guard, Wyatt pulled him into a tight hug and then shoved him back again. "I can't do that. I *won't* do that. I'm not going to risk you getting hurt. I'm not going to risk anyone getting hurt." He picked up his clothes and slung them back over his shoulder before heading out the bedroom door with a somewhat stunned Furlough following slowly behind him.

At the bottom of the stairs, he turned and met the old man's gaze. "I'm going to disappear for another year or so. That's all. I give you my word. And then we'll try it again."

Furlough's eyes narrowed, and he folded his arms across his chest. Silhouetted at the top of the stairs, with his canine guard flanking him, Wyatt could almost imagine the man holding the mountain against any and all comers. But Furlough was the closest thing he had to a father, after his own father had failed so miserably at the job, and he would not risk the man getting hurt.

"I'll see you soon, old man," he said sadly, turning his back to leave.

"And what about your friend… Adrian? You just going to leave him without a word of explanation?"

Did I say father?

Damn, but Furlough could sling guilt better than any mother he'd ever met. Frozen in the doorway, Wyatt hung his head. "I called him from Deer Park to say I couldn't make it and I had to leave town."

"Did you tell him why?"

Wyatt threw a frown over his shoulder. "Of course not."

Furlough leaned against the wall and clucked his tongue. "This guy you've been mooning over for weeks now, this guy who finally got you thinking enough to go into the big house and imagine the possibilities, *this* is the guy you're just going to run out on with no real explanation whatsoever? Just a quick 'see ya later' from a bar phone?"

"I know. I know," Wyatt groaned.

"And this scenario doesn't remind you of anything? A phone call is so much better than a single piece of monogrammed stationary left on a hall table, right?"

Wyatt gasped and reeled back like Furlough had slapped him. He stared in shock at the man for a long time, but Furlough only jutted his chin stubbornly and wouldn't look away.

"That was a low blow, old man," Wyatt growled, anger replacing shock.

"Just sayin'."

"It isn't the same thing! That was my *father* who left his only son holding the bag and didn't have the decency to say good-bye to my face. I'm leaving to try to keep both of you safe, not throw you to the wolves, like he did with me. Besides, I've barely known Adrian for a month."

"Long enough to have you skipping around like you're walking on daisies," Furlough pointed out as he made a big show of studying his nails.

All four dogs turned back to Wyatt, like they were watching a tennis match, and a noise escaped Wyatt's chest that was somewhere between a laugh and a groan. "I gotta go. I'll be in touch. You know I will."

He stepped outside into the crisp autumn night and shrugged his leather jacket a little tighter. There would be frost on the grass by morning. He could feel it.

"I love you, old man," he whispered to the door before stomping to the garage to stow his gear.

As he cranked the engine and pulled out onto the driveway, he glanced back at the lighted windows of Furlough's cottage, thankful Furlough hadn't come out to continue their argument. His resolve had already started to weaken around the edges, and he didn't know how much longer he would've been able to hold out.

The gate clanked closed behind him with a finality that hurt, and Wyatt pulled onto the road with the same hollow feeling in his chest he always had when he left home, only made worse by the fact that he was leaving more than just home behind this time. When he reached the main road, he stopped, ostensibly to scope the area for anything suspicious, but it was more than that. He turned his wheel to the right, south, but didn't squeeze the throttle. Looking back to the north, he brooded for a long time, unable to make a move.

Furlough's words had cut, and while Wyatt believed the situations weren't the same, he still couldn't make that turn. Piled on top of his own guilt, the old man's words ate at him, and the hurt and confusion in Adrian's voice rang in his ears. It was his own fault for letting things with Adrian go too far. He never should have agreed to that second date, let alone the third or fourth… and they had been dates. He could fool himself all he wanted, but it didn't change the fact that he didn't just hook up with Adrian. He cuddled with the man and ate and talked. It wasn't just fucking. It never had been. He glanced south one more time before turning his bike north and hitting the gas.

In the two hours it took him to reach Elizabethtown, after stopping for directions, he never once spotted a car that might be following him. Granted, it was hard to tell in the dark, but the roads he took were pretty empty at that time of night, so he should've seen something.

He'd had plenty of time to think on the drive and replay his conversation with Furlough, and he was starting to feel a little silly for freaking out the way he had. Maybe Furlough was right. Maybe the guys in the car didn't have anything to do with him. Maybe he'd been jumping at shadows for so long he couldn't tell the difference anymore.

Maybe he was finally going off the deep end.

What he really wanted was to hide in a bottle of Maker's Mark for about a month.

No. That wasn't true. What he *really* wanted was to get to Adrian's and hole up with him there, until neither one of them could walk and the rest of the world went away.

He stopped at a gas station just outside of Elizabethtown. After borrowing their phone book and buying some coffee and a map of the area, he climbed back on his bike for the last leg. He had no idea what he was going to say when he got there, absolutely none. Half of him wanted to just say fuck it, get on his knees and beg Adrian to keep him. The other half was still in flight mode and was screaming at him to keep on driving and not stop at all, for both their sakes, but he couldn't be that guy. He couldn't leave Adrian hanging like that.

By the time Wyatt reached the street where Adrian's apartment complex was supposed to be, he was a little calmer. He was a grown man, after all. They hadn't exchanged vows. They'd dated, and now Wyatt had to leave. He just needed to do the decent thing and explain as much as he could face-to-face.

After spotting the sign for Adrian's apartment complex, he was about to signal his turn when he caught sight of a dark sedan with tinted windows parked across the street from the complex. A ghostly light, like from someone's cell phone, emanated from inside and then quickly cut off. Frozen, with his heart in his throat, he drove past them, circled the block, and pulled into the parking lot of a donut shop that backed to the wooded area behind the complex. Nearly hyperventilating, he cut the engine and shoved his shaking hands under his armpits.

The reason he hadn't seen any kind of tail was because they must have followed Adrian when he didn't show, or maybe they'd followed Adrian another time and already knew how to find him.

Fuck!

There was no question now. He wasn't imagining things.

Pacing the parking lot in a panic, he tried to think. He couldn't leave, not without at least warning Adrian. He could try to find a phone and call Adrian's cell again, but he wasn't sure Adrian would answer. Searching the area, he spotted a hole in the chain-link fence, and that decided him. He climbed through and cut across the wooded area to the back of the apartment complex, fighting panic the whole way. Sticking to the tree line, he searched through the open stairwells between each building until he spotted Adrian's car. The buildings were small, with only four doors per floor—two on each side of the stairwells—so he just had to figure out which door was Adrian's in the opening closest to his car.

He hoped.

He couldn't see the ominous dark sedan from where he was, so he prayed they couldn't see him either. He made a quick dash to the back of the building and studied the four doors on the ground level. One door had a messy pile of cardboard boxes sitting right outside, so he was pretty confident he could scratch that one off the list. He cut another based on the frilly fall wreath on the door. Adrian was into some of that kind of thing, but he didn't strike Wyatt as the "frilly" type. His wreath would be classy, if he had one. Unfortunately, the other two doors had no distinguishing characteristics at all.

The block of mailboxes in front of the building taunted him. Adrian's name would be on one of those boxes, and he'd know for sure, but he didn't dare risk it.

Worrying his lower lip, he quickly climbed the first set of stairs to the second floor and scanned the doors there, praying for a sign, any sign. Luck smiled on him when he spotted a spotless, tastefully scrolled welcome mat in front of a door with a numbered wooden plaque in place of the cheap stick-on apartment numbers the complex seemed to favor.

Hoping he'd chosen correctly, he snuck up and knocked on the door, glancing nervously over his shoulder the whole time. At least the apartment was at the back of the building, instead of the front.

CHAPTER FIFTEEN

ADRIAN SWORE as he sloshed his vodka and cranberry juice down the front of his shirt and pants in his struggle to get free from the couch. The room spun a little when he finally got to his feet, so he set his drink on the coffee table as the knocking started again.

"Okay. Okay," he grumbled.

He tripped and nearly fell over the picnic basket he'd left on the floor by the couch, but he managed to right himself just in time and stumbled the rest of the way to the door without further incident.

As a testament to how drunk he was, he didn't even bother looking through the peephole before unlocking the deadbolt and pulling the door open. Luckily, the chain was still on, so the door didn't fly back and bash him in the face with the force of him opening it.

"Wyatt?"

He blinked stupidly at the blurry vision in front of him, not sure if he should believe it.

"Hey, Adrian." Wyatt shifted from foot to foot and kept glancing back over his shoulder.

"How did you find me?"

There were a hundred other questions he should've asked, but that was the one that popped out.

"The parking sticker on your car. It has the apartment complex's name on it. It wasn't hard to find."

"Oh." Adrian swayed a little and had to grab hold of the doorjamb to steady himself. For the life of him, he couldn't think of anything else to say, and he just stood there frowning at the tops of the three letters tattooed on Wyatt's chest since that meant he didn't have to crane his neck.

"Can I come in?" Wyatt asked into the awkward silence between them.

Adrian pursed his lips, unsure how to answer that. His body wanted to say "hell, yeah!" but his heart wasn't on board with that.

Petulance won. "Why are you here?" he asked harshly, finally dredging the energy to tip his head back and glare into Wyatt's stupid, perfect face.

Wyatt—gorgeous, laid-back Wyatt—flinched and grimaced. "I need to talk to you. Please, let me in."

Rolling his eyes, Adrian closed the door and fumbled with the chain until it came loose. After letting Wyatt in, he shut the door again, squared his shoulders, and carefully placed one foot in front of the other, concentrating hard on not stumbling or falling, until he managed to reach the couch. With as much dignity as he could muster, he lowered himself to the cushions and motioned regally for Wyatt to take the small chair next to it.

"I thought you said all you needed to on the phone." He had to talk slowly or the words came out slurred. From the look on Wyatt's face, he wasn't fooling anyone.

"How many of those have you had?" Wyatt asked, pointing to the tumbler on the coffee table.

"Why do you care?"

He was pouting now, and his voice wobbled embarrassingly, but he'd had enough to drink that he didn't care. He'd heard the club music in the background when Wyatt called, and after he'd hung up, he'd googled the number just to make sure. Wyatt had gone back to Deer Park to see if he could find someone better than Adrian… and obviously he had.

Bastard.

Wyatt sighed deeply. "I do care, Adrian, a lot."

Adrian blew a raspberry with an amount of overspray that would have mortified him if he'd been sober. "Yeah, right. I checked the number, asshole. You called me from Deer Park. You were only ten minutes away from me, and you couldn't come and tell me in person?"

He was trying really hard to maintain his perfectly justified anger, but Wyatt kept looking at him with those amazing hazel eyes, brimming with regret and concern. In an attempt to hang on to his anger, Adrian lashed out with all the ugly thoughts that had been running through his brain since his long drive home. "I mean, I know I'm not the best you could do, but the least you could've done was tell me you were on the hunt for something better, before I drove all the way out there, only to get tossed aside for some other quick fuck you picked up. Was he as easy as me? Some other pathetic, desperate loser you knew would get down on his knees and thank God a gorgeous man like you was willing to give him the time of day?"

Wyatt reared back like he'd been slapped, and scowled. "That's not fair."

"Yeah? Well, sorry. I'm not feeling fair right now."

He reached for his glass for a little more fortification and completely missed it. Concentrating hard, he reached for it again, only to have Wyatt move the glass even farther away.

He lifted his head to glare at the man, but all he saw was black leather before Wyatt knelt on the floor between his legs and pulled him into a hard hug.

"I'm so sorry. I didn't mean to hurt you. I'd hoped we were keeping it simple enough that no one would get hurt, but I was fooling myself," Wyatt whispered into his hair as Adrian melted against the man's chest and breathed in the scent of leather, crisp air, and autumn leaves. "There are things you don't know about me. I wish I could stay and tell you all of it, but it's not safe. I have to leave. I don't want to. I *have* to. I wasn't lying to you. I don't know how else to deal with it. This cloak-and-dagger shit is beyond me. It sometimes feels like the only thing I know how to do anymore is run."

Adrian was trying to focus on every word, despite the man's warm, hard arms around him and the solidity of his chest, but Wyatt wasn't making any sense, and Adrian was supposed to be pissed off, dammit. Where the hell did his righteous fury go?

"What cloak-and-dagger shit?"

Wyatt sighed and squeezed him tighter. "I shouldn't say. It's probably better if—"

Oh wait. There it is.

Adrian shoved at Wyatt an embarrassingly long time before Wyatt finally let go and sat back on his heels. "You know what? I don't care. I don't want to hear it." He gave Wyatt's shoulder another shove, which did absolutely nothing, and glared at him. "I was the dumb one. You said from the start, and I was the one who was stupid enough to think that you could... you could...."

"Oh God, Adrian, don't do that. Don't cry." Wyatt dove back in, and Adrian was wrapped tightly in his arms again before he could put up any resistance.

Who's crying?

"I'm not—" Adrian began indignantly, but stopped when he felt something warm and wet trickle down his cheek.

Shit. Damned vodka.

He didn't cry. He never cried.

Well, okay, maybe that one time after his disastrous bathroom hookup, and he'd been a little weepier in general lately, but really, who could blame him when the world was falling apart?

"I'm sorry, Adrian. I'm so sorry. You weren't dumb. You were wonderful, and… there was something there. I just can't stay." He hugged Adrian tighter and pressed a kiss to his neck just below Adrian's ear. They were silent for a while as Adrian fought with himself, but then Wyatt sighed. "Look. A long time ago, my dad made some very poor choices. He pissed a lot of bad people off and then skipped out and left me with a big old target on my back, lots of men hoping to use me as leverage to get to him—not that it would have done any good, but they didn't know that… and I guess they still don't. It was a mistake to come home, my mistake. I honestly hoped they'd given up by now."

Reluctantly, Adrian pulled out of Wyatt's embrace so he could see the man's face, which wavered a little until Adrian shut one eye. "I still don't understand."

The smile Wyatt gave him held a wealth of sadness. "I know. I think it's better if you don't. Hopefully, they'll follow me when I leave town, but just in case, do you have somewhere else you can stay for a few days?"

Huh?

"Me? What are you talking about? Why would I need to go anywhere?"

"They probably won't bother you. They're probably just hoping you'll lead them to me, but if you have anyone you could stay with—"

"You're just going to leave?" A sudden jolt of fear was an excellent buzzkill, but Adrian's brain still hadn't quite caught up, despite the sudden pounding in his chest.

"Have you been listening to me? These are bad people."

"Then call the police."

With a huff, Wyatt let go of Adrian, jumped to his feet, and headed for the door. "The cops can't help, not with this. They didn't help fifteen years ago. All they wanted to do was try to pin things my dad did on me somehow, since I was the one left holding the proverbial bag… an *empty* bag, I might add." With his hand on the doorknob, Wyatt hung his head. He didn't turn to look at Adrian as he said, "I'm sorry, Adrian. I'm sorry for the mess. I'm sorry for hurting you.… I'm sorry for a lot of things. Just, be careful and be safe. It should blow over once I'm gone."

While Adrian stared stupidly, with his mouth hanging open, Wyatt opened the door and stepped through it. Before he closed it, he turned around and said, "Lock the door after I leave and don't let anyone inside that you don't know, okay? There's a car with tinted windows across the street from your complex. If you see anyone get out of it or anyone suspicious at all outside, call the cops. I don't think these guys are that dumb or that desperate, but just in case." He paused and dragged a hand through his stupid, perfect hair. "Good-bye, Adrian. Be safe."

With that, he closed the door, and all Adrian could manage was a slow blink for several seconds. Eventually his paralysis wore off, and he flopped back on the couch and groaned. "What the hell was that?"

The room spun a little, and he swallowed thickly against the sudden urgent pressure in his throat, but it was no use. He beelined for the toilet and barely made it in time as the drinks he'd pounded decided to make a sudden reappearance. He spent several long minutes praying to the porcelain god and only felt marginally better when the heaving finally stopped. His head pounded as he levered himself to his feet, washed his mouth out in the sink, and then stumbled to the kitchen for some water.

After his second glass of water and a few Tylenol, he thought maybe he was sobering up a little, but not enough to even try to make sense of what had just happened. His head and throat still hurt. His eyes were puffy. And there was no way he could handle that much weird right now, so he did the only thing he could. He locked and chained his front door again—"just in case"—stumbled to his bedroom, and fell face-first onto his mattress. He didn't even bother getting undressed.

The next thing he remembered was waking up to the most piercing ray of sunlight he'd ever experienced in his life, right smack in his left eye, and his bladder screaming at him for relief. His head swam when he sat up, but the need to pee overrode any other discomforts. It wasn't until he'd finished that the real pain started, and he moaned, clutching his head to try to keep it from cracking off his shoulders.

The coffeepot took forever to brew, since he hadn't set the timer for Sunday.

…and why hadn't he?

Oh yeah, because I was supposed to be getting my brains fucked out and going on a happy little hiking picnic in the mountains. That's why.

One thing was for sure, he was done with mountain hikes. He could take a hint. They weren't for him. He'd say he was done with drinking too, but he wasn't sure he could keep that promise with how shitty his life was becoming.

Slumped over his coffee, staring morosely out his apartment window, it slowly sank in that his happy little fantasy with Wyatt was over. He had no idea what to make of Wyatt's visit. What he could remember was a bit fuzzy and still didn't make any sense. But the end result was the same.

Did I totally miss that Wyatt had a screw loose somewhere?

He could have been lying, but why would he drive two hours just to lie to me? What would be the point?

And if Wyatt wasn't crazy, and he wasn't lying…. Adrian's chest tightened a little in anxiety as he moved to the window and peeked through his blinds at the small stretch of woods behind his complex. He didn't see anything out of the ordinary, no goons in tracksuits carrying baseball bats. A few of his neighbors were taking Sunday morning walks with their dogs. A few kids were kicking a ball around, but that was about it. For a second, he was tempted to put on a robe and go out to the front of the stairwell to see if that car with the tinted windows was still there, but he decided against it. He didn't want to know.

He didn't want to know any of it. He wanted the whole world to just go away for a while and let him nurse his wounds in peace.

With more ferocity than the task needed, he cranked the rod on the blinds until they were closed tight, trudged over to the coffeepot, poured himself another cup, and shuffled to the couch. He was hungover, hurt, overwhelmed, confused, and spooked enough that he was beyond functioning like a normal human being. Sunday was going to be a couch potato day. He would not be partaking in any hair of the dog, but he had a whole picnic basket full of fried chicken, potato salad, and fancy nibbles, conveniently resting next to the couch, and a whole queue on Netflix streaming to get through.

Maybe he'd mainline *Supernatural* again, or some other series he'd missed on its network run. He sure as hell wasn't touching any of the romcoms, not for a while, anyway. He could go full-on action movies all day, the big, loud, blockbuster kind.

Decisions, decisions.

MONDAY MORNING rolled around cloudy and gray, like Adrian's mood. He managed to drag himself out of bed and get ready for work on autopilot. He didn't really remember the drive, which was a little distressing, but he didn't have the energy to dwell on it. Numb was good. Numb didn't hurt. Numb didn't put any more cracks in his fragile ego.

But apparently numb wasn't working for Bev. After attempting to work on their résumés and LinkedIn pages for barely more than an hour, Bev called it quits and wouldn't let him do any more until he told her everything. He was proud of himself for keeping it together, though. He pretended it was someone else's story and his voice didn't quaver once.

"I'm so sorry, Adrian. He sounded so perfect too."

"You know what they say about things that seem too good to be true," he replied, propping his chin in his hands and frowning… pouting really.

"I'll take you somewhere nice for lunch, my treat…. And why don't you come to dinner at our place tonight?"

Looking into her earnest brown eyes, Adrian couldn't help but smile. Bev was a good friend, better than he deserved.

"Thanks, Bev. You're the best."

She smiled and shook her head. "Really, come over tonight. Isaac will make dinner, we'll hang out, drink a little wine, and totally not talk about what's-his-name."

He managed a weak chuckle. "I'll take you up on lunch today, but I'd better take a rain check on dinner. I'm not the best company right now. I think I need to take a little alone time. I mean, I jumped right in with Wyatt on the rebound from Martin. I shouldn't have done that. Obviously I wasn't thinking clearly. I should've known better than to stray so far from my comfort zone. I'm just not that guy. I never was."

She frowned at him like she wanted to disagree but didn't know quite what to say. After a short silence where she squeezed his hand reassuringly a few times, she cleared her throat and said, "Well, what about what he said, though? Do you think he was serious? Should you be worried about 'bad guys' coming to get you?"

Adrian moaned. "I don't know. The whole conversation is kind of a blur. He was really freaked-out. He didn't seem like the guy I knew at all… but maybe that's the point. I guess I don't know him as well as I thought I did. I thought I knew the important stuff, like he was kind and funny and so damned good to me when we were together. He made me feel—God, he made me feel so good about myself and… shit."

He couldn't say any more or he'd get weepy again, and that was so not happening in his office, even if he was pretty sure Bev wouldn't think less of him for it. She opened her mouth, but whatever her response might've been was interrupted by the ding of the elevator. They both turned to look through his open door as Perretti stepped out, lifted a hand in greeting, and hurried into Adrian's office.

"Oh good, you're both here," he puffed.

The man looked even more harried than he had the week before, and Adrian and Bev shared a look before giving him their full attention.

"I know this is short notice, but you'll thank me after you hear me out," Perretti began. "We have auditors coming in this week, an outside company. They're going to need access to your computers, and the file cabinets, so I need you to leave them unlocked." Perretti threw his biggest, somewhat painful-looking smile at them. "But the good news is, starting this afternoon, you can go home, on paid leave, for the rest of the week."

"But—"

Bev only got that one word out before Perretti rolled over her. "Spend some quality time with your families. Take a well-deserved break, on the company." He picked up Adrian's jacket and shoulder bag and handed them over before extending an arm for Bev and ushering her toward her office.

Bev threw a questioning look over her shoulder but allowed herself to be led out, while Adrian stood frozen, his bag and jacket hanging limply in his hands. A moment later, Bev emerged into the hall with her coat and purse, but she was no longer silent.

"Wouldn't it make more sense for us to be here when the auditors arrive… to explain or help them find what they need?"

Perretti shook his head. "No need. I'll be here if there are any questions. It's just routine, to satisfy some possible investors. Nothing to worry about."

They both tried to get more out of him on the short elevator ride down, but Perretti just threw more empty assurances at them and walked them out to the parking lot. "I'll call you when they're done. It shouldn't take long. I know both of you do fine—make that *outstanding*—work. Enjoy this well-deserved break. You've earned it!"

Perretti beamed at both of them, and Adrian had the sinking feeling that the whole world had suddenly gone mad. They were both left speechless as the man did an about-face and headed back into the building with a quick wave.

"Did he just kick us out?" Bev asked.

"Uh, yup."

"At least we should be able to depend on him for a good reference," she quipped somewhat dazedly.

"Lunch?" Adrian asked, still staring after Perretti.

"Yeah," she chuckled. "Although I think I might need a liquid lunch, at this point."

They debated various theories for Perretti's weirdness throughout the meal, each more fantastic than the last, but weren't any closer to understanding than they'd been before they started. After lunch, Adrian somehow managed to convince Bev he would be fine enough on his own that night, but it wasn't easy. She let him go, but first he had to promise to call tomorrow and come to dinner at least once that week.

With a last concerned look at his office building, Adrian climbed in his car and headed home for some peace and quiet. It now looked like he had a whole week to wallow in his misery uninterrupted by work.

Yay.

At least the car with the tinted windows was gone when he arrived home, replaced by a regular, boring white work van. Maybe Amanda's boyfriend had managed to reclaim his spot, though Adrian couldn't see anything special about the van that warranted so much concern over its safety as he drove by it.

Once in his apartment, he hung his jacket and bag on the hooks by the door, kicked off his loafers, flopped onto his couch, and stared blankly up at the ceiling. Now that he was alone, he expected to be freaking out, but he was surprisingly unfazed by the day's events. Maybe he was just in shock from the general theme of upheaval in his life lately, and there was a major freak-out somewhere on the horizon, but right now he was pretty mellow. He glanced around his plain little apartment with dull, tired eyes. Maybe he was just done with emotions for a while. That would be nice.

Maybe he should get a cat?

Martin had been allergic, but he didn't have to worry about that anymore. Cats were quirky, unpredictable, rebellious... all the things he wasn't. A cat would make this place homier, and he'd have someone he could depend on, to come home to, but a cat wouldn't be so dependent he'd worry about leaving it alone every day. A cat would be nice.

He'd almost dredged up the energy to retrieve his laptop from his dining table so he could search for the nearest animal shelter when his phone started ringing. It took him a couple of rings to fish the thing out of his pocket, and when he finally saw the screen, he almost dropped it.

Wyatt's name was on his caller ID. He contemplated letting it go to voice mail for about a half a second, but who was he kidding? He was still pathetic enough that his heart had leapt in his chest.

"H-Hello?"

"Is this Adrian?" a gravel-filled voice asked.

Frowning and feeling his heart race for a different, less pleasant reason he said, "Yes."

"This is John Furlough. I'm a friend of Wyatt's. Don't know if he ever mentioned me."

Guessing the man expected some sort of answer, given the silence on the other end, Adrian replied, "No. Sorry. Uh, he said he was staying with a friend, but…."

Mr. Furlough grunted. "That was me. You seen Wyatt recently?"

Feeling a sudden jolt of anxiety he couldn't quite explain, Adrian asked, "How do you know Wyatt again?"

The gravelly voice on the other end chuckled. "Good answer. You don't know me from Adam. I got that. And maybe Wyatt gave you a bit of a scare before he ran off. I know you got no reason to trust me, son. I wouldn't, if I were in your shoes. But I'm running out of options here, and I think maybe you're just the thing I need to get that boy to stop running from the boogeyman and fight for what's his."

Shaking his head, Adrian slumped back into the couch cushions as the beginnings of a headache started between his eyes. "I'm sorry, Mr. Furlough, but I don't know what you're talking about, and I have no idea why you'd think I could be any help."

"You don't, huh?"

His skepticism was pretty clear, and Adrian flushed, wondering what Wyatt had told the man. He cleared his throat and tried again. "Listen. I don't know what Wyatt may have said to you, but he already said his good-byes to me. Whether you are who you say you are or one of the men Wyatt warned me about, the truth is, I don't know where he is or how to get in contact with him, and he made it sound like he definitely had no intentions of coming back here."

It hurt to say the words out loud, but Adrian needed to say them, and he needed to keep saying them until his heart believed them.

"He'll be back… and soon, if I know my boy."

"Well, I'm glad you think so," Adrian said a little more snidely than he'd intended.

Mr. Furlough just laughed again, the sound like tires on a gravel road. "You got spunk. I like that. You might need it."

Rolling his eyes, Adrian was about to say good-bye when the man cut him off, his voice much gentler now. "Listen, son. You don't know me. I don't know you. But Wyatt's important to me. The whole family was, once upon a time, and he's the only one left... or at least the only one left who's worth a damn. The question is, is he important enough to you to take a chance?"

Sitting up, Adrian raked a hand through his hair and sighed. "Mr. Furlough—"

"It's just Furlough," he interrupted.

"Furlough, then. I don't know what you want from me. If you know about me, then you know Wyatt and I only just started seeing each other, and... well, we didn't exactly exchange vows of undying love or anything, if you know what I mean. I obviously didn't know enough about him to see any of this coming, and I have no idea how I could possibly be of any help to you."

"You may not, but I do," Furlough answered, infuriatingly sure of himself. "Look, all I'm asking is for you to come see me. I have something I want to show you. And if you do that and you listen to what I have to say and still don't think my boy's worth fighting for, I'll lose your number and leave you be from now on. You have my word."

"You have my word."

His heart twisted painfully as those words echoed in his head in Wyatt's voice.

"I mean what I say and I say what I mean."

Adrian had a bad feeling his meltdown was closer than he originally thought, and now he sure as hell wasn't going to be able to stay in the quiet of his apartment tonight.

"Where are you?"

"You got a pen?"

Furlough rattled off the address and then proceeded to give him detailed directions. "Don't trust that GPS or Google too much. Once you get into the mountains, they tend to get a little confused. Just follow my directions and call this number if you get lost. What kind of car you got?"

"A beige Honda Civic."

Furlough grunted. "I'll keep an eye out for you and buzz you through the gate when I see you pull up."

"Oh, okay."

"You comin' now?"

"I, uh…."

What the hell am I doing?

I'm being totally insane. That's what I'm doing.

"Yeah. It'll take me a little over two hours to get there, though."

"That's fine. I'll be waitin'." Furlough hung up without saying good-bye while Adrian tried not to hyperventilate.

With shaking hands, he texted the address to Bev's cell.

She texted back immediately.

What's this?

Where I'm going. I'll call you tonight. Just keep the address in case you don't hear from me.

His phone started ringing a second later, and he smiled. "Really, Bev, it's fine. I just wanted someone to have the address."

"But this is out where you met Wyatt, right? Did something happen?"

"Nothing yet. I'm going to meet a friend of Wyatt's. His name's John Furlough. I don't know. He seems more like a dad or a grumpy uncle than a friend. He kept calling Wyatt 'my boy,' but not in a weird way, more like in a dad or grandpa way."

"And you think it's a good idea to drive all the way out there by yourself? After what Wyatt said about bad people being after him?"

Adrian sighed as he grabbed his loafers from beside the door and brought them back to the couch. "I know. But he called from the same number Wyatt used, and, I don't know, I feel like I need to do this. I need some kind of closure, or I'm going to go crazy. Besides, that's why I'm telling you where I'm going. Plus, I had an idea. One of the bartenders at Deer Park—the bar where I met Wyatt—is the sheriff down there. So I'm going to swing by on my way and see if I can talk to him before I go up. See there. I'm using the old noggin'."

"Or, you could just not go at all and tell both Wyatt and this Furlough guy to take their bullshit and hit the road," she threw back at him.

He laughed, mostly because that's probably the smartest thing he could have done, but he was tired of being smart, and he had to admit, now that the initial panic was wearing off, he was dying of curiosity, dying to learn more about Wyatt. Also, a tiny part of him wanted to believe Furlough when the man said Wyatt would be back soon.

Stupid? Probably. But there it was.

"I'll be okay, Bev. And I'll call you later. I promise."

CHAPTER SIXTEEN

THE HUGE, ornate wrought-iron gate in front of his car slowly swung open with a clank of metal and the whir of a motor as soon as Adrian pulled up next to the keypad and rolled down his window. The sun was setting behind the mountains, so he couldn't see much more than the faint outlines of nearly leafless trees and a winding gravel track running through them, off into the darkness beyond his headlights.

"The beginning of every horror movie *ever*," he grumbled.

It was just his luck that Deer Park was apparently closed on Mondays too, so Bev was the only one who knew he was up here. And, of course, his phone had no signal.

"You gonna sit there all night, or are you gonna come up?" Furlough's rough voice crackled over the speaker, making Adrian squeak and nearly jump out of his skin.

"Yeah. I'm coming."

He rolled up his window against the cold and took his foot off the brake. Once through the gate, the enormous thing swung closed behind him, and he swallowed nervously as it banged loudly and with finality. He really should have waited until daylight for this. He wouldn't be as creeped out if he had… maybe.

The road seemed to wind on forever in the narrow beams of his headlights, up and up into the darkness. It probably only felt like forever because he was driving about five miles an hour, but he was too nervous to go any faster, and when he first spotted the roof of the house, silhouetted in the twilight, he nearly pulled his foot off the gas entirely and slammed on the brakes.

Roof? No. He should have said roofs. There were several.

"It's a goddamned castle."

As he pulled into the circular drive, complete with fountain, several spotlights came on, nearly blinding him. Blinking away the spots, he put the car in park and slowly got out. Furlough was nowhere to be seen, no one was, so Adrian was free to gape his fill.

The mansion in front of him was enormous. Flanking the ornately carved stone archway above the impressive front doors were two double-storied wings that continued off into the darkness beyond the lights. Despite their being mostly in shadow, he could see the faint outlines of numerous turrets and chimneys. He'd never exactly paid much attention to architecture before, but the arched windows and carved stone detailing around every opening and along the roofline reminded him of some Catholic churches he'd seen. The turret roof caps ended in needlelike points he could barely see the tops of, and he thought there might even be a few more on the back of the building that he couldn't quite make out.

He was so enthralled, squinting at the place and trying to take in every detail, he nearly had a heart attack when a gruff voice spoke in his ear. "Nice place, ain't it?"

Adrian bit back a yelp and smiled weakly at the man while he tried to get his pulse under control. After finally putting a face to the voice, Adrian felt a little less like he'd been invited to Dracula's keep, and he relaxed marginally.

Furlough was a brick of a man, broad in the chest and shoulders, but not much taller than Adrian. His plain jeans, serviceable boots, and quilted flannel shirt were what Adrian had been expecting, even if the man's square, stubbled jaw, hard lips, and piercing gaze hinted at a sort of caged power, despite his thinning gray hair and wrinkles.

Furlough extended a hard, calloused hand, and Adrian shook it. "It's nice to meet you in person, Mr.—I mean Furlough."

The man's craggy face split in a grin that helped settle Adrian's nerves even more. "I'm glad you decided to come. Real glad. Come on. It's cold out here. Let's go inside."

He lifted an arm, indicating Adrian should precede him up the stone steps to the giant wooden doors. Adrian was on the second step from the top when he froze at the sound of dogs barking in the distance… lots of dogs with deep, scary barks. Or was it wolves? Did they have wolves up here?

He turned a wide-eyed stare to Furlough, but the man just smiled reassuringly and motioned for Adrian to continue. "Nothing to worry about. I sent the pack on a perimeter check, just in case whatever got Wyatt so spooked was more than just in his head. That's most likely excitement over your arrival or maybe some deer."

Furlough reached past him and put a big iron key in the lock. The door swung slowly open, but if Adrian had been expecting a squeal of hinges, like in the movies, he was disappointed. The door glided open silently, and he stepped into the entryway with only the sound of their footsteps echoing off the marble floor into a large space beyond. Furlough flipped a couple of switches by the door, and an awe-inspiring crystal chandelier lit up the grand staircases in front of him. Beyond the marble columns, the staircases dominated the room in more marble and red carpet, coming together on the second floor before splitting off again toward the two wings. Massive windows flanked the top of the stairs, and a large tapestry depicting some sort of battle hung between them.

As Furlough stomped off to the left, leading away from the stairs, Adrian trailed behind, spinning in circles so he didn't miss anything.

More tapestries, gilt-framed paintings of stoic-looking people, stained glass windows and lamps lined the rooms Furlough led him through. Most of the furniture was draped in white, so the place had a spooky, unused feel about it, but it was obviously clean and well cared for. What he could see of the décor seemed to be a mishmash of styles, from Victorian ornate and gilt to blockier, darker medieval-looking items, complete with a suit of armor in one dark corner—not the kind of things one usually would expect from a house in the mountains of Maryland.

Furlough finally stopped in what looked like an office, where a fire burned brightly in the marble hearth, and Adrian went to it gladly. Despite his jacket, the air was much colder in the mountains, and the house was only marginally warmer than outside.

"I'd offer you something to drink, but the kitchen is as empty as the rest of the place. If you want, we can take a walk back down to my place in a bit, and I'll fix you up there," Furlough said as he settled into what looked like a leather wingback chair, draped in a white sheet.

Still feeling a bit overwhelmed, Adrian sat in the one opposite. "Are you going to tell me what this is all about now?"

Furlough pursed his lips and waved a hand. "You're looking at it. It's about this place."

"But what is this place?"

"It's a home, *Wyatt's* home. He belongs here—if the nitwit will only stop running long enough to realize it." He frowned at Adrian and clucked his tongue. "I'm not going to live forever. I need to get him settled while I still can. I won't leave those bloodsucking lawyers to pick my replacement. They don't love this place like I do. They don't know what it means, what it represents. Besides, it needs to be a home again, not just a damned dusty museum. I need you to help make that happen."

"Wait." Adrian held up a hand. "This is Wyatt's house? Like he actually owns it?"

"In a manner of speaking. It's his to use, if he wants it."

"He left all this behind, and you think I'm what would make him come back?"

A broad smile warmed Furlough's craggy face as Adrian stared at the man like he'd lost his mind. "Like I said, I know my boy. He just needed the proper motivation. A kick to the pants has never seemed to work, so I'm hoping a kick to the heart will."

Adrian flushed. "I still think you're vastly overestimating my influence."

"He drove out to say good-bye in person, didn't he?"

"Well, yes, but that doesn't mean...."

At a loss to explain the obvious, Adrian just trailed off while Furlough settled back into his chair with a smug smile. "He'll be back. All you have to do is give him a reason to stay once he does."

Suddenly agitated, Adrian shot to his feet and started pacing in front of the fire. This conversation was so ludicrous it was laughable. Maybe he should pinch himself to make sure he wasn't asleep on his couch, dreaming.

Furlough let him pace in silence until Adrian couldn't take it anymore and rounded on the man. "You know, I really do think the whole world has gone completely crazy. I mean, barely more than a month ago, I was a boring accountant, with a boring apartment, and apparently a perfectly unsatisfied boyfriend. Now, my boss has gone off the deep end, I'm probably going to lose my job, my new boyfriend—scratch that— *lover* suddenly skips town because he thinks bad guys are after him, and I have a complete stranger telling me my lover is actually what? A prince from a secluded castle, and only I can get him to return? Oh wait, Wyatt's last name is Prince, if that isn't just effing hilarious."

His chuckle sounded a little hysterical, but he'd never coped well with change, and his breakdown was definitely on the horizon.

Dropping his head back to stare up at the play of light against the dark wood tray ceiling, he tried to catch his breath and calm down. The mess of his life wasn't Furlough's fault. He wasn't going to lose it in front of a complete stranger, particularly since that stranger had the air of someone who could end him with his pinkie or something.

Another slightly hysterical giggle escaped him, and he clapped a hand over his mouth.

"You know, his last name isn't really Prince," Furlough murmured. "My boy's got a twisted sense of humor. It's actually Everett."

Adrian let his hand drop and tipped his head down to glare at the man. "Well, that's just great! He didn't even trust me enough to tell me his last name, and you think what? He's going to come back and face whatever it was that could possibly force a six-and-a-half-foot mountain of a guy like Wyatt to flee with his tail between his legs? And then what... sweep me off my feet and vow to stay forever?" He huffed out a breath, turned, and headed for the door. "I think I need to go home now."

He didn't quite make it out the front door before Furlough caught up with him. Of course, the four giant German shepherds with tongues lolling out of gaping maws full of big, pointy teeth between him and his car might have had something to do with it.

"Hold on there, Adrian. Just give an old man a minute, please?"

Adrian took a quick glance over his shoulder before turning his nervous gaze back to the dogs. "Sure. No problem. I got nothing but time." He was proud to note there was only a tiny tremor in his voice, but Furlough's quiet chuckle let him know the sarcasm had come through loud and clear.

"Come down to my place, and we'll have a little talk. I'll make you some tea."

Furlough was obviously making an effort. The man's voice sounded as unused as the house behind him, and Adrian got the impression he didn't invite just anyone to tea. For some unknown reason, this was very important to Furlough, and Adrian was a sucker for anyone who made him feel special. He could admit that about himself. And he could also admit that there just might be enough of a pretty-pretty princess buried inside him somewhere that wanted to believe he could be the guy Furlough thought he was, that he could be the reason the prince wanted to return to his castle. It was stupid and completely unrealistic, but what did he have to lose by hearing the guy out, right? He'd already driven the two hours; what was a few more minutes?

He also had to pee in a major way, and he didn't look forward to returning down that gravel road with a full bladder, nor relieving himself against a tree in the cold mountain air.

"Okay. I'll stay a little longer. But I have to tell you, I kinda think you're a little crazy."

Furlough chuckled as he gripped Adrian's shoulder in the vise of one hard hand and steered him away from his car. "You wouldn't be the first."

Adrian accepted a steaming mug of tea and gratefully cupped his frozen hands around it as he settled back into Furlough's lumpy plaid couch. By the time they'd finished the walk from the house, his teeth had started chattering, and though Furlough's house was clearly heated and he'd started a fire in the small hearth, Adrian still hadn't thawed out quite yet.

Furlough's cottage was a stark contrast to the grandeur of the big house. It was small, only two stories, and barely wide enough for a room on either side of the door. The inside was decorated plainly in a hodgepodge of styles from the fifties, sixties, and seventies, if Adrian had to guess. Everything seemed a little worn, but still clean and serviceable, like Adrian remembered his grandparents' house being when he was a kid, before they'd sold everything and moved to Florida.

He could feel his guard going down even as he told himself appearances could be deceiving, but the warmth from the fire and Furlough's solicitousness were definitely getting to him.

Just as Adrian's eyelids started to droop a little, Furlough sat in the small rocking chair next to the couch and cleared his throat. "Now, I ain't much of a storyteller, but I get that you need some answers, and I'm pretty sure Wyatt hasn't told you any of this, so here goes. More than a hundred years ago, Wyatt's great-great-grandfather started building this place. He made buttloads of cash in steel and coal and all kinds of other things—had houses all over the place—but the story goes that he and his wife fell in love with this mountain and decided to waste some of those buttloads on that great big thing over yonder." He flapped a negligent hand in the direction of the big house before taking a sip of his tea.

"After he died, his son and then his son's son, Wyatt's granddad, added to it and took care of it. Wyatt's granddad was a good, solid man, did his part to keep the family fortunes together, to keep the *family* together. But somewhere along the line, he screwed up with Wyatt's dad. I don't know if it was Wyatt's mom dying, or the man was just a bad seed to begin with, but whatever happened, Wyatt's dad dropped the ball." Furlough set his mug on the end table between them, leaned forward, and pierced Adrian with his faded blue eyes. "You'll never hear me say this in front of Wyatt, but that man didn't deserve to be called a father. What he did to Wyatt... what he would've done if Wyatt's granddad and great-granddad hadn't started the trust that made sure he couldn't touch this place." He growled and slumped back in his rocker. "The man was useless from day one, didn't know how to do nothing but waste his money... only managed to get a law degree because Wyatt's granddad forced him to. Then what did he do with that degree? Makes me sick to think about it. Lawyers. Feh. Shoulda known when he decided to become a lawyer."

Adrian had kept silent, trying to follow along, but he was lost. "I'm sorry. I don't understand."

Furlough's lips twisted in a wry smile, erasing the dark scowl that had been there. "Sorry. Told you I weren't much of a storyteller.... The reason our Wyatt has some trust issues is because of his daddy—the reason he's afraid to come home for good, the reason this old place is empty, and that poor boy spends his life running instead of living." He grabbed his mug and took another swallow before sighing. "Anyway, Richard Everett, Wyatt's dad, blew through his trust fund quicker than water, particularly after Wyatt's mom passed away and he married that... *woman*, Wyatt's stepmother—although you never could've called that woman any kind of mother in my opinion. So when the trust fund was bled dry, Richard went to his dad begging for money. I was just the head groundskeeper here at that time, you see, so I only got it from Phyllis the housekeeper secondhand. But there was a big hoo-hah—yelling and carrying on. Wyatt's granddad wouldn't give the bastard a red cent. So what did Richard do? He went out and got himself a job. But not just any job. I don't know if it was spite or something else, but he used his connections and joined a law firm with some of his other trust-fund buddies. And who was their biggest client? Johnny Bianchi, that's who."

Furlough paused there, looking at Adrian expectantly, but Adrian had no clue who he was talking about.

"The mob guy. The gangster," Furlough said with a huff, when it was obvious Adrian wasn't getting it.

Adrian suppressed a laugh. Furlough had had him riveted until he'd used that word, but now Adrian felt like he was entering the land of the absurd again. Was James Cagney going to come out in a pin-striped suit, carrying a tommy gun? Or maybe Marlon Brando would give him an offer he couldn't refuse? Or Tony Soprano?

"Are you serious?"

Furlough scowled at him, and Adrian tried to school his expression, but he wasn't very successful. "Gangster, crime boss, gang leader, whatever you want to call bad people who get their money illegally and don't mind hurting other people to do it. Yes, I'm serious. Yes, they still exist, and Wyatt's dad stole millions from them and skipped the country, leaving his son with a big old target on his back from both the feds and Bianchi."

"Wait. What?"

"You heard me. The asshole stiffed his mob buddies, and his so-called business partners, grabbed the cash, and disappeared. He left his son behind with only a good-bye note that said little more than 'so long, have a good life' and skipped the country with his wife, leaving a lot of angry men with guns behind, searching for a way to get at him."

"Jesus."

"Yeah," Furlough agreed. "Wyatt and his dad, they were never close, particularly after the stepwitch came into the picture and Wyatt's granddad died. But that was cold. The man had to have ice in his veins to throw his own son to the wolves like that. But now you see where our boy Wyatt might have a little trouble with trusting people."

Adrian set his mug down and stared at the man, the tea a cold weight in his stomach. "So, uh, let me get this straight. If I'm understanding you correctly, Wyatt actually does have people after him. There's a real reason that he's afraid, and those people might be after me now too?"

"No. I mean, yes, there *was*, at one time, a possibility that these guys could come after Wyatt and either try to get him to tell where his dad was—which he had no idea—or try to use him to coerce his dad into coming back... or possibly just gun him down in revenge—"

"Oh, is that all? And here I thought we were talking about something horrible," Adrian threw in, at Furlough's casual tone.

Furlough frowned and rolled his eyes. "I'm trying to tell you that this was fifteen years ago. The money is long gone. Richard Everett is long gone. Even if they never managed to recoup any of it from Richard's former partners, which I highly doubt they did, there's no way they're still staking out this place in the hopes Wyatt might someday return... or even less likely, that Richard might. Fifteen years is a long time. I think it's more likely Wyatt has been jumping at shadows so long he doesn't know how to stop."

"But...." Adrian strained to remember what Wyatt had said. "He said he saw them... that he was being followed. Are you saying he's hallucinating?"

Furlough's bushy eyebrows knit. "Not exactly. But maybe he's seeing what he expects and not what's actually going on. Maybe there's another explanation. Or, even if they are who he thinks they are, maybe it's time he stopped running and faced them, once and for all."

Adrian shivered and wrapped his arms around his chest. This conversation had gone into territory that was so far beyond anything his life experiences had prepared him for it was laughable. The ferocity with which Furlough had spoken that last sentence made Adrian uneasy to say the least.

"Look. Thank you for telling me all this. At least now I have some idea of what's going on, why he left. But honestly, I don't know what this has to do with me. I mean, not to go into intimate detail or anything, but my relationship with Wyatt was not exactly deep, if you know what I mean. He didn't tell me this himself. If, as you seem to think, he had actual feelings for me, he would have invited me here to see his home, wouldn't he? He would have talked to me about some of this. He would've told me *something*." He jumped up and headed for the door. After grabbing his jacket off the hook in the entryway, he said, "Thank you for the tea... and the stories, but I think I should head home now. It's over a two-hour drive, and it's already pretty late. I need to get home before I fall asleep."

The dogs stirred from their puppy pile in the corner, and four pairs of eyes watched him as he tugged on his jacket.

Furlough sighed from close behind him. "You don't have to drive home. Like you said, it's late. I got a spare room you can sleep in, and then you can leave in the morning."

"Thanks, but I think I'll sleep better at home."

Furlough folded his arms across his broad chest and pursed his lips, but when Adrian reached for the doorknob he said, "Wait. Just think about what I said, okay? He's a good boy, Wyatt. He deserves a life and a home with someone like you."

"You don't even know me."

"I know enough. I know how Wyatt's been since he's been seeing you, and while I asked you up here to show you the place, I also wanted to get a look at you and see for myself, see your reaction to the old place. I like what I see. You look like you belong up there."

Adrian couldn't hold back the bark of laughter. "No offense," he said with a chuckle, "but I think maybe Wyatt isn't the only one seeing what he wants to see, Mr. Furlough. I grew up in a double-wide, in the back end of coal country, Pennsylvania, with my parents and two sisters. There is no way I could possibly ever belong in a place like that."

Furlough didn't stop smiling. "You came all the way out here, didn't you? You wouldn't have done that if you didn't care."

Adrian didn't have anything to say to that. He wanted to stick his tongue out at the man, but all he did was shake his head.

"Just tell him to come home, when he calls," Furlough said quietly.

A blast of cold air hit Adrian as he opened the door. "I don't think he's going to call," he said over his shoulder.

"He will," Furlough said before closing the door and leaving Adrian to make his way back up to his car alone.

The floodlights were still on at the house, and Adrian couldn't help but take another long look at the place, but that's as far as he was willing to let himself dream. He was a grown-up who lived in the real world, and he had messes of his own he needed to get back to, including possibly pounding the pavement and skimming want ads.

CHAPTER SEVENTEEN

AFTER GETTING home close to midnight, Adrian went straight to bed but slept fitfully. He'd like to blame the cup of coffee he'd picked up on the way to make sure he stayed awake enough to make it home in one piece, but it had more to do with the fact that he couldn't stop thinking about Wyatt. Sleeping in Wyatt's arms, Wyatt's smile, his hands, the worry and sadness on his face the last time Adrian had seen him, all of it played through his mind, making sleep damn near impossible.

In the morning, he stumbled to his kitchen and nearly cried in relief when a full pot of hot coffee greeted him. Thank God, the timer on the pot was still set for a regular weekday. He was probably going to have to refill it and make another pot before he felt human enough to face the world.

He needed an IV drip.

He'd just finished pouring his second cup and was reaching for the creamer when someone knocked on his door, making him jump and spill hot coffee over his hand. Hissing in pain, he wrapped a towel around it and hurried to the peephole as the knocking became more insistent.

A man and a woman, both in dark suits, stood outside his door. They must have heard him by the door because the woman pulled a wallet from her pocket and flashed a badge at the peephole. "Mr. Walnak, this is Agent Truitt and Agent Walker with the FBI. May we speak to you?"

With shaking hands and his gut twisting, Adrian opened the door but left the chain on. "Yes? Can I help you?"

"Are you Mr. Adrian Walnak?" Agent Truitt asked.

"Yes."

"Sir, if you don't mind, we'd like to come in and speak to you for a moment."

"What is this about?"

"Please, sir. We just have a few questions for you. May we come in?"

Adrian looked down at his T-shirt and pajama bottoms and grimaced, but he figured he was decent enough. He closed the door, took the chain off, and opened it for the two agents. "I wasn't exactly expecting company," he said by way of apology as the agents came in, and he shut the door behind them.

Fidgeting nervously, he fell back on the manners his mom had grilled into him. "Can I offer you a cup of coffee?"

Agent Truitt gave him a small smile and shook her head. "Thank you, but no. We're fine."

"Then, uh, p-please, sit down."

He waved a hand to indicate the couch, wincing at the stutter. He'd like to blame the weirdness of the past few weeks for his nerves, but the truth was authority figures—particularly cops of any kind—made him nervous. He never knew whether he'd done something wrong without realizing it. He blamed his mom for that deep-seated guilt.

The agents took up positions between him and the door and watched him closely as he sat in the small chair across from the couch.

"So what is this all about?" Adrian asked.

"We'd just like to ask you a few questions, sir. You work for Pacciano Bros construction, correct?"

Truitt seemed to be the talker of the two, so Adrian tried to focus on her, but the other agent, Walker, was scanning his apartment with such intensity Adrian had a hard time ignoring him.

"Yes."

"In their accounting department?"

"Yes."

"Your direct boss is a Mr. Jim Perretti, correct?"

"Yes, he is. Is there something wrong? Is Mr. Perretti okay?"

Truitt raised one gold eyebrow a little and searched his face. "Why would you ask that?"

Swallowing his nerves, he shrugged. "I don't know. You mentioned him. I was just trying to figure out why you were here and—" He stopped there as a sense of loyalty made him a little reticent to blab the man's personal business to the FBI.

"And?" Truitt pushed.

"I don't know. I guess he's been acting a little weird lately. I just wanted to make sure he was okay. Now, will you please tell me what this is about?"

"You weren't at work today or yesterday afternoon, Mr. Walnak. Can you tell us why not?"

Frowning, Adrian said, "My boss gave us paid leave while an independent auditing team was supposed to come into the office. Wait. How did you know I wasn't at work?"

Truitt exchanged a glance with her fellow agent and leaned forward. "So Mr. Perretti sent you home?"

"Yes. But—"

"Did he tell you why he didn't want you there?"

Frustrated that she wasn't answering any of his questions, Adrian started to get a little annoyed. "He said we'd be in the way and that he could handle any questions the firm might have. It was supposed to be for some investors who wanted an independent review before they'd agree to invest in the company, I think. Now, please, just tell me what this is all about. Is there something wrong with the company or Mr. Perretti? Did something happen at the office?"

Adrian hadn't heard anything on the news or seen anything online, but he also hadn't been paying much attention to the world outside his own drama the last day or so. A small jolt of fear ran through him as his imagination started to supply him with every horror story in recent memory of people going postal in offices and schools, and bombs going off.

"Do you have any travel plans, Mr. Walnak?" Agent Walker asked, finally turning his piercing gray eyes away from his inspection of Adrian's apartment and spearing Adrian with them.

"What? No. Why would that even matter?"

"And have you taken any out-of-town trips recently?"

Now Adrian's fevered imagination immediately jumped to Wyatt and the things Furlough had told him last night. "Why would you ask me that?"

"Please, Mr. Walnak, just answer the question," Walker said, his heavy brows lowered and his lips pinched in a severe line. If the man was going for intimidating, it was working. But Adrian hadn't done anything wrong, and he wasn't going to be bullied in his own apartment when they wouldn't answer a single one of his questions.

Straightening his shoulders and wishing he was dressed in something other than a ratty T-shirt and plaid pajama pants—and that he couldn't feel his cheeks heating—Adrian said, "Look. I don't know what's going on here, but my personal life is just that, *personal*—as in no one's business but mine. If you want me to answer questions about it, you're going to have to give me a good reason to do so."

Truitt was the one who leaned forward this time, her smile conciliatory. "Of course, Mr. Walnak, and we don't mean to intrude. We're in the middle of an investigation. We're just making sure there are no loose ends, and we want to understand where you fit in."

"Fit in to what?"

Truitt and Walker exchanged another look, and after a short pause, Truitt sighed and said, "As we speak, Mr. Walnak, warrants are being served for Pacciano Bros financial records, all of them. We expect to begin making arrests very soon. What we need to determine is on which side of those arrests you would like to be."

Up until that moment, Adrian had been thinking Truitt was the nice one, but now he wasn't so sure. Her words slid like ice down his spine. Adrian tried to breathe against the vise around his chest. "I-I don't understand. Why w-would I... I mean, why would you.... Jesus. What the hell?"

Wincing at his sudden lack of verbal skills, he glanced back and forth between the two of them, hoping one would take pity on him and answer his poorly vocalized questions. The two agents continued to study him impassively as he floundered. Adrian wasn't sure what they were looking for, but eventually Truitt's expression softened a little and she said, "Mr. Walnak, are you saying you can't think of any reason why we would be here talking to you?"

"No," Adrian blurted out, finally managing to find his voice. "I don't know anything about this. I mean, things have been a little weird at work lately, with new policies and Mr. Perretti acting pretty odd, but... no, I have no idea why you'd be investigating the company. I don't know what you're looking for. But I can promise, you won't find anything wrong with the financial records."

"Oh?" Walker was the one who spoke, but they both perked up at that. Adrian had the queasy image of two predators sensing prey, and he swallowed hard.

"No. Bev and I, we do our jobs. We're good at our jobs." Neither agent had lost that predatory look, so Adrian cleared his throat. "I mean, we do our jobs *honestly*. We report everything to the IRS, we pay our employees and withdraw and report wage taxes. Everything's aboveboard and legal. We're accountants, every column adds up, every t is crossed and i is dotted. Both Bev and I stand by our work.... Wait, are you guys questioning her too?"

They seemed a little disappointed at his speech, but Truitt at least shook her head in answer. "We will be conducting interviews as

the process continues, but we haven't as yet spoken to Mrs. Tullman...
unless you think we should."

Oh, good God, I'm so over my head right now it's not even funny.

"No! No. I just wondered why you were talking to me. I promise
you, Bev and I haven't broken any laws. If you're getting the records,
then you'll see that."

Both agents seemed to relax a little as they studied him again. At
least Adrian felt like some sort of curious bug under a microscope now,
instead of a rabbit staring down two wolves.

"Mr. Walnak," Truitt began after the silence became a little too
awkward. "Based on information we've already gathered, we were
prepared to believe you had no part in the crimes we've been investigating.
However, your recent behavior has led us to question that decision. To be
frank, when someone we believe to be an innocent bystander starts acting
strangely and out of character, just as we're wrapping up an investigation
that has taken months, if not years, it makes us a little nervous. You
see, we like to dot our i's and cross our t's as well, particularly in an
investigation of this magnitude." As Adrian continued to stare with his
mouth hanging open, Truitt cleared her throat and leaned toward him
again, her expression severe. "We were led to believe you and Mrs.
Tullman were merely innocent bystanders, but then you started making
sudden trips out of town and having what one might call *clandestine*
meetings in a motel. Add to that the fact that you were seen entering
the property of a man with known mob ties, and you can see where that
might make us question the information we've been given."

"Uh, no, wait... that was... that was personal. It didn't have
anything to do with the company."

"Then what did it have to do with?"

Flustered, Adrian flapped his hands around uselessly, and when he
managed to speak again, his voice had gone up at least an octave, and it
cracked embarrassingly. "I told you. It was personal. I was just meeting
a—a friend. It was just a long-distance, weekend thing. That's all....
Wait. You guys were following me?"

He felt like an idiot because it took him that long to figure it out,
but despite the shocked and offended look he gave them, neither agent
seemed the least embarrassed or bothered by it.

Truitt shrugged. "Like I said, we like to be thorough, and when
someone in the periphery of our investigation begins to act out of

character, we like to know why. You need to understand the scope of this investigation, Mr. Walnak. This isn't a game. This isn't just some minor tax evasion case. This is serious. The people you work for have major crime ties, and your company is a front for that. We find it difficult enough to believe you and Mrs. Tullman could deal with the finances of such a company for several years and not be involved, but it isn't impossible. However, if there's something you would like to tell us, before things get really messy, now would be the time to do it."

It's a fact. The world has gone absolutely batshit insane.

"No. No. I don't have anything to tell you, because I don't know anything about this. I shuffle paperwork. I pay bills and taxes. I write invoices and make sure all the columns add up. That's all I do."

Truitt's smile was kind and understanding, though Adrian wasn't so sure he could trust it now. "We understand that, Mr. Walnak. We do. You're not a bad person. You're not a violent criminal. The men you work for are way out of your league, and maybe you don't know all the things they get up to—out of sight, out of mind, as it were. But it's guys like you, Adrian, the guys who handle the money, they're the ones who are the biggest help to us in our investigations. They're the ones who know about the bank accounts and the money trails. They're the ones who help us catch these guys who do the real crimes, the violent crimes. And when they help us to stop these real bad guys, we help them too."

He might have been completely blind to what was apparently happening at his company, but he wasn't an idiot, and right now he was done being shocked.

"Look. I get what you're saying, but I'm really not your guy. Believe me, if I'd had any idea that Pacciano Bros was doing anything illegal, I would've quit a long time ago. I'm sure you hear this all the time, but I'm not lying to you. I don't know anything useful. Whoever told you that Bev and I weren't involved wasn't lying either. We're just accountants, doing our jobs as well and honestly as we can. You'll see that when you go through our work. And as for that whole going to someone's house with mob ties thing, I was just going to see a friend. I didn't know anything about the rest of that."

He felt a twinge of guilt for not revealing all he knew about Wyatt and that whole business with Wyatt's dad, but honestly it didn't have anything to do with whatever was happening with Pacciano Bros, and it wasn't like he knew anything of the specifics.

Truitt and Walker exchanged one more glance before Walker nodded and they both stood up. Adrian scrambled to his feet as well. "Thank you for your time, Mr. Walnak. We appreciate you speaking to us." Truitt pulled a card out of her suit jacket and handed it to him. "If you do happen to think of anything pertinent to our investigation, don't hesitate to call, anytime. We have a lot of long nights in our future, and anything you might think of would be helpful."

He could still hear a slight warning in her voice, despite her words, and he had to wipe his palm on his pants before offering it to them. "I don't think there's any way I could possibly help you, but I'll definitely let you know if I think of anything."

He went around them to open the door. Walker stepped out first, but Truitt paused in the doorway. "I do recommend you take your boss's advice and stay away from your office for the time being. I think it would be better for all concerned, though I wouldn't recommend any big trips in the near future, in case we need to question you again."

With that, the two agents left, and Adrian closed the door and collapsed against it. God, he was tired, but he needed to make a call. He picked up his cell, only to find the battery had died. After hooking it to the charger, he plopped down on his bed, quickly swiped past his notifications, and dialed.

"Hey, you!"

"Hey."

"I tried to call you a couple of times this morning. I was worried."

"Forgot to plug it in last night after I got home."

"You were kind of out of it. It's a good thing you called me on your way so I could help keep you awake. Anyway, guess who called me first thing this morning. The big boss, Eddie Pacciano himself."

"What?"

"Yeah. I know, right? I've barely ever said two words to the man, and he's calling my cell. But that's not the weirdest part. He wanted to know where I was and why I wasn't at work. How would a member of the crack-of-noon club even know we weren't there? And he asked about you and Perretti too. Although, why he'd expect Perretti to be there that early in the morning, I have no clue."

"That's why I called, Bev. The FBI were just here."

"What? Why?"

"They're investigating Pacciano Bros. They told me they were serving warrants as we spoke."

"Jesus, Adrian! What the hell is going on?"

"I wish I knew. The agents were too busy asking me questions and treating me like I'd done something wrong to fill me in on the details. All I got was that they think Pacciano Bros is a front or something for some very bad people, and they've been investigating for months, maybe even years. I kept telling them you and I didn't have anything to do with it, but I'm not sure they believed me."

"Holy shit! Oh my God. Oh my God." She gulped. "We haven't done anything wrong, though, so there's no way we could be in trouble, right?"

"I don't think so. I hope not."

She groaned. "You're supposed to be more reassuring than that."

"Hey, I'm trying. But it's not every day the FBI comes knocking on my door. I'm a little freaked-out right now… on top of already freaking over everything with Wyatt and all that. I'm telling you, I don't think I can handle any more surprises. I'm gonna lose it."

"Okay. Okay…. Whew! Let's just take a little breather here. We haven't done anything wrong. So, in theory, that means we have nothing to worry about. Who knows? Maybe this is just some big mistake, and it'll all get cleared up in no time."

"Thanks, Pollyanna. Would you like a rainbow with your silver lining?"

She tsked at him. "Don't get snippy with me. I'm trying here."

He sighed. "You're right. I'm sorry. It's just been a weird few weeks, and I didn't get much sleep last night."

"Don't worry about it. Hey, at least losing my job is the least of my worries now. There's a bright side for you."

He laughed. He couldn't help it. He took a breath and forced his shoulders to relax. "We don't know anything concrete, and we haven't lost our jobs yet, so let's agree to not panic until we hear something official, okay? *And*, it's only a couple of months 'til Christmas, and then only a little longer 'til tax season is in full swing, so you know we can definitely find something then to hold us until we get new jobs, even if we lose this one," he reminded both of them.

"Yeah. Keep going. I think my panic attack is fading."

He laughed again. "Um, okay. Uh, this could be a good thing for us too. Who knows? Maybe there's an even better job waiting out there just for us, with a raise and more vacation time and—"

"Okay, stop. You've gone too far into happy la-la land now," she interrupted.

Rubbing his aching head, Adrian settled a little deeper into his pillows and closed his eyes. "It's going to be okay, for both of us."

"Yeah, it is."

"Call you later?"

"Yeah. Get some sleep. I need to get hold of my husband and try to figure out a way to break this to him gently, so he doesn't make me panic again."

"Bye, Bev. Good luck."

"Bye."

He must have passed out, because his watch said it was after one o'clock the next time he looked at it. Still a little groggy and out of sorts, he took a shower and got dressed for real this time. He didn't have any plans to go out, but somehow he felt more prepared to search the Internet for any news on Pacciano Bros, read through want ads, and figure out what the hell he was going to do now with actual clothes on.

Lucky for him he'd made the right decision getting dressed—otherwise he would've been on his way to meet Edward—Eddie—Pacciano in his pajamas. A very large man in a chauffeur's uniform and cap knocked on his door at about five. Adrian had barely made it through a couple of pages of online want ads at that point. He shouldn't have gone with the guy, but he couldn't think of any reason to refuse a meeting with the owner of his company, particularly when he was technically still being paid. Also, he didn't see the other hulking brute in a suit until he'd already made it out to the waiting vehicle, and by then it was too late to come up with an excuse not to go.

The trip in the large black SUV was nerve-racking, mostly because the men who'd come to get him weren't much for small talk. They didn't seem overly menacing in their attitude, but they were big and silent and serious, and the agent's words from earlier, like *violent* and *criminals*, kept swirling around in his head.

The SUV pulled up in front of a quaint little Italian restaurant in downtown Harrisburg, and Adrian felt some of his tension ease. They were in a public place, with plenty of people walking up and down the street.

Edward Pacciano stood as Adrian came in, followed by the men in suits. The smile the owner of his company gave him was broad and welcoming.

"Adrian, come in. Sit down."

He knows my name?

"Thank you, sir." Adrian took the seat Edward gestured to after shaking the man's hand.

"Don't bother with the sir. Call me Eddie, please."

"Okay." Adrian tried to smile, but it wasn't easy with the nervous fluttering in his stomach and the hint of an impending breakdown hovering at the edges of his consciousness.

The big men in suits, still looming behind him, weren't helping either.

"I know this is a bit strange, Adrian. I'm guessing you've heard by now that our little company is under federal investigation."

Eddie wasn't a large man, maybe a few inches taller than Adrian, but not much. His auburn hair, brown eyes, and open smile had always given Adrian an impression of warmth whenever the man had deigned to come into the office. In the past, Adrian had always wondered why everyone, including Perretti, was so tense around Eddie. But now, sitting close to him and being the center of his attention, Adrian was starting to get an inkling. It wasn't anything overt, just an underlying coldness or sense of power in the man. Or maybe after everything he'd heard, Adrian was becoming paranoid. He'd always thought he bought into the whole "innocent until proven guilty" thing, but apparently his gut wasn't particularly concerned with being fair.

"Yes, sir—I mean, Eddie. I heard."

He wasn't sure what he expected Eddie to say next, but he sure as hell wasn't prepared for the man to relax against the back of his seat and laugh like he didn't have a care in the world. "Don't look so worried, Adrian. There's obviously been some sort of mix-up somewhere. My lawyers are sorting it out now. Things will be back to normal again soon. I'm sure." He signaled a waitress. "Would you like something to drink, or maybe something to eat?"

"Maybe just a glass of water," Adrian croaked. His nerves were getting worse, not better. If Eddie was trying to soothe him with that speech, he wasn't doing a very good job.

The waitress brought a jug and filled the water glasses on the table. When she left, Eddie sat forward again and said, "Look. I know this is a bit odd, talking here, but since things are obviously a little crazy at the offices right now, I figured this was a better place to chat. Mostly, I'm just curious why you and your colleague and boss weren't at work today when all of this started."

Adrian gulped down some water and couldn't help a furtive glance at the men behind him. "Mr. Perretti told us to go home yesterday. He said an independent auditing firm was coming in for some investors, and we should take paid leave and get out of their way for the rest of the week."

"Did he? Interesting."

At that moment, Adrian wasn't sure how he could've ever associated the word warm with Eddie Pacciano. Eddie's eyes looked more black now than brown, and Adrian shivered.

"And do you know where Jim is now?" Eddie leaned forward as he spoke, bracing his elbows on the table, and it was all Adrian could do not to scoot his chair back to put more distance between them. The men still looming behind him were motivation enough to stay put.

"No. I haven't seen him since he sent us home."

"Have you heard from him at all?"

Though Eddie's voice was still calm, and his expression only betrayed a bland interest, Adrian's heart was beating a mile a minute, and he could feel a prickle of sweat at his temples and down his back.

"No. I—"

His phone started ringing in his pocket, and he jumped. Fumbling it out, he checked the screen, but didn't recognize the number. He was about to hit Ignore when Eddie waved a hand at him and said, "Please, go ahead."

"No, it's okay. I don't have to—"

"Answer it," Eddie commanded.

Swallowing, Adrian hit the screen. "H-Hello?"

"Adrian? It's Wyatt. I just wanted to check in to make sure you're okay… and to apologize again for running out on you like that. I feel terrible about it."

Under any other circumstances, Adrian would have danced a little jig that Furlough was right and Wyatt had actually called him again, but the fact that the goons behind him had moved closer so they could hear both sides of the conversation made him want to panic and run, not dance.

"No big deal." He forced a laugh. "I'm sure I'll catch you next time, Wyatt."

There was a pause on the other end of the line, and Adrian felt all the eyes in the room boring into him as a bead of sweat trickled down his jaw to the collar of his shirt.

"Are you okay? You sound odd," Wyatt finally said.

"No! I'm fine!" he replied a little too cheerily, and winced at his volume. Clearing his throat, he forced his voice into a more normal register. "Just work stuff. You know, the usual. Listen, Wyatt, I gotta go. I'm out with some people, and I don't want to be rude." He flashed Eddie an apologetic smile. "But before I let you go, Furlough asked me to tell you he wants you to come home. You should maybe call him, okay?"

"You talked to Furlough?"

"Yeah. Sorry, but I really should go now. I'll talk to you soon. Bye."

Doing his best to hide his shaking hands, Adrian blindly fumbled behind him to stuff his phone in his jacket pocket as the goon nearest him sneered. "Who was that, your boyfriend?"

The other goon chuckled, making Adrian flush, but Eddie cut a withering look at his men, silencing them. He turned his dark eyes to Adrian and studied him a moment before he said, "Since you don't appear to be hungry, Adrian, let's cut to the chase. I sent my friends here to check in with you earlier since I hadn't been able to get you on the phone, to make sure you were okay and to see if you knew where Jim Perretti was. He didn't show for work today, and with everything going on, we were understandably concerned, especially since none of us has heard from him." He pursed his lips and frowned. "But here's the thing, Adrian. When my friends here came to talk to you, they saw you were already talking to a couple of very official-looking people in suits, and when they came back to tell me this, I was understandably surprised."

Adrian fidgeted but met the man's intense gaze. "The FBI wanted to talk to me."

"What did they have to say?"

"Only that they were serving warrants at the office today, and they'd been running some sort of investigation for a long time."

"And what did you say?"

"Nothing, really. I mean, they acted like I'd done something wrong, but I told them I didn't know anything. I just did my job to the best of my ability. I never cut corners. I never did anything illegal."

Eddie nodded along as Adrian talked, unnervingly calm considering the topic of conversation was a huge federal investigation into his company. "Did they ask you about Jim?"

"No, not really. They just kept insinuating that I had something to hide and that I should tell them now, rather than later. But I swear, if someone was doing something illegal, I didn't have anything to do with it."

He was practically hyperventilating now, and Eddie's expression softened, though the smile he gave Adrian didn't reach his eyes. "I believe you. You seem like a very honest man. I've always thought so. Therefore, I'm going to ask this just one more time. Do you know where Jim Perretti is, or where he might have gone?"

"No. I have no clue."

Eddie nodded. "Okay. Well, since you don't seem hungry, I'll just have the boys take you home."

"But—" One of the men behind him began to object. Another look from Eddie silenced him.

Eddie stood up, and Adrian scrambled to his feet. "Thank you for coming to meet with me, Adrian. I appreciate your taking the time."

As if I had any choice.

Adrian forced a smile and shook the man's hand. When he drew his hand back, he found Eddie had given him a card.

"This is the direct line to the company's lawyers. Should the FBI wish to speak to you again, please call and wait for them to send someone, on our dime. We don't want the feds bullying you without someone on your side."

Adrian nodded and tried not to look like he was running for the door.

"And don't worry," Eddie called after him. "This little misunderstanding should blow over in a few days, and we should all be back at work in no time. Enjoy your vacation, Adrian."

"Thank you," Adrian wheezed as he pushed through the door, the goons following closely behind him.

The drive home was possibly even more nerve-racking than the one there. Too many episodes of *Law & Order* had Adrian watching every turn the SUV made to make sure they were indeed headed back to his apartment. He was sweating so hard he had to take his jacket off for fear of overheating and passing out, despite the chill in the air now that the sun had set.

Just let me get home. Please, just let me get home.

He had no idea who he was praying to, but at this moment, anyone who'd listen would do. When the lights of his apartment community came into view, Adrian almost wept with relief. They stopped in front of his building, and the men didn't even look at him as Adrian let himself out of the enormous SUV.

As he passed the mailbox, he considered getting his mail but decided it could wait until morning. He desperately needed the relative safety of his apartment, and he was definitely *not* going to be opening his door again tonight, no matter who knocked on it.

He'd just reached the top of the stairs when he noticed a shadow by his door. For a brief second his heart leapt in his chest, thinking it might be Wyatt, but then he heard the squeal of tires from the parking lot behind him and saw Jim Perretti's balding pate as it caught the overhead light. One panicked glimpse over his shoulder revealed the goons pouring out of their vehicle and the glint of something shiny and black in each of their hands.

"Run!" Adrian shouted as he did the same.

There was no thinking, only panic. Fight or flight kicked in, and he sprinted down the stairs and barreled out the opening between the buildings and into the woods behind the complex. He could hear Perretti's labored breathing behind him, and he slowed enough to grab the older man's sleeve and drag him along. The woods weren't very deep, just big enough for a little dog walking and to block the view of the ugly donut shop beyond. A chain-link fence ran along the perimeter, but Adrian knew there was a cut-through everyone used to satisfy fried dough and sugar cravings. The only problem was, at this hour, the shop was very well lit, and they'd be spotted easily if they headed for it.

He heard a crashing off to his left, not too far away, and he dragged Perretti down a small drainage ditch and clapped a hand over his mouth to muffle his heavy breathing. Fumbling with his other hand, he searched his pockets for his cell, and that's when he realized he'd dropped his jacket in his headlong flight.

Fuck!

Screaming a few more obscenities in his head, Adrian fought down his panic. They'd barely gone a hundred yards, and Perretti was already wheezing. What the hell were they going to do?

When the crashing moved off a little ways, Adrian leaned close to Perretti's ear and whispered, "I need your phone to call the police."

Perretti shook his head. "It's in your bag," he gasped.

"What?"

"That's why I'm here. I—"

"Shit. Later," Adrian hissed, holding up his hand to silence him.

Creeping up from their little gully, Adrian spotted a tiny square of light in the woods and whimpered. Leaning close to Perretti again, he whispered, "They're calling someone, probably more people. We need to make a run for it."

"My car's over there," Perretti wheezed, pointing to the back of the apartment lot.

Adrian thanked the weather gods it had rained sometime the night before and the leaves on the ground were damp as they shuffled as silently as they could toward the end of the complex. Once or twice they had to hide behind a tree as the goons got a little close for comfort, but, miracle of miracles, they managed to sneak through another opening in the buildings without being spotted.

Poking his head around the side of the building, Adrian scanned the parking lot. When he didn't see anyone, he motioned Perretti forward and then followed him to a burgundy sedan Adrian didn't recognize. The stickers in the window identified it as a rental. Adrian slid into the passenger seat and hunkered down, closing the door as quietly as he could. Perretti got in on the driver's side but didn't start the car right away.

"What are you doing? We need to get out of here!" Adrian hissed, though why he was still whispering, he hadn't a clue.

"I need your bag, Adrian. I need my phone."

"We can call the cops once we get somewhere. Just drive."

Perretti shook his head. "No. We're not calling the cops. He has them on his payroll."

"What are you talking about? Who has who on what payroll?" Adrian was beginning to wonder if Perretti had really lost it.

"Dirty cops," Perretti said, like Adrian was an idiot.

Yup. He's lost it.

But this was so not the time to be arguing. "Okay. The FBI, then. We'll call the FBI. But first we need to get out of here. Those guys had guns! We need to find someplace safe and call the FBI."

"No FBI. I need my phone."

"Jesus, Perretti! Forget about the stupid phone! I'll buy you a new one. Just get us out of here so we can call someone."

Adrian made a grab for the keys Perretti still had in his hands, but the man lifted them out of reach and pulled a gun from his pocket. In mute shock, all Adrian could do was blink as an actual firearm was pointed at him for the first time in his very boring life.

"I need my phone, Adrian."

Sweat poured down Perretti's temples and glistened on his bald spot. He was flushed and still heaving in breaths like he was going to have a heart attack, but as soon as that gun started wavering in front of him, that was all Adrian could see.

"What the hell?" Adrian croaked.

Perretti sighed and wiped his forehead on his sleeve. "I'm sorry, Adrian. I didn't want it to be like this. I tried to keep you and Beverly out of it, but they left me no choice. I had to get my phone away from the office, and the feds were picking me up to take me to a safe house, where they would've taken it away from me. It has very important information on it, Adrian. I can't leave it."

Trying not to hyperventilate, Adrian forced himself to blow out a slow, calming breath before he managed, "Okay. It's important. I got that. But if they were taking you to a safe house, then you're working with them, right? So we just have to get to a phone, call them up, and they can get here, and we can all get my bag together. That's a good plan, right?"

"We're not calling the FBI. I'm not going to testify. Moira and the kids are already on a plane out of the country, and I'm going to be joining them as soon as we get my phone."

"Mr. Perretti, you can't just—"

"It's not up for debate," he said, holding the gun a little more firmly. "All I need is that phone, Adrian, and I'll be gone."

Stifling a groan, Adrian spotted movement out of the corner of his eye and swung his head away from Perretti in a panic, but it was just a couple of his neighbors heading for their car. He desperately wanted to wave, to signal them somehow, but he kept still. He was scrambling for some sort of plan or something he could say to make Perretti change his mind when he heard the loud rumble of a motorcycle entering the parking lot. Recognizing the sound, Adrian turned toward it, half hoping, half fearing what he'd see.

Wyatt!

Even in the dark, there was no mistaking Wyatt's powerful six-and-a-half-foot frame as he pulled up in front of Adrian's building and climbed off his bike. Wyatt paused next to Adrian's car, and once more when he seemed to catch sight of the SUV double-parked and still running a little way off. Adrian's heart leapt when Wyatt suddenly scanned the parking lot more closely.

"Do you know that man?" Perretti asked as Adrian fought with himself about what to do.

"Uh...."

How the hell did he answer that? He had thugs with guns combing the area for them, and his boss holding a gun on him in the car, his boss who refused to leave until Adrian somehow magically managed to get the phone that was stashed in a bag hanging behind the door in his apartment.

Insanely, Adrian kind of wished the FBI was still suspicious of him, so they'd still be tailing him and a whole army of men in suits would come barreling down on them any second.

"Get him over here," Perretti ordered, cutting that little fantasy short.

But Wyatt had already turned away and was climbing the stairs to his apartment.

"Shit," Perretti swore. "Come on, we're going over there."

"Are you crazy? Hello? Bad guys with guns are out there!"

Perretti motioned with his gun, and whining in the back of his throat, Adrian climbed out of the car.

Did he think his boss might actually pull the trigger on him?

Not really.

Was he willing to take that chance with his life?

Absolutely not.

They huddled against the side of the building just as Wyatt reached the bottom of the stairs again. When Perretti poked Adrian in the ribs with the gun, Adrian hissed as loudly as he dared, "Wyatt!"

"Adrian." Wyatt's relief was palpable until he got close enough to see the look on Adrian's face. "What's going on? Are you okay?"

"Forget the small talk," Perretti hissed as his head whipped in all directions, searching for their pursuers. "Give him your keys, Adrian. Tell him where to find your bag."

Wyatt must have spotted the gun, because his face hardened, and he glanced nervously between Adrian and Perretti.

With a wince of apology, Adrian pulled his keys out of his pocket and handed them to Wyatt. "Please. Go inside my apartment and get the bag that's hanging just inside the door and bring it back here."

Wyatt took the keys, glanced once more at the gun, and hurried back up the stairs as Adrian and his captor kept to the shadows. Wyatt returned less than a minute later, carrying Adrian's bag, and Adrian blew out a relieved breath. He took the bag from Wyatt and offered the whole thing to Perretti, but Perretti shook his head. "Back to the car, both of you."

"No. You have the phone. Take it and go," Adrian objected, but Perretti shoved the barrel painfully into Adrian's ribs.

"Stop arguing. Both of you in the car now. I can't have you calling the cops until I get a decent head start."

They scuttled back to the rental, and after forcing Adrian into the driver's seat and Wyatt into the passenger's, Perretti climbed in the back. As they were pulling away, Adrian spotted the two goons coming out of the woods and heading toward their SUV, but if the goons spotted them, they were too far away to do anything about it.

"What the hell is going on? Who are you?" Wyatt demanded as soon as Adrian pulled out onto the highway.

"I'm so sorry, Wyatt. I didn't want to involve you in this.... This is my boss, Jim Perretti."

With his face screwed up in what Adrian could only describe as a WTF expression, Wyatt swung around to glare at Perretti. In the rearview mirror, Adrian saw Perretti actually smile and give Wyatt a little wave with the hand not currently holding a gun. "Nice to meet you, Wyatt."

Apparently unimpressed with the introduction, Wyatt scowled at the man. "Where are we going?"

"Only a little farther," Perretti answered, his good humor seemingly returned now that he had the phone he'd been desperate to retrieve.

"And what happens when we get there?" Wyatt growled.

"Don't worry. As soon as Adrian here gets us a suitable distance from civilization, I'll drop you two off and be on my way. No harm, no foul."

Wyatt fell silent then, though he placed a hand on Adrian's thigh and squeezed. Now that some of the adrenaline was wearing off, the only thing Adrian wanted to do was find someplace warm to curl up in Wyatt's arms and never climb back out.

"Perretti, what's going on?" Adrian asked when the silence in the car got too much and his hands started slipping on the wheel from how much they were sweating.

"You mean right now or in general?" Perretti seemed way too calm for someone holding a gun.

"In general."

"I really didn't want to involve you or dear Mrs. Tullman. I promise you that was never my intent. But the feds changed the plan for picking me up at the last minute and I needed to sneak the phone out of the building."

Adrian frowned at him in the rearview. "Well, I'm involved now. I think you owe me at least a little explanation. The FBI showed up at my door. Thugs with guns chased me. Then you pulled a gun on me too. I mean, what the hell?"

Perretti nodded and settled against the back of the seat with a sympathetic smile. "I'm sorry, Adrian. I know it's a lot to take in. Ever since I married Moira, she's been pushing me to get out, to cut ties with the Pacciano family. I have kids now, and I'm just too old for this shit anymore. When the feds approached me with what they already knew, I caved. I had to turn state's evidence to save my own ass."

"So it's true, then, that stuff the FBI said about the company?"

"Let's just say all the money the company handled was not from construction. I just made it look like it was. But it isn't anything you need to worry about. I was the one who doctored the paperwork and made the money come out squeaky clean on the other side. You and Beverly only dealt with the numbers I gave you. They can't pin anything on you. I'm the one they want. But no way in hell was I going into witness protection so I could be an insurance salesman in Boise or something. I earned this money. I'm getting out no matter what it takes." He patted the pocket where he'd put his phone.

"That's why you needed it?" Adrian asked, trying hard to ignore the 'no matter what it takes' part of his statement.

"Yes. It's my insurance policy—bank accounts, passcodes, all the numbers I need to start a new life. The great thing about being the one to hide the money is that you know where to find it too."

There didn't seem much else to say, so after casting one nervous and apologetic glance at Wyatt, Adrian went back to concentrating on the road and praying that this would all be over soon. About an hour outside of town, Perretti had Adrian pull off onto a dark, deserted stretch of road and made him and Wyatt get out of the car.

"I'm going to need your phone, Wyatt, and any cash the two of you have on you," Perretti said.

"He doesn't—" Adrian began as he pulled out his wallet, but he stopped when Wyatt handed a cell phone to Perretti.

At Adrian's look, Wyatt shrugged. "I picked one up on the way out of town. It's what I called you from earlier, figuring you could put it in your contacts if you, you know…."

"How very sweet. This one's a keeper, Adrian," Perretti said cheerfully as he accepted what little cash Adrian had and the stack of bills Wyatt begrudgingly handed over. "Now all you boys have to do is head back the way we came. It shouldn't take you too long to reach that gas station we passed a while back, and I won't even bother asking you not to call the cops. I'm sure you will anyway. Good luck, Adrian. I'm sorry about how all this turned out. I tried to keep you out of it, but I needed someone to sneak this baby away from the feds."

Perretti patted his jacket pocket again and hopped into the car. Then he peeled off, spraying gravel and dirt on them as he went.

As soon as he drove away, Wyatt rushed to Adrian and grabbed his arms. "Are you okay? Did he hurt you?"

"I'm… I'm fine. Just a little shaken up."

He was a *lot* shaken up, actually, but he still had some pride left.

"What the hell is going on? What was that?" Wyatt demanded.

In fits and starts, Adrian told Wyatt about his colossally awful day as they walked back toward civilization. It wasn't long before he was huddling against Wyatt for warmth.

"So those two men I saw at the motel and your apartment were feds watching *you*?" Wyatt asked incredulously.

Adrian shivered, and Wyatt stopped long enough to unzip his leather jacket, allowing Adrian to slide partly underneath. Perfect as he was, Wyatt had already offered to give Adrian his jacket and go without, but Adrian had manfully refused.

Masculine pride was a bitch sometimes.

Wyatt's question sounded rhetorical, but Adrian answered it anyway to break the sudden silence as they started walking again. "Yeah. I guess so."

With a bark of laughter and a shake of his head, Wyatt pulled Adrian tighter against his side. "Furlough was right. I was running from shadows. I'm an idiot."

Adrian managed a weak smile and a chuckle too. "Yeah. Joke's on you. The accountant is the one who has mobsters after him."

Wyatt stopped again and pulled Adrian into a bear hug. "I'm so sorry. This must have been terrifying. I'd know better than anyone."

Adrian buried his frozen face against Wyatt's chest and just breathed him in. "I can't even imagine doing this for fifteen years," he mumbled. "One day, and I'm about ready to fall apart."

"It wasn't really that bad. I had a few close calls at first, ducking out of bars and a couple motels. The men my dad screwed over were pretty pissed and *really* wanted to know where their money was. I was too good at running though… but maybe that's more of a curse than a blessing these days."

With his hands and his face buried in Wyatt's warmth, Adrian really didn't want to get moving again, but the lower half of his body was turning into a Popsicle, so he reluctantly pulled away. "I'd love to continue this conversation, but my lips are going to freeze pretty soon, so let's find us someplace warm."

Luckily, hypothermia was averted by the timely arrival of a friendly flower delivery truck driver on his way home from work. After Adrian and Wyatt flagged him down, the man drove them to the nearest gas station, and they called the police from there. The police contacted the FBI, and after Adrian and Wyatt's second cup of blessedly hot coffee, Truitt and Walker showed up to drive them back into town.

Wyatt was tense and uncharacteristically sullen and hostile with the agents from the moment they stepped out of the car, but it took Adrian's exhausted brain until they were tucked into the back of the sedan to figure out why.

"You okay?" Adrian whispered.

Wyatt nodded, never taking his eyes off the agents in the front seat.

"You sure?" Adrian pressed.

At last Wyatt's lips curved slightly, and he turned to meet Adrian's concerned gaze. "Yeah. Just bad memories, I guess. The last time I was in the back of an official vehicle, they were dragging me in to interrogate me about my father, and every mobster on the East Coast was after me. It wasn't a good time for me."

With the agents not-so-subtly eavesdropping, it was hard to think of what to say to that, so Adrian grabbed his hand and squeezed, hoping the gesture conveyed his sympathy and understanding.

"It wasn't the feds I was running from, anyway. I didn't do anything wrong, and while they sure as hell didn't help matters any, I'm not a scared kid anymore. I'll be fine," he continued loud enough for the agents to hear every word.

Luckily—at least for Wyatt—the agents quickly began pumping Adrian for information once it became apparent Adrian and Wyatt were done talking. They pretty much ignored Wyatt. Adrian had to rehash the whole day on the hour drive back, and then again when they got to the FBI field office in Harrisburg. Throughout both recitations, the agents seemed almost disappointed that Eddie Pacciano himself hadn't actually done anything to Adrian that could be construed as a crime, but they were very interested in anything Adrian could tell them about Perretti and what was on the cell phone he wanted so badly. Despite his obvious animosity toward the agents, Wyatt was of more help with the details, like the license and actual make and model of the rental car. Which was a good thing because Adrian had been too freaked-out to remember anything useful like that.

After the feds were done pumping both of them for information, Adrian was about ready to pass out. He hung on Wyatt's arm like deadweight, and all he wanted was a bed somewhere close by, never mind the fact that the clock on the wall said it was barely ten o'clock.

"Thank you for your cooperation, Mr. Walnak, Mr. Everett," Truitt said as she and Walker led them out of the building. "We recommend that you not return to your apartment for a few days. We have a sinking feeling Jim Perretti is long gone, but the men who chased you are still out there. The police will issue warrants, of course, but the best we might do is gun violations and perhaps some menacing charges. We have nothing else right now."

"Especially since our star witness has apparently flown the coop after committing a felony," Walker added bitterly.

A pronounced vein in the man's temple had been throbbing since they'd picked Adrian and Wyatt up, and Adrian had been unable to stop staring at it in morbid fascination.

"I'm sorry," Adrian mumbled, trying to pry his tired eyes away from it. He had no idea what he was sorry for at this point, but it seemed the right thing to say.

Both agents grunted.

Stepping out onto the sidewalk in front of the enormous gray concrete building, Adrian glanced around him blearily. He had no idea what to do next. Apparently his brain had done all it could for one day. Thank God Wyatt was still there, because Adrian was in shutdown mode.

They stood out in the cold long enough for Adrian to gather some brain cells to lift his head and send a questioning glance up at Wyatt. But before he could vocalize it, the rumble of an engine caught his attention. Glancing to the side, he spotted a familiar rusty red pickup truck coming down the street. It pulled up to the curb in front of them, and Wyatt nudged Adrian toward it before reaching for the door.

"Get your asses in here. We got a long way to go," Furlough said as Adrian climbed in and scooted across the bench seat to make room for Wyatt.

"Are you sure you don't want me to drive?" Wyatt asked once he'd closed the door.

"I'm good with the bright lights of the city," Furlough grunted as he pulled back out onto the street. "I'll let you take over once we're out of town, where my night vision ain't so good."

Adrian had no idea where they were going or why Furlough had come to pick them up, but he didn't really care. He dimly noted the shotgun on the floorboard by his feet and the rifle in the rack behind his head, as well as Wyatt's strong arm wrapped around his shoulders, but that was all before sleep washed over him, dragging him under.

CHAPTER EIGHTEEN

"YOU OKAY, boy?" Furlough murmured over Adrian's quiet snores.

"You already asked me that on the phone, old man," Wyatt said around a yawn.

"Yeah, well, I'm asking again."

Wyatt chuckled. "I'm okay. And thanks for coming all the way up here to get us."

Furlough grunted as he navigated the truck onto I-81. "We got a couple of hours, so start talking. I need more intel than a three-minute phone call in the middle of the night."

Adrian slumped against Wyatt's shoulder as Furlough took the on-ramp, and Wyatt shifted to pull him more comfortably against his side. Adrian was already leaving a slight drool spot on Wyatt's shirt, but Wyatt just smiled.

He must have it bad if he found drool adorable.

"Well?" Furlough said crankily, breaking in on Wyatt's little moment.

"Sorry. It's been a long day."

"It's looking to be a long night too," the old man groused.

With a sigh, Wyatt stretched his legs as far as the space would allow. "I told you we could find a hotel for the night. You didn't have to come get us."

"Uh-huh. And what would the feds be doing about keeping you safe in that hotel?"

"Not much," Wyatt agreed. "We aren't exactly 'material' to their investigation. Those men were after Adrian's boss, not Adrian. He was just in the wrong place at the wrong time, from what I can tell."

Wyatt rattled off what little he knew of Adrian's situation and the investigation into Adrian's company before giving Furlough the blow-by-blow he seemed to require of the rest of their exciting evening.

"And you're sure he's not involved somehow?" Furlough asked, nodding toward Adrian's still-sleeping form.

"Yeah, I'm sure."

They might not have known each other long, but he'd shared enough heart-to-hearts with Adrian to get a feel for the man. No one could fake that kind of sincerity and sweetness, not enough to fool Wyatt, anyway. He'd been burned enough times to be able to tell the difference.

Shrugging out of his jacket, now that Adrian was asleep, he draped it over Adrian's shoulders with as little jostling as he could manage. Adrian shifted a little and grumbled but didn't wake, and Wyatt tucked him close again. "Besides," Wyatt murmured as he combed his fingers through Adrian's soft, dark blond hair, "I wasn't the one who invited him out to Everly for the grand tour, now was I? He must have passed the Furlough test to be allowed within its hallowed walls."

Furlough grumbled like the poked bear he was, and Wyatt grinned.

"He made a good enough first impression to see the place," Furlough admitted begrudgingly. "But that was mostly for your sake. He could have been a right bastard, and I still would've put up with him long enough to get you back where you belong…. I would've figured out some way to get rid of him down the line, if necessary."

Even after all these years, Wyatt could never tell if Furlough was kidding when he said things like that. The part of him that wanted a father figure who cared that much sometimes hoped he wasn't, but he was never brave enough to ask.

"Well, you don't have to worry about that. It's getting him to stay that will be the hard part, not the other way around."

Furlough's knuckles whitened on the steering wheel a moment before the old man cleared his throat. "Does that mean you're planning on sticking around this time?"

Wyatt could have hedged. He could have put him off with a "maybe" or "we'll see," like he'd done before, but Furlough deserved better than that. "Yes."

For a long time, Furlough didn't respond. Then he let out a breath that sounded like he'd been holding it forever. "I'm glad to hear it, son. Real glad."

"You want me to take over now?" Wyatt asked before their little moment together got too awkward.

Furlough snorted. "Naw. I'm good. Besides, your friend there looks pretty comfy, and I ain't gonna be the one cuddling him if you're driving."

With a chuckle, Wyatt closed his eyes and napped until they reached the gates to Everly.

Adrian wasn't easy to rouse, once they pulled into the garage next to Furlough's cottage, but with a few not-so-gentle nudges and lots of encouragement, Wyatt managed to get him through the door and all the way up the stairs to his room.

He switched off the light and was about to close the door on what he thought was a sleeping Adrian when the pile of blankets on the bed spoke.

"Where are you going?"

"I thought I'd leave you to get some rest."

"Alone?"

He sounded so pitiful Wyatt stepped back into the room and went to the bed. "I didn't want to assume, and you were kind of out of it."

A hand emerged from the pile of blankets and grabbed his, tugging him down. "All I could think about all day was how much I wanted to curl up with you someplace safe. Please, assume away."

"Okay. Just let me go say good night to Furlough, and I'll be right back."

"Hurry," Adrian ordered around a yawn.

Furlough wasn't in the living room when Wyatt came down the stairs, but it didn't take long to find him. Sure enough, Furlough was in his "control center," next to the kitchen, at the back of the cottage. Perched in his old wooden swivel chair, elbows braced on the desk, Furlough stared intently at one screen in the bank of monitors and clicked on his mouse. His shotgun lay on a side table within easy reach. He'd draped a plaid blanket across his lap, and a giant thermos rested on the desk next to him, like he planned to be there a while.

"Ready for the siege," Wyatt teased from the doorway.

"Yup."

"Where are the dogs?"

"On patrol."

Furlough didn't bother to turn around. He just kept clicking through, and Wyatt's good humor faded.

"You're serious, aren't you?"

Swiveling around in his chair, Furlough pierced him with a sober gaze. "You and your man up there were kidnapped tonight, *after* your man was chased by armed goons, and just *before* you were questioned by the FBI. Pardon me if I'm a little edgy."

The harshness in his tone and the lines of tension bracketing his mouth and forehead made Wyatt wince.

"I'm sorry, Furlough. But do you really think they'll find Adrian all the way out here?"

"No. Probably not. But better safe than sorry." He swiveled back and began clicking on the screen again. "I'm not going to stay in here all night, just 'til the dogs come back from their patrol. Right now, I'm changing some settings on the security, namely the motion sensors and alarms. Usually I keep the alarms off because every goddamned squirrel, raccoon, and deer sets off the sensors and the beeping drives me crazy. Tonight, though, I'll feel better with them on." Turning his head, Furlough squinted at him. "You should be in bed. I'll come get you if anything interesting happens."

"Okay." Wyatt stopped just outside the door. "And thanks, old man… for everything."

He would've hugged the old bastard, but Furlough wasn't so much into physical demonstrations of affection beyond the odd pat on the shoulder or punch in the arm. Wyatt had gotten away with one hug recently. He wouldn't push his luck.

"No more running," Furlough said gruffly, his back still turned. "This place is yours, and I'm gonna make sure it stays that way, whatever I have to do to make that happen."

Back in Wyatt's room, Adrian snored softly from beneath the covers, and despite the drama of the last few hours, Wyatt couldn't help the warm fuzzy that spread through his chest. He actually had the two men he cared about most under one roof, there for him. This was what he wanted more than anything, and he finally had hope that it could happen this time.

Shedding his clothes as quickly and quietly as possible, he slid into bed with a sigh of profound relief and contentment. Cuddling up to Adrian's back, he wrapped an arm around his waist, buried his face in Adrian's hair, and fell asleep almost instantly.

He slept so hard he nearly jumped out of his skin when Furlough shook him awake a few hours later.

"Get up. We've got company."

"What is it? What's going on?" Adrian flailed around and nearly clipped Wyatt in the jaw with an elbow as he tried to free himself from the blankets.

"Three men on foot, coming up the front drive. They left their car at the gate and climbed the fence," Furlough explained as both Wyatt and

Adrian scrambled to get dressed. "I only saw one rifle on the monitors, but I'm going to assume they're all armed."

"Oh my God," Adrian gasped, and Wyatt swore.

"How in the hell—"

"Never mind that now," Furlough cut in tersely. "I've already called the sheriff, but he ain't exactly close by, and we can't hightail it out of here in the truck, because they've blocked the gate, so we need to hunker down someplace safe until help can get here."

Furlough waited outside the door while they finished throwing on clothes. Once they were dressed, he came back in and handed Wyatt the shotgun he carried before turning to Adrian. "You ever fired a gun before?"

Adrian visibly swallowed. "No."

"I figured. I'll just hang on to this, then." Furlough slung the rifle he'd left by the door over his shoulder and hurried out again. "Come on. Let's get out of here quick before they find us."

By the front door, Furlough handed them heavy coats, hats, and gloves as the dogs paced nervously at their feet. "Bundle up. We might be out in the cold for a while."

"We're going out in the woods?" Adrian asked as he hurriedly donned the gear.

"Yup. Let 'em waste time searching the houses. We got a few hundred acres of land to hide in."

Adrian shot Wyatt a worried look, but Wyatt nodded and gave him as reassuring a smile as he could manage. Furlough knew this mountain better than anyone, and if they stayed in the houses, they'd be found eventually for sure. Hurrying out the door, Wyatt grabbed an extra pair of Furlough's boots because he suddenly realized the loafers Adrian had on were not going to cut it.

With the dogs fanning out around them, Furlough took off at a limping jog along the worn path behind his cottage, surprising Wyatt with his speed. Wyatt shoved Adrian after him and took up the rear, with Delta on his heels.

The moon was barely a sliver in the sky, which in some respects was a good thing since they'd be hard to spot, but it also meant they tripped over rocks and protruding roots as they hurried from the cottage. Eventually the trail leveled out, a good distance from the houses, and Furlough allowed them to stop for a break. Their panting breaths plumed in the chill mountain air as Wyatt set his shotgun aside and went to Adrian.

"You okay?"

"So far so good," Adrian huffed, his smile tight in the pale light of the moon.

"Let's get you into these and hope they fit," Wyatt said, holding up the boots. "Your shoes aren't going to last long if we leave the trail."

"Oh, thanks. My feet are killing me already from the rocks I've kicked."

He took the offered boots and hurried over to a downed tree by the side of the trail. While he pulled them on, Wyatt nervously searched the darkness around them and strained to hear any sounds beyond their little group. Furlough moved a short distance away from them and pulled what looked like binoculars out of his bag. As he lifted them to his eyes, Wyatt had to smile.

"Night vision?" he whispered after trotting over.

"Of course," Furlough grunted.

"You're loving this, aren't you?"

Furlough lowered the binoculars long enough to scowl at him. "Having someone I care about in mortal danger? Hardly."

"But?" Wyatt supplied for him.

With a harrumph, Furlough cracked a sheepish smile. "*But…* I can't say I'm not enjoying feeling the old blood pumping again. It's been a long time since Vietnam."

"Semper Fi," Wyatt chuckled.

Adrian joined them a moment later. "What's going on? Did you see something?"

"No," Wyatt whispered back. "It's nothing. You ready?"

"Yeah. They're a little loose, but not too bad," he replied, shifting nervously from boot to boot.

"Okay," Furlough whispered as he stowed the binoculars. "Let's head out. Keep to the path. Speed is what we want now, that and silence. All of us crashing through the woods will make a hell of a racket, so we'll only leave the trail if we think we've been spotted."

Falling in line behind him again, they continued to jog the path as it wound its way around the mountain, toward the road, until the faint sound of a siren echoed through the hills.

Heart leaping, Wyatt grinned as he heard Adrian wheeze, "Oh, thank God."

"We're not out of the woods yet, boys… literally," Furlough hissed as the siren grew louder.

The old man's teeth gleamed in the moonlight, and Wyatt couldn't help but roll his eyes. They hunkered down as the siren got closer, but then it seemed to stop some distance off for a while. They sat in silence waiting, their panting breaths pluming in the air and the dogs pacing restlessly around them, until the sound of tires crunching on the gravel filtered through the trees. Furlough opened his mouth to say something, but Sherriff Ian Morgan's amplified voice cut him off.

"Sherriff's department—drop your weapons!"

They couldn't see the road from where they were, but thin slices of bright white light suddenly stabbed through the trees not far from them, along with the occasional flicker of blue and red.

"I said drop your weapons! Freeze!"

The second order was followed by the crack of a gunshot, and that was apparently too much for Furlough's pack. At the sound of the shot, the dogs took off at a run.

"No!" Furlough shouted. "*Fuss! Fuss!*"

The dogs didn't stop, and a second later, Wyatt had to scrabble for a grip on Furlough's coat as the old man moved to go after them.

"Are you crazy?" Wyatt hissed.

"Let go," Furlough ordered, gripping Wyatt's hand hard and removing it from his jacket. As he took off at a jog, he shouted back to them, "They're my babies too. I won't let them get hurt. Stay down and stay put!"

"Shit!" Wyatt swore. Turning to Adrian, he grimaced. "I can't just let him go. I need you to hide until we tell you it's safe to come out."

"No. I'm going with you."

Shaking his head, he put a hand to Adrian's chest, stopping him. "Adrian, you're the only one here who doesn't have a gun. Please, just do as I ask and keep down and keep safe."

Furlough had already disappeared, and Wyatt needed to catch up to him before he did anything stupid. He didn't have time to argue. All he could do was pray Adrian would listen to him as he set off after Furlough at a sprint.

Chapter Nineteen

Adrian didn't stay put.

He couldn't. Cursing fate and anything else he could think of, he fought with himself for about two seconds before he started to run.

This is stupid. This is so stupid. What the hell am I doing?

What exactly he thought he could do in a situation so far out of his league it was laughable, he had no idea, but his legs wouldn't let him stop. Wyatt crashed through the woods ahead of him like a bulldozer while Adrian stumbled and tripped and flailed in his wake. At last he crested a rise, and he could finally make out the flashing lights from two police cars with spotlights aimed in their direction.

The blades of light that sliced through the tree trunks illuminated several shadows, but Adrian couldn't really make sense of what was going on. The sheriff was still shouting demands into the woods over his loudspeaker, but no one appeared to be listening. Then the dogs started barking and snarling, a man screamed, and another shot rang out, which was then closely followed by one more, much too close for Adrian's liking.

Oh God. Oh God. Oh God.

Like a lunatic, Adrian kept running until he skidded to a halt by a small clearing. In a panic, he could hardly comprehend what he was seeing. Two dark shapes lay still on the ground to his left. Standing above them, Furlough held his rifle on someone while three dogs stood guard just behind him, growling. To Adrian's right, two men wrestled on the ground, one of them unmistakably Wyatt. As Adrian watched, Wyatt and the other man broke apart, and Wyatt's opponent delivered a hard right to Wyatt's chin that made Adrian wince and clench his jaw in sympathy.

Appearing momentarily stunned, Wyatt's grip on the man must have slackened because the guy pushed off him and lunged away in Adrian's direction. A shaft of light illuminated the man's face for less than a second, but Adrian recognized him as one of Eddie Pacciano's men from earlier in the day. He registered this at the same time that he realized the man wasn't looking at him, but at something on the ground not far from him. Metal glinted in the flickering lights, and Adrian moved before his conscious mind could even form the word *gun*. He dove for it and wrapped around it like a receiver about to be dogpiled in a Steelers game.

A second later, that was exactly what he felt like too, as the goon landed on him and attempted to wrestle the gun away. Despite the blows and kicks raining down on him, Adrian stayed wrapped around that gun like an armadillo, his eyes tightly shut and his jaw clenched hard against the pain. He didn't even scream when the man broke his fingers. He did come close to blacking out, however, which probably would've been a relief, but before he could, the guy's hands fell away and the blows and swearing stopped abruptly.

Daring to sneak a peek, Adrian cracked open one eyelid and lifted his head. Silhouetted against the sheriff's spotlights, Wyatt looked like a giant guardian angel standing over him. He was holding his shotgun in front of him with the butt pointed at Adrian, and a quick glance to his right revealed the goon in a heap on the ground.

Yay! I can faint now!

But he didn't faint. He may have let out a whimper or two as he moved the gun to his uninjured right hand and tried to sit up.

"Adrian, are you okay?" Wyatt gasped. He now had the shotgun barrel trained on the guy on the ground, but he kept glancing worriedly over at Adrian.

"Mostly."

"What the hell is going on over there?" Furlough shouted, his voice sharp with fear or maybe anger. Adrian couldn't tell which. He was still holding his rifle on another guy, but his head kept turning to the dark shapes on the ground at his feet.

"We're good," Wyatt answered, sounding completely wiped out.

"Furlough? Is that you?" came a shout from the direction of the cars.

"Yes, goddammit, Ian! We're clear! Get your asses in here, now!"

The crunch of heavy footfalls through frosty leaves and branches soon followed, but Adrian's attention was riveted on the dark shapes on the ground across the clearing. Three dogs hovered nervously around one shape, nudging it, and Adrian thought he heard a whine.

Flashlights lit up the clearing as three men in uniform descended on them, shouting orders. Adrian dropped the gun he held and scooted away from it. Wyatt rushed to his side immediately after one of the deputies took custody of the man he was guarding, but Adrian couldn't drag his eyes away from Furlough.

As soon as the sheriff took over for him, Furlough rushed to the prone body of one of his dogs while the other deputy knelt by the man on the ground next to them.

"I just winged him," Furlough gritted out to the deputy as he lifted his unmoving dog into his arms. "Right shoulder. But if my Charlie here dies, I'm gonna be payin' him another visit."

The deputy radioed for an ambulance while Furlough stomped off toward the road, carrying Charlie, the rest of his pack at his heels.

"Furlough? Where are you going?" the sheriff shouted.

Furlough didn't answer. He didn't even slow down.

"Goddammit, get back here! You can't just leave me with this mess! Someone's going to have to explain all this!"

"It's your job, ain't it? And you know where to find me."

Furlough was obviously moving fast because Adrian could barely hear the last few words.

"We need to get you to a hospital too," Wyatt said worriedly.

"I'm okay, mostly," Adrian objected, still staring off where Furlough had disappeared. But when Wyatt took his elbow and helped him to his feet, the world spun, and Adrian came really close to throwing up.

"Yeah, you're right as rain," Wyatt said wryly. "Come on, tough guy. Let's get you some medical attention."

Everything was kind of a blur after that. Wyatt led him out of the woods while the sheriff and one deputy led the two goons still on their feet out in handcuffs and stuffed them in the back of their cruisers. The third deputy stayed behind with the man Furlough had apparently shot, and once the other two were safely locked in the cars, the second deputy ran back into the woods with a first aid kit while they waited for the ambulance to arrive.

Furlough's truck came flying down the driveway, swerved around the police cars, and kept on going as Wyatt helped Adrian to one of the cars and propped him against it.

"That man and I are gonna have words the next time I see him," the sheriff grumbled as he joined Adrian and Wyatt.

Wyatt smirked and shook his head. "Can he even get out? He said the road was blocked."

"Yeah," the sheriff sighed in resignation. "We pushed their car out of the way so we could get up here."

"Well, hopefully all will go well, and Furlough won't mind having that chat the next time you see him."

He didn't take his eyes off Adrian as he spoke, and Adrian wanted so badly to find someplace warm to curl his aching body into a ball and wrap Wyatt around him.

"You boys okay?" the sheriff asked.

He really was a mountain of a man. He even made Wyatt look normal-sized.

Jeebus they grow 'em big out here.

Adrian chuckled and then winced as pain shot through his ribs… and everywhere else.

"The guy got in a couple good licks when he jumped me, but Adrian got the worst of it, I think." Wyatt combed his fingers through Adrian's hair as he spoke, and Adrian's eyes drifted closed as he hummed his approval.

"Adrian?" the sheriff said.

"That's me," he murmured dreamily.

Sheriff Morgan chuckled. "Yes, it is. Adrian, where are you hurt?"

Without daring to look at it, Adrian lifted his throbbing hand, and Wyatt hissed and draped an arm around his shoulders, gently pulling him against that marvelous body.

"Anywhere else? Did you hit your head?"

Adrian chuckled. Maybe he was acting a little loopy, but it was mostly because he was trying not to cry or puke in front of all those oh-so-manly men. "No. But I think he managed to pummel every other square inch of me."

"Okay, well the ambulance will be here soon, and we'll get you checked out—you too, Wyatt. Then we'll all take a trip to the hospital before we drop these guys at the jail. I'm going to need statements from all of you. But as Furlough so pointedly demonstrated, it can wait until more important things are tended to."

At the reminder, Adrian bit his lip and stared off in the direction Furlough had gone.

"I hope his dog's okay."

Wyatt kissed his temple. "Me too."

BY THE time they all made it to the hospital, Adrian was dead on his feet. The ambulance took the guy with the gunshot wound—for obvious reasons—so Adrian and Wyatt were split between the front passenger seats of the two sheriff's vehicles, while the second deputy rode in the ambulance to keep an eye on the bad guy. The county apparently had limited resources, and waiting for help to arrive from elsewhere just wasn't worth it.

Unsure if his hand would require surgery, the EMTs didn't want to give him much for the pain, so the bumpy ride down the gravel road nearly resulted in Adrian painting the inside of a county vehicle. He kept the bile down, but only just barely, and Wyatt took one look at him in the parking lot of the hospital and insisted they find a wheelchair to cart him the rest of the way.

Adrian intended to make a token protest, but he was just too tired. The rest of his adrenaline had apparently worn off, because his entire body had turned into a throbbing ball of pain and misery. He'd never been in an actual fight in his life before now, and he was definitely sure he never wanted to be in another… not that he'd actually done much fighting, but that was beside the point.

He did end up passing out for a little while. The nurse gave him the good drugs and left him alone, but only after his X-rays and some rather personal poking and prodding of the rest of his body. Wyatt was by his side when he woke up, and he couldn't help the dopey smile that spread across his face. He was feeling good… at least until he saw the shiner Wyatt was sporting and the goose egg on his jaw, both blooming in ugly shades of purple and green.

"Ouch," Adrian said in sympathy, reaching to touch Wyatt's jaw with his good hand.

Wisely, Wyatt leaned away from Adrian's clumsy movement and took Adrian's hand between his own warm palms.

"How are you feeling?" Wyatt asked, his brows knit with concern.

"M'okay."

Adrian giggled, and Wyatt grinned. "Feelin' good, huh?"

"Not bad. You?"

"Not bad. The guy nearly cracked one of my ribs, and I have a few other bruises in addition to these," he replied, motioning to his face. "But I've had worse. I'd like to go a few more rounds with him, after what he did to you, but I guess I'll have to be content with sending him to jail instead."

"Uh-huh."

Wyatt laughed. "We can talk about it later. The nurse said they should be able to set your fingers tonight… or, I guess, this morning now. They called someone in, a specialist, and he should be here soon. Why don't you go back to sleep, and I'll wake you when he gets here?"

"You'll stay, though, right?"

That came out a little more pitiful and whiney than he'd intended, but Wyatt only smiled. "Yeah. I'll be here."

He dragged a chair next to the bed and dropped into it with a sigh before taking Adrian's hand again. Satisfied Wyatt wasn't going anywhere, Adrian allowed his eyes to drift closed.

CHAPTER TWENTY

A COUPLE of hours later, Wyatt paced in the waiting room at the sheriff's station until he was sure he was wearing a groove in the ugly vinyl tile. They'd been released from the hospital with prescriptions for pain pills and instructions for the care of Adrian's splint, but they hadn't been allowed to go home. Adrian had to be completely wrung out, on his last legs, and still the feds wouldn't let Wyatt take him home. At this point, Wyatt was so exhausted he wasn't sure he could make it home himself without passing out, but he'd manage something, if the assholes would just let Adrian out of that room.

"Can I get you some coffee?" Ian Morgan offered, his smile apologetic.

"Might as well," Wyatt gritted out. This wasn't the sheriff's fault.

Ian returned with a steaming cup a few minutes later. "If they don't let him out soon, I'll go in and check on him, okay?"

"He didn't do anything wrong. They should be harassing the assholes in the cells, not him."

"I know. They just need to dot their i's and cross their t's while everything is still fresh in everyone's minds. This way, you and Adrian don't have to wait around for the real interrogations to finish."

"I guess," Wyatt grumbled begrudgingly. "Your coffee sucks, though."

Ian laughed. "Cheney's shift doesn't start for another couple of hours. He's the coffee snob around here, and he won't let anyone use his fancy machine without him. Want another?"

Wyatt opened his mouth to say something pissy, but snapped it shut when he heard a familiar gravelly voice shouting down the hall.

"Where the hell is everybody? Wyatt! Ian! Where are you?"

Ian groaned. "Looks like we've got company."

Wyatt followed Ian into the hall as one of the FBI agents poked his head out of the room they were keeping Adrian in. "What's going on?" the agent asked.

Wyatt tried to peer around the man to check on Adrian as Ian answered, "Our other witness from tonight. I'll talk to him."

"Wyatt!" Furlough charged over to him and gave him a hard hug without even looking at Ian.

Stunned by the show of affection, Wyatt grunted at the stab of pain in his ribs but didn't pull away.

"I'm okay," Wyatt wheezed, and Furlough quickly let go and stepped away.

After clearing his throat self-consciously, Furlough said, "Good. Good. Where's Adrian?"

"In there," Wyatt replied, pointing to the closed door he'd been glaring daggers at for what felt like hours.

Furlough turned his frown on Ian, and Ian grimaced. "Don't look at me like that. Questions have to be asked and statements have to be made... including yours."

"How long has he been in there?"

"Too long," Wyatt answered.

"Right, then."

Without another word, and before the sheriff could try to stop him, Furlough stomped over to the door and started banging on it. "You in there, your time is up!" he shouted.

The door swung open. Two very disgruntled-looking agents stood in the doorway. "What the hell is going on?" the woman asked the sheriff.

"You got a sworn statement from our boy in there?" Furlough overrode anything the sheriff might have said. At their silent stares, Furlough nodded. "Right. You asking him anything he hasn't already answered at least once?"

Both agents simply sent disbelieving stares at the sheriff, and Furlough grunted. "I thought so. Here's what's going to happen. We're going to take Adrian home now, and you're going to go hassle the real criminals you have locked up in your cells. If you still feel like you don't have all the answers you need, you can call us at Everly... or better yet, call this number and speak to the Everett family attorneys." He handed a card to the female agent and brushed past both of them to get to Adrian.

Wyatt gratefully followed in his wake. He was exhausted, but Adrian looked worse. His beautiful blue eyes were dull and ringed in dark circles. He looked like he could barely keep his head up, and Wyatt felt a stab of guilt that he hadn't been the one to charge the door sooner.

"Come on, son, let's get you home," Furlough said as he and Wyatt helped Adrian to his feet.

"They kept saying just one more question," Adrian said dully.

"It's okay, baby. We got you. We're going home now," Wyatt murmured.

By the time they made it out of the room, the sheriff and the agents were having a heated exchange in the hallway, but Ian just waved them off. Satisfied they wouldn't be harassed, Wyatt concentrated on putting one foot in front of the other until they reached Furlough's truck. Thank God, Everly was only half an hour away from the sheriff's station. Wyatt was asleep barely five minutes into the trip.

As they stumbled into Furlough's cottage, Wyatt wasn't sure he'd ever seen a more pathetic crew. Adrian was a zombie, barely upright and not really conscious. Despite putting on a brave front, Furlough looked haggard and about twenty years older than he had only a few hours ago. Only three dogs came to greet them, their ears drooping and tails barely wagging. Despite his fatigue, Wyatt had to ask, "Charlie?"

Furlough's jaw ticked. "He's gonna be laid up for a while, but the vet says he'll heal. Bastard only winged him... which is why I only winged the bastard." His grin was more a baring of teeth, and Wyatt nodded. He knew the feeling.

"I'm glad to hear it. Where is he?"

"Animal hospital forty-five minutes from here. Don't know how long they're gonna keep him. I'll go check on him, once I've had some sleep. It's been a damned long night."

"Yeah. Good night, old man... and thanks."

At Furlough's nod, Wyatt helped Adrian up the stairs, and they barely took the time to shed their coats and boots before collapsing on the bed.

It was after one in the afternoon the next time Wyatt opened his eyes. He ached all over and couldn't wait to take a long, hot shower to ease some of it. Adrian still looked pretty pitiful when Wyatt scooted out of the bed, so Wyatt made the trip downstairs to get the hydrocodone the doctor had sent him home with and a glass of water first. Satisfied that Adrian was hydrated and drugged, Wyatt dragged his tired ass to the bathroom for that shower.

Afterward, he was really tempted to crawl back in bed with Adrian, but he needed to check on Furlough. The old man wasn't in his bedroom, and Wyatt hadn't seen any sign of him downstairs.

A little worried, Wyatt quietly slipped back into the guest room, got dressed in clean clothes, and grabbed his boots and coat. The truck was still in the garage, so Wyatt did a circuit around the cottage before heading up the hill to the castle. The front door was unlocked, but he wandered the house for a good half hour before he heard the furnace and generators cut on, telling him where Furlough had to be.

In the basement, he found Furlough crouched in front of the furnace, his toolbox open on the floor beside him.

"You know, after taking down armed felons, I think the estate would understand if you took the day off," Wyatt said wryly as he descended the last few steps. Delta came up and snuffled at his hands, and Wyatt buried his hands in the soft ruff as he crossed the room.

"Keeps me busy. Besides, I got a lot of work to do if we're going to have the place fully open by Christmas."

Wyatt rolled his eyes. "Let's not get carried away, old man. I've agreed to stay put, but give me a chance to ease into things before you go crazy."

Furlough merely grunted and continued what he was doing, so Wyatt huffed and wandered over to the half of the basement used for storage. Boxes and crates lined the walls, along with folding tables and chairs, and various other things draped in white cloths. Inside some of those boxes were holiday decorations that hadn't seen the light of day in over fifteen years. There was even an indoor fountain somewhere in the heap. It made him a little queasy to think of pulling all that stuff out again, but also just a little bit hopeful.

Memories of better, happier times filled his head. As a child, every year at Christmastime, his grandpa would open Everly up for a grand ball. People came from all over for it. The house was filled with music and light and life, not to mention the hefty chunk of change they collected in charitable donations for the foundation his grandpa had created.

After his grandpa died, his dad had kept the tradition going, but only to the extent that he threw the party. The guest list altered significantly. No longer were any locals, or the underprivileged children and their families from the Everly foundation invited. Richard Everett only wined and dined his society friends on the foundation's dime. And when the board cracked down on his spending and the money ran out, so had he.

Wyatt scowled at the boxes.

"It's good to see you back here," Furlough said gruffly behind him.

Rolling suddenly tense shoulders, he sighed. "It's good to be back here… I guess. I'm just not sure I'm ready for all this yet. Can't I hide out at your place for a while and work up to it?"

"Nope," Furlough said flatly, and when Wyatt glared at him over his shoulder, the old man grinned. "Pull up your bootstraps, boy. You've been on vacation too long. It's time to get to work."

Wyatt snorted. "Yeah. It's been a blast. I've just been chilling on a beach somewhere with my feet up, just like Dad," he said sourly.

Furlough growled at him. "You know what I mean. This is your home. It's incredible and beautiful and completely paid for… and it's yours as long as you want to live in it… not exactly something to shake a stick at."

Wyatt laughed. "You mean, first-world problems? Poor me, I have a castle to live in?"

Furlough gripped his shoulder. "Exactly."

"It's a lot of work, though, living up to Grandpa's legacy. And it's not exactly easy for me, being here again," he argued.

"Never said it was. But you're not alone now. Hell, you weren't alone then… and that was my fault for not making sure you knew that. You got people to help you. Speaking of which, where's your young man?"

"In bed still… and he's not mine."

Furlough smirked at him before heading back to the furnace. "He's yours," he said over his shoulder. "Last night, he could've run away… or better yet, both of you could've done what I told you and stayed hidden. But he ran toward danger for you, not away from it. Scared as he was, unprepared as he was, he came running. He's yours."

"How many ex-wives do you have?" Wyatt jibed. "Why should I be taking advice from you on this subject?"

Furlough gave him the finger. "Fine. Don't take my advice. You find out for yourself. Go on. Quit pussyfooting around and ask him. Then tell me I'm wrong."

Wyatt's smirk fell away as butterflies took flight in his stomach. He wanted it. He wanted it all—Adrian, Everly, Furlough, everything. That "one day" he'd always promised himself was within sight.

Furlough turned around and got back to work, though his words still echoed in the room, leaving Wyatt with a sense of urgency. After a deep breath and one last scratch of Delta's ears, he headed out of the basement and straight for Furlough's cottage with a sense of purpose.

It seemed so simple. All he had to do was ask.

His chest was tight by the time he stepped through the front door, and he was panting despite the easy walk. At the bottom of the stairs, he froze, trying to catch his breath.

Shit.

Furlough had freaked him out with his all-or-nothing talk, goading him, and now he was a mess. It didn't have to be all or nothing. They'd just been through a traumatic experience together. He didn't have to jump in right now. They could go slow, continue to date. The thought of Adrian going back to his apartment, and to possible danger, made him queasy, but no major decisions had to be made right now. With everything Adrian had going on, the last thing Wyatt wanted to do was add to the stress. He could start with just convincing Adrian to stay until he was feeling better, and the possible danger had passed. After that, he'd find some other excuse to keep him there for a little longer. Then after that….

Chapter Twenty-one

"Hey."

Wyatt jumped about three feet off the ground, clutching at his chest, and Adrian hid his smile behind his coffee cup. Giving Wyatt a chance to recover, Adrian said, "I hope you and Furlough don't mind, but I helped myself to the coffee."

"No, no, that's fine. You found everything okay?"

Wyatt still sounded a little breathless, and guilt wiped the smile off Adrian's face. He'd been watching Wyatt hold a silent conversation with himself at the bottom of the stairs for several minutes before he'd made his presence known. With everything that had happened the night before, sneaking up on Wyatt had been a little cruel. Wyatt probably wasn't on the verge of a freak-out, like Adrian was, but he obviously wasn't unaffected either.

Adrian's good hand shook as he gripped his mug a little tighter, trying really hard not to think about last night. "Yeah. The pot was still hot… and thanks to whoever left the mugs and sugar out."

Feeling awkward and shaky, he moved to the couch, where Wyatt joined him.

"How are you this morning?" Wyatt asked. A deep V seemed permanently etched into his forehead as he searched Adrian's face, and a little more guilt trickled through Adrian's already shaky emotional landscape.

"Okay, I guess," he answered, trying to put on a brave front. "God, I thought those agents were never going to let me go. I don't even remember what I said toward the end. I hope I didn't confess to anything."

"I should've gotten you out of there sooner. Thank God Furlough showed up when he did."

"He is pretty cool." They shared a smile before Adrian set his mug aside and squeezed Wyatt's hand. "But don't beat yourself up about the rest of it. I'm a grown man. If I'd been thinking, I would've told them to shove it earlier. You were just as tired and bruised as I was. Don't feel bad."

They sat in silence, just gazing at each other for a bit, until Adrian started to blush. Clearing his throat, he grabbed his coffee and took another sip before he asked, "So what happens now?"

"You mean with the sheriff and the investigation, or…?"

"You know what? I don't even know." Adrian chuckled. "Except—oh shit! I need to call Bev. She has to be going crazy by now!"

He jumped to his feet, making his ribs scream and sloshing coffee over his good hand and onto the embarrassingly baggy T-shirt and boxers he'd borrowed from Wyatt's dresser. "Ouch! Dammit!"

Flailing about, Adrian plunked the mug on the coffee table, making an even bigger mess, and stuffed his hand in his mouth. He was going to run to the kitchen for a towel, but a firm hand on his shoulder pushed him back down on the couch.

"I got it. You just stay there," Wyatt said with a hint of tired humor.

If Adrian hadn't been so grateful that he wouldn't have to drag his aching body back into the kitchen, he might have been grumpier about being laughed at. But the truth was, everything hurt, and he wasn't sure he could make it there without another disaster occurring.

He accepted the cool, damp rag Wyatt gave him to wrap around his hand with all the dignity and graciousness he could muster. Then he sat regally on the edge of the couch as Wyatt mopped up the mess he'd made on the coffee table.

"Thank you."

"You're welcome," Wyatt replied as he handed over a cordless phone.

Adrian took it, smiling his gratitude, then groaned.

"Yes?" Wyatt asked with a smile.

"I need my cell. I don't have her number memorized."

Luckily, the sheriff had given him his phone back that morning, after he'd identified it among the things confiscated from the thugs, but it was upstairs, in his jacket pocket, and that seemed a million miles away.

"I'll get it for you," Wyatt offered, already on his way to the stairs.

"You're a saint," Adrian called after him, and Wyatt chuckled.

When Wyatt brought the phone and a charger back, Adrian kissed him before plugging the thing in and retrieving Bev's number.

"Hello?"

She sounded awful.

"Bev?"

"Adrian! Thank God. I was worried sick about you. What the hell is going on? Where are you?"

"Sorry. It's been a night. I hardly know where to begin."

"Well, last I heard you were being hassled by the FBI. Why don't you start there?" She sounded pissed, but the little warble in her voice hit harder than the anger.

"Yeah. Things got interesting after that. Eddie Pacciano sent some guys to pick me up so he could talk to me."

"What?"

Adrian winced at the screech, and he could tell by the look on Wyatt's face that he'd heard it too. In as detached a manner as he could manage, Adrian related the tale of his day from hell. He was trying for calm, but Bev nearly hyperventilating on the other end of the line wasn't helping. Thank God, Wyatt started rubbing a big warm hand in soothing circles on his lower back, or he might have lost it too.

"But you're okay now, right?" Bev asked breathlessly, when he'd finished.

"Mostly. I have a couple of broken fingers, and a lot of bruises, but I'll be okay."

"And you're someplace safe?"

"As safe as I'm going to get, I suppose. Hopefully by now, everyone has figured out I don't know anything about—well, *anything* really—and they'll leave me alone."

"Hopefully? Can't the FBI or the police put you in protective custody or something?"

"The FBI still isn't completely sure I'm not involved," Adrian answered sourly. "But I'm not exactly their star witness either. I just apparently have the worst luck in the history of mankind."

Wyatt slid a little closer, and with a sigh of relief, Adrian slumped against his shoulder.

"If you and Wyatt went back to his place, how did they even find you?" Bev asked.

Casting a sour look at his cell phone, now resting on a lamp table by the wall, Adrian said, "My cell was in my jacket when I dropped it. They must have found it, and I guess they hacked in or something, checked the recent calls, and found this number, Everly's landline."

"Who's Everly?"

He chuckled. "Not who, where. God, you should see the place, Bev. It's incredible."

Wyatt gave him a little squeeze for that, and Adrian smiled.

"Oh, I intend to. Don't you worry about that. But let's get back to the almost being killed by mobsters part for now," she finished, sourly.

"Hey! It wasn't my fault Perretti turned out to be a liar and a thief. He's the only reason those assholes came after me. They were looking for *him*, or whatever was on his phone, and desperate enough to try anything. The feds said they spotted guys at the airports, train stations, and bus stations they were staking out. Seems like everyone's looking for him, but they hadn't caught him as of this morning... at least the FBI hasn't."

"Not sure which team I should root for at this point, the bastard," she said harshly.

"Yeah." He snuggled deeper in Wyatt's arms, resting a cheek on his chest as his agitation faded, leaving only exhaustion in its wake.

"But you think you're pretty safe now?"

"Mm-hmm," he murmured. He just needed to close his eyes for a second.

"And you don't think I have anything to worry about?"

"They want Perretti, not us," he mumbled around a yawn. "I'm pretty sure Mr. Pacciano believed me when I said neither one of us was involved... at least until they saw Perretti hanging out in front of my apartment."

"Okay." She blew out a long breath. "Isaac and I might take the kids away to see my folks for a bit anyway, just in case. Is Wyatt there with you now?"

"Yup."

"Good. Get some rest, stay safe, and call me if you hear anything, okay?"

"Yup."

"Have a good nap." She chuckled before hanging up.

He didn't really intend to nap, but he woke up a while later stretched out on the couch with Wyatt, using Wyatt's chest as his pillow.

With a cringe, he wiped his chin and stared down at the drool spot he'd left on Wyatt's shirt. Hopefully it would dry before Wyatt woke up.

"Feeling better?" Wyatt rumbled.

"Yeah." Adrian met Wyatt's sleepy hazel gaze, hiding the wet spot under his palm. "You?"

"A little stiff, but I'm good."

Adrian glanced down to where Wyatt's knees were bent because he didn't quite fit on the couch, and winced. "Sorry. That looks really uncomfortable." He slowly and painfully detangled himself and slid off the couch. Bracing his good hand on the arm of the couch for balance, it took him a good few seconds to stand fully upright. He was actually pretty proud of himself for not releasing a single whimper as every muscle in his body protested and his damaged hand throbbed.

"Don't apologize," Wyatt replied. "It was a nice nap. Besides, I'm used to it. My feet have hung off the end of nearly every bed I've slept in since I was sixteen."

His smile was warm and sexy, familiar and comforting. He looked so good, all rumpled from his nap, Adrian wished he didn't feel a hundred years old… and like he'd been hit by a bus. His mind was definitely willing to take Wyatt up on the promise in that smile, but his flesh was also most definitely weak.

When Wyatt sat up and swung his legs to the floor, Adrian carefully eased down beside him again and cleared his throat.

"So, uh, about what I started to ask earlier—you know, before I spazzed and spilled my coffee all over everything—we should probably figure out what happens now, huh?"

"Yeah. We probably should talk about some things at least."

Unsure how to read Wyatt's tone, Adrian huffed out a breath and shook his head. "I don't even know where to start." Groaning, he dropped his face into his palms. "Nothing is what it seemed only a month or so ago, and I'm trying not to flip out. I really am. But I don't do so well with change on a normal day, and *this*, this is craziness."

"Things have been kind of crazy," Wyatt agreed.

"Kind of?" Adrian reared back and gaped at him like he'd lost his marbles. "We were chased by men with guns… like, real guns that can put holes in you. We were interrogated by the FBI. My boss kidnapped us at gunpoint and stole our cash. My boss's boss sent thugs after us! Armed thugs!" Adrian could hear his voice getting louder and more strident, but he couldn't seem to stop now that he'd started. "Not to mention, my company is under investigation by the FBI, so I probably don't even have a job anymore! And I don't think the mob offers severance packages, particularly when the guy who signs the checks might be going to jail! Does unemployment even cover that contingency? And if he is guilty, does that mean my salary was paid with dirty money? Do I have to give that back? My rent check is due in a few days, and I don't even know if I can go back to my apartment! I don't think I even want to! What the hell am I going to do? I—"

"Breathe, Adrian. Come on, just breathe." Wyatt's deep voice cut through Adrian's panicked gibbering enough for him to realize he was the one hyperventilating now.

Wyatt's big warm hand rested on his back again, a soothing weight, and Adrian closed his eyes and tried to focus on the simple act of drawing air in and out of his lungs at a more appropriate pace.

"It's okay. You're going to be okay," Wyatt continued gently. He scooted closer to Adrian's side and slid an arm across his shoulders. "Last night was scary, but it's over now. Furlough and I aren't going to let anything happen to you."

"And what if something happens to either of you? How am I supposed to live with that?" Adrian countered, in a slightly more normal register. "Charlie got shot, for God's sake. He could have died, and it could have been you or Furlough instead, and that would have been my fault."

"Charlie's going to be fine. Nothing is going to happen to any of us. The FBI have the bad guys in custody, at least on trespassing and assault charges, and they're working on more. We showed them we aren't the kind of people they can bully without consequences, and I'm sure Furlough already has plans for how we can beef up security, and Ian's going to be keeping an eye out for us too."

Adrian swallowed and nodded, a little mollified. "Okay."

"And as for the rest of it, about your job and your place, you know you can stay here as long as you want."

Adrian stopped breathing altogether and stared.

"I do? I mean, I can? You wouldn't mind?"

Wyatt cupped his jaw and tugged until Adrian lifted his head and met his gaze. "I want you to stay… and not just because we can look out for you here, but for selfish reasons too."

Adrian pulled away a little and frowned, despite the fluttering in his chest.

"You were on your way out of town the last time I talked to you."

With a deep sigh, Wyatt closed the distance between them again and buried his face in Adrian's hair. His warm breath ghosted against Adrian's neck as he murmured, "I'm sorry for that. I thought it was a way to keep both you and Furlough safe, while keeping me safe at the same time. I thought all they wanted was me. You notice I didn't get very far, though, right?"

"I guess I kind of messed that up for you."

"No, you didn't mess anything up… or I guess you did, but not in the way you mean. I was in a motel when I called you, just sitting there because I couldn't bring myself to hop on my bike and go any farther away from you." He punctuated that last incredible statement with a nibbling kiss to Adrian's neck.

"Really?" Adrian asked breathlessly as he eased farther into the couch cushions and Wyatt continued to kiss and nibble and suck.

Wyatt chuckled against his skin, that deep, gorgeous sound that always stroked something deep inside. "Really. Furlough was right. It's time I stopped jumping at shadows and stand up for what I want."

"And what is that?" Adrian asked, shamelessly digging as he threw his head back to allow the man more room to work.

"I want you," he answered, followed by more kisses and the rasp of his stubble over Adrian's throat. "I want a home, family, this place… to stay put and live my life, hopefully with a partner who wants the same things."

Adrian had to close his eyes because the stars in front of them were too distracting. He needed to be practical. He needed to think, but his heart leaping for joy behind his ribs and yelling, *Yes! Yes! Take me! I'm yours!* was making that difficult.

He must have been silent a beat too long, because Wyatt pulled back and cleared his throat. His face was flushed, but his gaze seemed nervous. "Of course, there's no pressure or anything. I know we haven't really talked about this stuff before, and you've obviously got a lot on your plate. We can take this as slow as you want. I just figured I'd, you know, put it out there and… I mean, I didn't really intend to say all that. It just kind of came out but…."

He trailed off, looking uncomfortable, and the utter absurdity of a man as beautiful, charming, and kind as Wyatt waiting with bated breath for someone like Adrian to accept what he was offering smacked Adrian in the face.

"Why?"

The question slipped out, and Wyatt's gorgeous face scrunched up. "Why what?"

"Why me?"

Wyatt frowned, all hesitance gone. "I thought we already had this conversation."

"We did. But it's been a shitty couple of days, kicked off by you riding off into the sunset without me, so humor me, okay?"

"I came back," Wyatt defended.

"You did. I just need to hear it again. After everything I went through with Martin, I just need to know where I stand, that's all. I need it all out in the open, no hiding, no more lies. So why?"

"You know, if I ever meet this guy, Martin, I'm going to have a hard time not punching him in the face. Why *not* you?"

Adrian barked out a laugh as his cheeks flamed, but he was the one who'd asked the question, so he needed to see it through. "I really can't blame it all on Martin. I mean, I'm a realist from way back, and, honey, you're at least a ten while I'm—"

"What?" Wyatt interrupted sharply. "Hot? Funny? Sweet? Generous? Caring? Brave? I could keep going." Leaning close again, Wyatt draped himself carefully over Adrian and kissed him hard. When he broke away, his expression had softened again, and he said quietly, "I get that you don't see it... *yet*... but you gotta trust me, it's there. That's what I see when I look at you." He paused and worried his lip a little before continuing. "I see someone I want to roll the dice with, someone I want to wake up with every day, not just every weekend. And if it's too soon for you to say the same, that's okay. You can just stay until you're feeling better, and we can talk about it again. Everly's a big place. You can have your own wing while things get sorted out with the feds and your job, if that's what you want. Hell, if you're worried about work and your bills, I could hire you to audit the estate's accounts and my trust fund, while we do the long-distance thing, once the coast is clear. Whatever you want."

"You have a trust fund?"

Why his brain latched on to that one part of Wyatt's speech, he wasn't sure. Maybe because it was practical, concrete, and didn't make him feel so embarrassingly needy and afraid to hope.

After looking a little nonplussed, Wyatt smiled and shrugged. "Yeah. Haven't touched it in years, not since the early days after I left here. I wanted to make my own way, and I had mixed feelings about my family for a while." He chuckled. "I guess I still do."

"You're saying you just left it?" Adrian asked, aghast. "Please tell me you've checked statements, or you at least have a financial advisor you trust looking after it."

"Uh." His guilty look was enough.

"Oh my God. What's the name of your bank? We need to call them like now."

Adrian struggled to get up, wincing as pain shot through everywhere, but Wyatt's warm hands cupping his jaw stopped him. His eyes were soft and his smile wide as he leaned close and kissed him again. "That's probably the sweetest thing anyone's ever said to me."

"You need to get out more," Adrian grumbled, but he wasn't too upset to still be pinned under the man.

Wyatt shook his head. "I'm serious. You want to take care of me. How could I not love that?"

Love?

He was going to get mental whiplash if he kept this up. He needed to concentrate on one thing at a time.

Cautiously, he relaxed into the cushions again and stared up at the man on top of him. "You'd do that… let me take care of you?"

Something eased in Wyatt's expression, and he nodded. "We can take things as slow or as fast as you want to, but God yes, I would love it if you wanted to stay here and take care of me… as long as you maybe let me take care of you a little too."

Even battered and exhausted as he was, having Wyatt on top of him was making it very hard to be levelheaded and realistic, especially when he was saying everything Adrian wanted to hear. He pulled back as far as the cushions would allow and took a breath. "And that whole discussion we had before, about how you didn't have anything but a sexual relationship to offer, that's off the table? This is a real relationship you want, with dating, and sharing with each other, and staying in one place, and—" He swallowed. "—monogamy?"

Wyatt's smile grew. "Yes. All of that. You and me. I give you my word, I'm not going anywhere. I have something to stick around for now."

"Oh come on, you had a friggin' castle. That wasn't enough?"

"Nope."

"You had Furlough."

His smile turned sad. "Yeah. I guess I always took it for granted that he'd be here when I finally decided to come home. That wasn't fair of me. But now I have you both."

Wyatt toyed with a lock of Adrian's hair as his smile turned hopeful again. "Take a little vacation from the craziness back home and stay here with me. We'll spend some real time together. And if you like it—which I very much hope you will—we can go from there. What do you say?"

Adrian melted. He couldn't help it. The man was a gorgeous, warm, solid weight on top of him, and Adrian wanted to believe.

God help the utterly besotted.

"I say, yes."

Epilogue

I THINK *I'm in love.*

Three weeks after the most horrible and frightening day of his life, Adrian sat alone beneath the gorgeous leaded glass dome in Everly's solarium, warming himself in the early morning sunlight and trying to come to terms with the nervous fluttering inside his chest. He'd woken only an hour earlier in the massive dark wood four-poster bed he shared with Wyatt, so happy just to watch Wyatt snoring openmouthed next to him he could barely stand himself. Even after three weeks of spending nearly every waking moment together, he was still disgustingly besotted.

It had to be love.

He took a sip of his coffee and lifted his gaze to the play of sunlight through the dome above him. The lead-traced designs of vines and flowers probably cost more to make than anything anyone in Adrian's family had ever owned… possibly put together. Sitting in his ratty bathrobe, flannel pajama bottoms, and T-shirt seemed like an insult to his surroundings, but Wyatt never once let him feel like he didn't belong. Adrian still wasn't quite sure how he managed it. Some sort of magic the man wielded… or possibly it was the sex—*probably* it was the sex. Despite both of them still being a bit tender, they'd left their mark, so to speak, on several of the rooms already. It was a damned good thing Furlough had a place of his own to go to at night, or Adrian would've probably died of embarrassment by now.

The first week, they hadn't done much other than sleep. At least Adrian hadn't. Pain and pills that made him a little loopy saw to that. He'd spent a lot of time curled up on the couch with Charlie in a brand-new dog bed all his own on the floor next to him. Furlough grumbled endlessly about Charlie getting spoiled useless during his recuperation period, but Adrian had seen him hovering over Charlie and fawning over the dog like a mother hen with one chick when he thought no one was looking. Wyatt had hovered over Adrian in similar fashion, but Adrian wasn't complaining. Wyatt was a damned sexy nurse, and the sponge baths had been a lot of fun.

When he was finally feeling up to it, he'd helped Wyatt and Furlough around the big house, one room at a time. Mostly he pulled furniture covers off and dusted with his good hand while Wyatt and Furlough either helped or inspected for termite or water damage. It amazed Adrian the amount of dust that could accumulate in a house that had seen almost no activity for fifteen years.

The thugs had broken a window in the kitchen to gain entry, but luckily they hadn't done much damage other than leave muddy footprints all over when they'd searched the houses. Adrian closed his eyes and shuddered. He got queasy every time he thought about that night, and he'd tried very hard to block it from his mind.

At the end of the first week, they'd received word that Perretti had been caught trying to fly out of JFK with a fake passport, so at least the FBI had their witness back. Adrian might still have to testify in the assault case against the thugs, but hopefully that would be the extent of his involvement with organized crime from here on out. The trial could take years, but he wasn't going to think about that. The FBI wasn't particularly interested in him, so he would just hope Eddie Pacciano and his associates wouldn't be either.

He gripped his mug tightly and took another sip to distract himself from that line of thought. He was supposed to be freaking out about falling in love, not about the scary men with guns who might or might not still be after him.

One thing to panic about at a time.

As if summoned, a very rumpled and sexy Wyatt shuffled into the solarium with a steaming coffee mug in hand, providing all the distraction Adrian might need. Wyatt was shirtless, despite the frost on some of the windows. To Adrian's continued delight, Wyatt's body ran hot most of the time, so he was happiest in as little clothing as possible. His only concession to the fact that Furlough might join them at any time was a pair of low-slung, soft, knit shorts that left most of his rippling muscles and gorgeous tattoos on display and very little to the imagination.

"Mornin'," Wyatt rumbled as he slid into the chair next to Adrian and tugged him over for a kiss.

"You're up early."

"I was going to say the same thing about you. Figured you'd be worn out after last night. Guess I need to try harder."

The man could still make him blush like a virgin. "Maybe my stamina's improving," he fired back with a smirk.

"Oh it is… not that I had anything to complain about before." Wyatt took another sip of his coffee, and when he set the mug down, his grin had faded to a look of concern. "Everything all right?"

"Yeah. Just thinking."

"About?"

"Everything, I guess."

"That's a lot," Wyatt deadpanned, and Adrian snorted. When Adrian didn't say anything more, Wyatt scooted closer and took his hand. "Does everything include what we talked about last night?"

"Yeah. I don't know if I can make looking after your finances my permanent job, but you know I'm honored you trust me enough to check into them for you."

"That's good enough for me."

Adrian rolled his eyes. "I still can't believe you were working ten-to fifteen-dollar-an-hour jobs when you had thirty million just sitting in a trust fund." He'd had a mini-anxiety attack over it when Wyatt had dropped that bombshell on him.

"I don't need much," Wyatt drawled with his usual disinterested shrug.

Adrian narrowed his eyes and pinched his lips, and Wyatt chuckled. "If you think that's bad, just wait until you see the trust set up for Everly and the Everett charitable foundation."

"Oh God," Adrian groaned.

Wyatt's smile grew. "You see, I'm useless without you. You have to stay and take care of me."

At Wyatt's plaintive gaze and pout, Adrian rolled his eyes again. The man was as far from useless as you could get. From everything Furlough and Wyatt had told him over the last weeks, Wyatt's grandfather had spent plenty of time teaching him the family "business." He was perfectly capable of handling all of it, if he set his mind to it. He just didn't want to.

That was unfair. There was a lot to deal with, apparently. There was a board of directors for the foundation and the trust, which Wyatt was a senior member of, by virtue of birth. If he took on the house, he'd be expected to be deeply involved in both. Slipping on the family yoke wouldn't be all winters in Aspen and cocktails on the yacht.

Does Wyatt even have a yacht?

Maybe he should ask that sometime. Not now, though.

"I said I'd check into it. If I can, I'd like to hire Bev to help me until she finds another job."

"Is it official, then? Is your company out of business?" Wyatt asked around a bite of one of the blueberry muffins Adrian had baked once they'd gotten the kitchen cleaned up and functioning again.

"Don't know for sure. But Bev says everyone she's talked to is bugging out like rats abandoning a sinking ship."

"Sure. You know you can hire anyone you want. I trust you." Before Adrian's little heart did a flip over that, Wyatt said, "Speaking of Beverly, we need to get dressed and get going."

"We do?"

"Yup." His smile was just a little bit mischievous, and Adrian frowned.

"Uh. Okay. You guys made plans?"

"Yup."

"When was that?"

"Yesterday."

"Do I get to know what they are?"

"It's Sunday. Bev invited us to brunch, and I figured we could pick up some more of your stuff on our way back."

They'd already made one trip to his apartment. Wyatt had done most of the packing and carrying, since Adrian only had one good hand. Wyatt had also loaded way more than Adrian would have into the back of Furlough's truck, but he hadn't complained. If they brought much more, there wouldn't be anything left in the apartment but Adrian's crappy furniture—which would never darken the doors of Everly, if he had anything to say about it—and some of Martin's stuff that he still hadn't bothered to pick up. Which would mean Adrian would be all but moved out.

He wouldn't mention that to Wyatt, though.

After putting their dishes away, they didn't spend as long in the shower as Adrian wanted. He'd finally gotten used to being naked around Wyatt, with the added benefit that whenever Adrian was naked, Wyatt was too, and Wyatt usually couldn't keep his hands to himself. Adrian had never in his life felt this sexy and desired. It was another in the long list of reasons he was falling head over heels for the man.

Though they took Adrian's car, Wyatt drove. It was easier because of Adrian's hand, but he soon realized that wasn't the only reason Wyatt took the keys, when they drove past the exit for Beverly's side of town. Adrian spoke up, just in case Wyatt had missed it, but Wyatt smiled and said he knew where he was going.

Adrian's stomach flipped a little when they took the exit for midtown, but he didn't get really nervous until Wyatt parked up the street from The Sturges Speakeasy and got out.

"Why here?" Adrian asked, trying to keep his voice regular.

Wyatt smiled as he joined him on the sidewalk and wrapped an arm around his shoulders. "It was Bev's idea. She said you really liked this place."

His reply was innocent enough Adrian couldn't tell if he knew this was where Martin and his friends hung out, or if it was just Bev he needed to have words with.

Adrian hung back, making Wyatt go in first. Using Wyatt as a shield, he scanned the room until he spotted Keith and then Martin and a blond he didn't recognize. He felt a slight twist in his gut at seeing his ex again, but he couldn't really put a name to the feeling.

The rest of Martin's friends had their backs to the room, but the minute Martin spotted Wyatt, all heads turned in their direction. Adrian waited the space of a few heartbeats, but not a single face registered recognition, probably because not one of them was actually looking at *him*. All eyes were on Wyatt, boldly raking every inch of the man. Adrian was invisible… again. The realization hit him like a punch to the chest, and he was gearing up for a real wallow in poor me when Wyatt took his hand, distracting him.

"Is one of them Martin?" he asked, following Adrian's gaze.

"Yeah, the redhead," Adrian answered, starting to get pissed that Wyatt had obviously known who might be there.

"Huh."

Wyatt didn't give him a chance to try to figure out what that meant. He pulled Adrian into his arms and kissed him for all he was worth, right there in the middle of the restaurant. Adrian tensed initially—given the whole public place thing—but when Wyatt set his mind to it, he could make Adrian forget anything in the world outside existed, and Wyatt had definitely set his mind to it.

"All right you two, break it up," Bev broke in, pulling a dazed Adrian into a quick hug before doing the same to Wyatt. "Nice one, by the way," she said as she led both of them by the arms to a table where Isaac was waiting.

"I think Martin's eyes are about to pop out of his head, and he's turning an ugly shade of green. It really clashes with the ginger hair."

Adrian risked a glance over his shoulder, and sure enough, all eyes were on both of them now, and recognition had definitely dawned.

"Should we go over and say hi?" Bev asked gleefully.

You evil bitch.

You fabulously evil bitch.

Wyatt answered, though. "Better not. If we get any closer, I might say or do something I shouldn't."

He had enough growl in his voice that Adrian glanced at him in surprise and put a hand on his shoulder. "That won't be necessary."

Wyatt took the hand, kissed it, and his face split in his customary sexy smile again.

"So whose idea was this anyway?" Adrian asked.

"Mine," Bev answered unapologetically as she climbed in next to her husband.

Adrian tried to glare at her, but he couldn't hold it. While he liked to think he never would've done something this catty on his own, he had fantasized a similar scenario, and he was enjoying the look on Martin's face… just a little.

"You're kind of a bitch when you want to be," Adrian said as he and Wyatt took the seats across from them.

"I don't know what you're talking about," Bev replied with a smile. "You used to tell me how much you loved their Sunday brunch here. It's not my fault if your ex just happened to show up."

"Mm-hmm."

"You mad?" Wyatt asked softly.

With a sigh, Adrian shook his head. He wasn't mad. He actually felt kind of good… happy. It was hard not to do a side-by-side comparison with Martin and his friends only a few tables away, and despite the twinge of a little unresolved hurt and the slight blow to his newly bolstered ego, he was sure, beyond a shadow of a doubt, that he'd gotten the better end of the deal with the people he had at his table.

In a backward kind of way, he actually had Martin to thank for where he was now. If the asshole hadn't kicked the feet out from under him, he never would've gone crazy enough to head out into the middle of nowhere to pick up a guy at a bar. He probably would've just moved on and settled for another guy who thought he was mediocre at best, instead of someone who made him feel like he hung the moon.

Throwing caution to the wind, he leaned close to Wyatt and whispered, "I'm not mad. I'm in love."

He pulled back enough to meet Wyatt's gaze, bit his lip, held his breath, and waited. The broad smile that slowly spread across Wyatt's face lit up the whole restaurant.

"I love you too."

For once, Adrian didn't care who might be watching. The rest of the world might as well have disappeared. He kissed the gorgeous man sitting next to him and rested his forehead against Wyatt's cheek.

"Oh my God, that's so adorable," Bev squealed, and Adrian burst out laughing. His cheeks flamed as he buried his face in Wyatt's shoulder.

"Can we eat now?" Isaac asked plaintively.

Wyatt slid an arm around Adrian's shoulder, scooted his chair close enough that their thighs touched, and grinned. "Absolutely."

ROWAN MCALLISTER is a woman who doesn't so much create as recreate, taking things ignored and overlooked and hopefully making them into something magical and mortal. She believes it's all in how you look at it. In addition to a continuing love affair with words, she creates art out of fabric, metal, wood, stone, and any other interesting scraps of life she can get her hands on. Everything is simply one perspective change and a little bit of effort away from becoming a work of art that is both beautiful and functional. She lives in the woods, on the very edge of suburbia—where civilization drops off and nature takes over—sharing her home with her patient, loving, and grounded husband, her super sweet hairball of a cat, and a mythological beast masquerading as a dog. Her chosen family is made up of a madcap collection of people from many different walks of life, all of whom act as her muses in so many ways, and she would be lost without them.

E-mail: rowanmcallister10@gmail.com
Facebook: www.facebook.com/rowanmcallister10
Twitter: @RowanMcallister

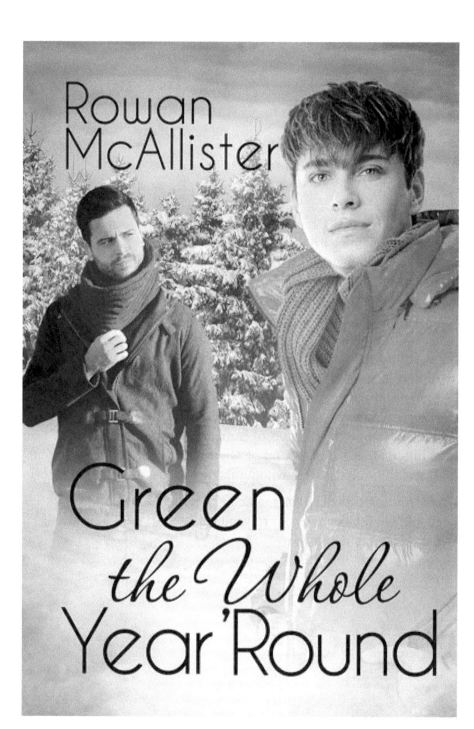

Rowan
McAllister

Green
the Whole
Year 'Round

Couples counselor Ted Freeman is still reeling six months after his partner left him. He desperately hopes a week of peace and quiet at a quaint mountain cabin will be just what he needs to regain his personal and professional confidence.

Neil Kelly is a computer programmer who just got promoted to full time and is celebrating over Christmas by going on his first real grown-up vacation at the Cabins in the Pines Inn. When he runs into Ted, his longtime crush, Neil can't believe his luck, and he vows to do whatever it takes to make Ted see him as something other than the dork next door.

Neil wasn't part of Ted's plan for the holidays, but he might turn out to be exactly what Ted needs.

www.dreamspinnerpress.com

Too much partying and self-inflicted trouble have left Cameron Lacey's life a complete mess. But he's determined to change, and he'll do anything to keep a roof over his head until he gets himself together. When he's introduced to Sam Powell, he can't believe Sam will let him stay without expecting anything in return—in Cameron's world, nothing is free. Realizing Sam's bleeding heart is exactly as it appears throws Cameron for a loop… and completely head over heels. Unfortunately, old habits die hard.

Cameron's demons rear their ugly heads, leading to a series of backsliding disasters and fumbled attempts by Sam to save Cameron from bad choices. As Cameron struggles to become who he wants to be instead of who he is, he also comes to hope Sam will discover that what's right for him might not be what he's looking for—but who he already has.

www.dreamspinnerpress.com

Lost in the Outcome

Rowan McAllister

When Nathan Seward wakes up in a cheap hotel with a stranger, unable to remember the night before, unscrupulous plots and clandestine schemes are the furthest thing from his mind. True, he's in Houston to bid on his biggest contract yet, one that will put his software development company on the map, but he's the underdog at the table, not one of the big players. Unfortunately someone out there sees him as a threat and isn't above drugging and blackmailing him to put him out of the running. Luckily for Nathan, the man in bed next to him couldn't be further removed from the corporate world.

Tim Conrad is scraping the bottom of the barrel. He left college during his freshman year to take care of his dying mother, and life and lack of money prevented him going back. Now twenty-seven, his dreams are long buried, and he's scraping by with dead-end jobs and couch surfing because he can't afford a place of his own.

As Nathan tries to run damage control and figure out what the hell happened to him, he and Tim discover a connection neither was looking for, as well as dreams they've both forgotten.

www.dreamspinnerpress.com

My Only Sunshine

Rowan McAllister

Tanner Wallis is nearly at the end of his rope the night Mason Seidel finds him lying next to the mangled body of a cow on the back pastures of the Seidel family's Wyoming ranch. Recently out of the hospital after he and his boyfriend were brutally beaten, Tanner is jobless, homeless, and almost penniless. His desperate hope is that Mason will believe he's innocent of the senseless crime and give him a place to heal, both physically and emotionally, until he can get on his feet again.

But Mason already has enough on his plate. He's only been back on the ranch a few months, ten years after his father kicked him out for being gay, and only because his sister begged him to come help after the man's disabling stroke. With all his responsibilities—running the struggling ranch and keeping his sister and father off his back—Mason can't really afford the distraction Tanner represents. But he can't just abandon the attractive young man either. There's trouble in spades on the ranch, but if they face it together, Mason and Tanner might find a future with a little sunshine.

www.dreamspinnerpress.com

ROWAN MCALLISTER

AIR AND EARTH

Elemental Harmony: Book One

When absent-minded video game developer Jay Thurson impulsively follows his intuition westward, he never expects his rideshare to turn out to be a gun-toting madman. In an act of desperation, Jay turns to the gift he's long neglected and feared for help and leaps from the moving car on a dark and deserted back country road.

Running for his life leads him to the doorstep of Adam Grauwacke, a roadside nursery owner and sometime vegetable farmer, whose affinity for the earth goes far beyond having a green thumb. Adam's world is ordered and predictable, dependable and safe, but despite having his dream farm and business, he's always felt something's missing. When he welcomes Jay into his home, life seems to click for both men, and together they explore their gifts and their attraction.

But harmony has no value if it is easily won, and a crazed gunman and volatile ex might be their end if Jay and Adam can't learn to trust the strength of their bond.

www.dreamspinnerpress.com

ROWAN MCALLISTER

WATER AND FIRE

Elemental Harmony: Book Two

Aiden Flanagan has spent his entire life fighting who and what he is. After losing control of the power within him one time too many, Aiden flees to his parents' vacation home on Nantucket to lock himself away as punishment and to protect the people he cares about. Getting nowhere on his own, Aiden fears he'll never have enough control to join the world again—and perhaps he doesn't deserve to—until an act of kindness brings Murphy Mizuuchi into his life.

Though still grieving the loss of his partner, Murphy's own gifts won't allow him to ignore the strongest projector he's ever encountered or deny the beautiful soul behind Aiden's drama. Drawing on his own recovery, his empathy, and years of practicing meditation, he shows Aiden not only how to find a safe outlet for who he is, but to value his abilities.

But Murphy isn't the only one drawn to Aiden's fire. Someone from his past followed Aiden to the island, and it will take both Murphy's and Aidan's powers to protect him from a man who won't stop until he takes all Aiden has.

www.dreamspinnerpress.com